"An unforgettable portrait of a young woman at war with the world and herself. Protagonist Del can be hard to like, but she remains easy to love. This is a brilliant and exciting debut."

—Karen Joy Fowler, *New York Times* bestselling author of *We Are All Completely Beside Ourselves*

"A wry and unexpectedly tender story of finding the family we need when we least expect it. Perfect for fans of *Olive Kitteridge* and *The Good House*."

—Eleanor Brown, *New York Times* bestselling author of *The Weird Sisters*

"Deliciously witty and deeply poignant. Sharp, surprising, and memorable, this is a book I know I'll keep mulling over for a long, long time."

—Emma Hooper, bestselling author of *Etta and Otto and Russell and James*

"Darkly funny and brimming with pathos. . . . For fans of Elizabeth Strout [and] Ottessa Moshfegh . . . this is a humorous and life-affirming trip through the fraught, weird heart of America, exploring the granular details that make and break a life."

—Sharlene Teo, award-winning author of *Ponti*

"A keenly observed and achingly real story of grief and loss and the extraordinary lengths one woman goes [to] to make sense of her past and discover who she might become."

—Dana Reinhardt, author of *Tomorrow There Will Be Sun*

Housebreaking

COLLEEN HUBBARD

Berkley
New York

BERKLEY
An imprint of Penguin Random House LLC
penguinrandomhouse.com

Library of Congress Cataloging-in-Publication Data

Names: Hubbard, Colleen, author.
Title: Housebreaking / Colleen Hubbard.
Description: First edition. | New York : Berkley, 2022.
Identifiers: LCCN 2021032947 (print) | LCCN 2021032948 (ebook) |
ISBN 9780593337028 (trade paperback) | ISBN 9780593337035 (ebook)
Subjects: LCGFT: Novels.
Classification: LCC PS3608.U227 H68 2022 (print) | LCC PS3608.U227 (ebook) |
DDC 813/.6—dc23
LC record available at https://lccn.loc.gov/2021032947
LC ebook record available at https://lccn.loc.gov/2021032948

First Edition: April 2022

Printed in the United States of America
1st Printing

For my children

September

Chapter One

ON AN UNSEASONABLY WARM AFTERNOON IN LATE SEPTEMBER, Del did something that she could not explain to herself and would not explain to others. In the months to come, when she considered the moment that changed everything, she would reach no conclusion as to why she did what she did. In the short term, it was stupid; but in the long term, it was nothing less than catastrophic.

The cleaning of South Elm started as it normally did. Del picked up the keys from the agency and checked the paperwork to see if there were any add-ons. Sometimes the owner wanted the fridge cleaned or the oven scoured. Other cleaners wouldn't do that sort of filthy work and tried to trade jobs, but Del didn't mind. She got paid fifteen dollars out of the agency's fifty-dollar fee for extras. On this occasion, a note indicated that she needed to change the sheets in the top-floor guest suite.

South Elm was fairly straightforward. She had cleaned it twice a week for more than a year without ever meeting the occupants, but she knew them from her intimate involvement with their stuff. The owner was a single mother with twin boys and, judging from her Japanese knife collection and elaborate home cinema, a serious amount of cash. They lived in a five-bedroom brick town house overlooking a small gated park.

As Del let herself into the house and went to the cleaning cabinet in the kitchen, she thought that the owner's man must be coming. She wasn't sure who he was, or the nature of his relationship to the homeowner or her sons, but she had picked up enough details to piece together the scenario. He visited every other month or so. Del was always asked to set up the guest bedroom for him, perhaps for propriety's sake, but at some point, he ended up in the owner's bed. His sheets were mussed but didn't have the stink of having been slept in overnight, and Del had found his plaid boxers bunched at the foot of the owner's bed.

Del took the bucket and cloths out of the cabinet and then removed the cleaning solutions and spray bottles from the drawer beneath the kitchen sink.

She started with a spritz around the living/dining area, which opened to a huge bay window that overlooked the park. Walking around in her socks on the wide-planked walnut floor, she wiped down Lucite chairs, straightened the photos on the mantel, and made sure that a pebbled glass whiskey decanter was centered on its platter. Then she started to clean the floor. Plunge, wring, mop, repeat. She liked this type of work because it allowed her mind to drift. Del thought about *Night Must Fall*, which she had watched on TV last night with her roommate, and wondered if they would get pizza for dinner. She moved to the kitchen to get to the good stuff, like the greasy stove hood filter. Putting on gloves, she filled the sink with Palmolive and hot water.

Later, with an hour left of the clean, Del leaned the mop against the wall on the third floor, across from the children's skylighted playroom, and felt a drop of perspiration roll from her throat down to her bra. Her chapped hands burned from being soaked in cleaning fluids. It was late afternoon, and the sun shot like a dart through the blinds at the end of the hallway and went directly into her skull. The turbo vacuum cleaner still roared in her ears though she had unplugged it at least twenty minutes earlier. And that was when Del did something she had never done before: she went through the house room by room, touching the owner's belongings as if they were hers. The silky pearl nightgowns that Del herself had tucked into the marble-handled chest of drawers, a toy aircraft carrier with guns that popped, a small gold compact that clicked open to reveal a cake of raspberry gloss. She touched her fingertip to the gloss, felt it melt to a semiliquid state, and pressed it to her lips. Then she turned on the tap, took off her clothes, and got in the tub.

Del wasn't cleaning the tub; she had done that already. She was submerging herself, a boiled lobster color to her skin. Just as she reached for the cork-topped glass container of bath salts, a woman with straight black hair appeared in the bathroom door, a crumpled paper grocery bag under one arm. The green tops of carrots hung limply from the bag.

Del expected screaming. It was the owner of the house, and she had never seen her cleaner before. But she didn't scream. She simply put down her bag, threw over a towel, and watched as Del put on her bleach-stained jeans and loose gray T-shirt. The woman was wearing a crisp white lab coat with her name stitched in blue above where her heart must be. Del had laundered that coat before. It had to be washed with like colors.

In silence they walked through the long white hallway and down the stairs, where Del slipped on her shoes and went to the door. She wanted to apologize, but the words didn't come. Shame pulsed through her body. The woman in the lab coat stood at the top of the brownstone steps and watched as Del retreated to her bus stop.

By the time Del got to the agency to drop off the keys, there was already an envelope on the desk with her name on it. It was her final paycheck with a yellow Post-it Note stuck to it.

On the Post-it Note were two words handwritten in black ink.

Get lost.

Chapter Two

THERE WERE SEVERAL REASONS DEL DID NOT PLAN TO SHARE THE change in her employment status with her roommate, Tym. She needed to think through how she'd cover up her mistake.

Del and Tym had made a deal that her dirt-cheap rent was contingent on maintaining steady employment. There was no way she could afford to live anywhere else. Also, she was certain that she could find another job before he even noticed that she was around the apartment at unusual hours, such as all day long every day of the week.

Four years ago, on her twentieth birthday, Tym had brought a box of supermarket cupcakes to the apartment Del had shared with her father. Her father, Stan, had died several weeks earlier, and she had not been able to keep up with the rent. She had no experience with eviction and wasn't sure how quickly it would happen, so she had simply stayed inside the apartment, eating through her father's collection of spicy ramen, waiting for an authority figure to show up and kick her out.

By the time Tym arrived to check in on her, the utilities had shut off one by one. She was living in the dark, ignoring the huge pile of mail by the door.

Among her father's friends, she was well known for skipping out on jobs. It had become a joke. Since she moved in with her dad at age seventeen, she had worked at a restaurant, a café, a video rental place, and several temp agencies. Her longest stint had been a six-month placement at a dentist's office. She had liked that job: the dentist gave her a year's supply of toothpaste, and she always got to leave at exactly 4:30 p.m. But she got bored and irritated with the regularity of it, and one day she had simply stopped going in.

Tym had known the whole story, and so when he told her in her father's dark apartment that she could come and live in the spare room of his place, he stressed that she would need to get a job and keep it. He wasn't a charity worker, and she wasn't a strong candidate for late adoption. She would need to behave like an adult. She agreed and went on various long-term placements for a temp agency before being hired as a cleaner.

Being a cleaner didn't appeal to a deeper calling, but what did? Not the dentist's office. Not the video rental place, either. She had worked steadily since she was thirteen, when she earned a paycheck at a jewelry store where she used a bent paper clip to dip necklaces into an electrified vat of blue ooze until they shone. Work existed to provide her with food and rent money, that was it. Keeping her expectations low was the key to a minimal level of life satisfaction. And for a while, she had been satisfied. Her father had become a friend, despite everything that had come before, and she became friends with his friends, too. It was a new period in their lives, and everything that had happened previously was safe so long as they never talked about it.

Now that she had been fired, she felt sure that she could find something else pretty quickly. Cleaning for a different agency. Maybe back to temping. Perhaps something steady, like managing a coffee shop. She would go out the next morning and begin filling out applications.

After leaving the cleaning agency with her check, she took a subway home. The car slipped underground into a dark tunnel. When it arrived at her station, a billboard advertising vacations in Mauritius distracted her. Where was Mauritius? How long did it take to fly there? What language did they speak? The cost of the flight was double what she had in her savings account. When she came out of the station, the sun was shining, and she forgot all about it.

"Home early," Tym said as she walked into the kitchen. Tym had buzzed gray hair and ropy calf muscles from riding a bike six days a week to his job at the drugstore. Del had never seen him wear pants; he said that he didn't feel the cold and that shorts were therefore the only appropriate year-round wardrobe item.

He had been one of Del's father's closest friends, along with Dave and Bruce the Moose. Her father and Bruce were dead now, and Dave had moved out west, so it was just the two of them, Del and Tym, holding down the fort.

It was sauce day. Tomato dotted the kitchen wall as well as the apron he was wearing, which had a life-size image of Michelangelo's *David*, with a neck that ended at the top of the apron.

"I guess," she said, with, she hoped, an air of nonchalance. "Everyone's going on vacation next week and not getting their houses cleaned. I've only got a couple of my usuals."

"Weird timing, September. I would have thought people would take vacation in August, before school starts."

Del sat at the table, on a retro red chair that Tym had picked up off the sidewalk. "If you're really, really rich, those kinds of rules don't apply to you. Some of those kids probably don't even go to school. They probably have governesses, or whatever."

Tym dipped a wooden spoon into a pot of bubbling sauce on the range and tasted it. "Makes sense, I suppose."

He made a huge pot of pasta once a week and packed it into individual Tupperware containers to bring to his job where he worked as a photo processor. He didn't use a recipe and the ingredients never changed, yet he was always convinced that the previous week's sauce was better than the current version.

He offered the spoon to Del. "Taste this. Too much salt?"

She fanned the spoon, but even so the boiling sauce singed her tongue. "No."

"Too much meat?"

"Never. It's great."

"There's something," he said, turning worriedly back to the stove. "Something not quite exactly one hundred percent right."

He hummed as he stirred more oil into the pot. "Too much onion, maybe?" he mumbled to himself.

The phone on the wall rang. It was never for Del, so she didn't bother.

"Yellow?" Tym said into the mouthpiece.

He listened to the caller on the other end explain something. Maybe it was a sales call.

"She sure is." Tym held out the phone.

Was it the cleaning agency? The woman who owned the
house? Feeling her color rise, Del took the phone. How was she
going to cover this?

"Hi?" she said tentatively.

"Adela? Is that you?"

She didn't go by that name anymore. The voice was a man's
and had the forceful positivity of a sales pitch.

"Who's this?"

"I thought it was you. Funny. You sound just like yourself.
It's Greg. Cousin Greg. You'd never believe how long it took to
find your number. If you were trying to hide, you couldn't
have done it better." He chuckled as if he had said something
particularly funny.

Greg was the youngest of the Murrow brothers. She hadn't
seen him since her mother's funeral seven years earlier, when
she was a senior in high school. Greg's father, Chuck, was her
mother's brother. Del hated Chuck. She hated Greg a little bit
less.

She didn't say anything, so Greg continued, like idiots always do. "Well, it's good to talk to you. It's been such a long
time! I was just saying—seeing as I'm coming into the city—
that it would be good to meet up. You know, catch up. I can't
wait to hear what you're doing. Big-city stuff. I've got some
business on Friday; d'you think we could meet then?"

"Friday," Del repeated slowly, as if thinking. "Friday I'm
busy."

Friday she needed to steal a car and drive it into the ocean. Friday she needed to bring a match and a can of gasoline to the office of the White Pages so that no one could look up anyone's number ever again. Friday she needed to hijack a radio station and play Electric Light Orchestra on repeat for fifty hours until the feds broke in and shot her to death.

"That's alright," he offered genially. "I can do Saturday, too."

"Hm. Might be going out of town."

Tym was staring her down.

"Who is it?" he mouthed. He gestured wildly with the spoon, which flung tomato flecks on the wall.

"My mom was really excited to get back in touch. She said to tell you Auntie Jeanne says hi. We never get to hear anything about you. Adela! It's so funny to hear your voice again. Blast from the past."

Greg's mom, Jeanne, was alright. She always kept butterscotch candy in her purse. Jeanne had come over to visit Del's mother, Louise, even after things got bad and everyone else had left them to rot. Hearing Jeanne's name, Del felt a strange ache from somewhere below her rib. Tym was going into meltdown.

"Fine. I can do Friday. I'll move the thing I was supposed to do."

They agreed to meet at four forty-five. Greg needed somewhere with parking. She told him the name of a chain diner just off the highway.

"What the fuck was that?" Tym asked when she had returned the phone to its cradle. "You haven't had a phone call since you finally paid off that damned credit card. Was that a date? Boyfriend?"

"It was my cousin."

Tym smirked. "Knowing the backwater you come from, I'll ask again. Was that a date?"

"All of my clothes smell like garlic. Can we get a fan in here?"

Del didn't want to be hounded. How had Greg found her number? Why was he calling her out of nowhere?

Tym shoved open the narrow window by the sink that faced into a brick wall. "There, fixed. I'm leaving in ten minutes to buy drugs from a nice young man called Duncan. I'm not going to be late, so if you have something to say, go ahead and say it. The invitation has been officially extended."

"My cousin wants to meet up. I don't know why. I haven't heard from him in years."

"Which one? Claudio? Gilberto? Roberto?"

"No, those are my dad's cousins. This is one of my mom's relatives from back home."

He turned the burner off. "Sounds juicy. Meet me at the gates by the park in an hour."

After Tym walked out the door, she did a quick wipe of the kitchen. Neither one of them liked to clean up the apartment, but they both preferred the place to be clean and complained that the other one was the source of the constant mess. Tym had told Del she should take a professional interest in cleanliness; she told him that she was off the clock, unless he planned to start developing her photos in the bathroom.

Tym had lived in this third-floor walk-up for thirty years, renting from ancient Italian landlords who never visited, never fixed anything, and rarely adjusted the rent. They were called the Verdiccis, and she and Tym paid the rent every month by dropping off a check at the corner store where someone knew someone who knew someone who knew the Verdiccis.

If Tym found out that she had lost her job for such a stupid reason and he kicked her out, where would she go? She couldn't afford to live anywhere on her own. Roommates seemed unlikely. Most of the people her own age were in college or had recently graduated, whereas Del had a GED and no ability to talk about her recent backpacking trip to Thailand or her job in advertising. For the first two years living at Tym's, she had trod carefully: making her bed every day and restricting her belongings to a small closet as if he might forget she was there and never remember to kick her out.

She checked her watch. Twenty-six minutes until she had to leave to meet Tym. She flicked on the TV, adjusted the rabbit ears, and punched the remote through the seven channels that usually had decent reception. At the White House, Bill Clinton was giving a speech about Saddam Hussein. Politics had nothing to do with her. She flicked the news off. Stepping over piles of clothes on her bedroom floor, she flopped onto her comforter.

Her furniture was the same as it had been when she moved in. A chest of drawers that had been her father's. A single bed that her dad had bought for her when she moved into his place weeks after her mother died. Four crystal rabbits that her mother had collected, one with a chipped ear. Next to her bed was a wooden whiskey crate that she had had since she was a little girl. The inner lid was lined with ripped blue fabric.

When she was a little girl, she used to play a game with the box. Del would set an egg timer to one minute. When the timer started, she'd yell, "Fire!" and race around the house, picking up her belongings and packing them into the box. Anything left outside the box after a minute would have been destroyed in the imaginary inferno. At the end of the minute, she'd write an inventory of what she had packed and comment on what she should have done differently. Her collection of clay animals that came free with her mother's boxes of tea was an often-pondered choice. Clay became hard in a fire. Could she leave them out and yet count on seeing her leopard and gorilla again?

On one occasion, her parents had observed her playing this game, and her father had remarked that Del needed a sibling. Her mother had laughed so hard the ice cubes in her glass laughed along with her.

Now she used the box as a bedside table. On it sat a white lamp with a blue shade, a red glass bowl where she put her cheap silver rings at night, and two library books, both romances, that her mom had had on loan when she died in the wreck. Over Del's bed was a map of the world that her father had given her for her eighteenth birthday. She had been out of the country one time, on a trip to Canada to see a choir with her middle school. She had marked Quebec City on the map with a small red dot.

When she had started working at the dentist's office, she opened a savings account for travel. She saved $473.12 and intended to go to Germany because a patient had told her that visiting Germany was like looking at the future and the past at the same time. She couldn't imagine what that was like, so she wanted to go and see it for herself. She thought it might involve mountains or a water feature.

Lying on her bed, Del breathed deeply, the scent of Tym's cheap sandalwood incense stinging her nostrils.

She wanted to find the person who had given Greg her number and send him shit through the mail. Who would have her number? The cleaning agency? Was this their revenge? Her high school friends had all lost touch when she left town. Probably they went off to college and majored in subjects like art history or sociology, whatever that was. After her mom died, Del showed up at her dad's apartment and never went back to her hometown. She got her GED by mail. Her dad had no desire to return, either—he was happy in the city with Dave and Bruce and Tym, with the five-dollar night at the repertory cinema with crushed popcorn on the floor. He wanted to be away from those people just as much as she did. They never discussed going back even though the house was theirs.

But it wasn't just her arrival at her dad's apartment that closed down any sentimental feelings about the place where she had grown up or about her family there. It was before that. It was a million things. It was when she was eleven, at the annual Easter party at Greg's parents' house. Pink and yellow eggs dotted the hill over the field that they used as a pumpkin patch in the fall. Greg and his brothers tugged at the ties their mother made them wear. As everyone lined up for the buffet, Del's mother dropped a vodka and cranberry over the newly laid floor. The finest oak, Greg's father, Chuck, had told them earlier. You couldn't even imagine the cost. Obscene. The looks on the faces of her aunt and uncle and cousins as her mother knelt down to wipe up the spill, the cranberry soaking into the white chiffon dress she had bought at the Goodwill as a special treat. She looked like Elizabeth Taylor in *Cat on a Hot Tin Roof*. No one helped. They never did. Del and her mom knew they were embarrassing, sliding down the ranks of social acceptability when everything for Uncle Chuck and his family was looking up, up, and up.

Just after six p.m., the air was thick with pollen. The summer had been unusually hot. People were dying in the Midwest. Crops withered. In the park, blades of grass had gone crisp as if the whole thing had been microwaved.

Tym inhaled deeply from a one-hitter painted to look like a cigarette. "Gregory." He drew out the syllables as if it were the name of a weird fruit.

Del felt dizzy and slightly manic. Her fingers itched as she and Tym walked along the concrete path that made a figure eight through the park. They passed a storage shed where the park warden kept his tools, the green of the door charged and electric. Nearby, men on folding chairs clicked dominoes into white chains. She and Tym took a seat on a bench near a small fishpond.

Del took the lighter. "Greg is an asshole and a loser, and he's probably married to someone named Gwyneth but fucking someone called Kimberly. You wouldn't even believe these people if you met them."

"Dire," Tym pronounced.

"Dire," Del agreed.

Greg was a couple of years older than Del. He had two older brothers, Mitch and Kevin. Their father, Chuck, owned a construction firm in her hometown and had created a development company from the farmland that Del's grandparents left to their son. The land amounted to about twenty percent of the town. To Del's mother, her parents left nothing but the house where she had been raised. A simple old farmhouse, a shack, really: two bedrooms under a leaky roof, with a coal stove Del's father had installed for warmth when they couldn't afford oil heating during the energy crisis.

Del once overheard Uncle Chuck saying it was Del's father's job to provide for his wife and that's why the parents left everything of value to their sons. Del's mother had been a pretty girl once; she could have married lots of guys, guys who would have provided. Instead she had married Stan. Who should be blamed but herself?

"Fuck him. Don't meet him. Never call him back. Ignore him. What the fuck's he gonna do? We'll change the number."

Tym didn't put up with bullshit. It was one of the things Del admired about him. When something or someone irritated him, he walked away immediately. Tym had few friends, no savings, and changed jobs every year or so. He very rarely dated someone for more than a couple of months. Over the summer, he had taken up with Marcus, a trainer and former Marine he had met at the gym. Marcus hadn't irritated him yet, but Del knew his time would come.

"Greg's mom is nice. She did crafts."

Nice moms made things with hay and ribbons. Nice moms baked cakes for fundraisers, put money in the church collection, chaperoned school trips.

"Nice is boring. You don't want to be nice. Do you know what I saw today?"

"What?" she asked.

Tym described a strip of photos of an ordinary-looking suburban couple and their kids followed by frames of a party where the couple were having sex with other people while in costume as pieces of fruit.

He was required to flip through the photos that he printed to see if there was any child pornography. Twice he had had to call the police, and an officer had come in to collect the negatives and the order form.

Now he opened his satchel to show Del a print. A white woman with big kneecaps was dressed as an apple. She wasn't wearing tights, and the snaps at the bottom of the apple were open, revealing a thick patch of hair. Behind her on the couch, a banana was kissing some grapes.

"Let's never live in the suburbs," Del said.

"Never ever ever. Living death. Everyone who seems nice has corpses piled under their front porch."

"How's Marcus?"

"He's good. I made him put on his old uniform the other day. Set off all my Captain von Trapp fantasies."

"Edelweiss . . ." she sang.

Tym laughed. "Something like that. But much, much filthier."

It was dark and quiet by the time they decided to go home. In their neighborhood, narrow brick buildings leaned into each

other, and plastic supermarket bags of trash were piled in the
street. Potbellied Antonio from the corner shop waved as they
walked past. Del watched as Tym packed up his cold spaghetti
and stacked it in the fridge. After he went to see Marcus, she
sat on the couch watching *The Trouble with Angels* until she
fell asleep.

Chapter Three

SHE WAS TWENTY MINUTES LATE FOR MEETING GREG. SHE HAD taken a streetcar from a café where she had put in a job application, but a broken train at the next stop had held it up. On the opposite track, a silver streetcar rattled past. The reflected sunlight flickered intermittently like a filmstrip.

Greg was sitting in a corner booth by himself. The diner was empty except for a college-aged waitress with half a cigarette tucked behind her ear. The place had a truck-stop theme, but it was in an upscale neighborhood, the sort of restaurant that families went to for lunch after church on Sunday.

"I'm sorry I'm late," she said to him.

She was wearing a pair of black capri pants that had been washed too many times, black Doc Martens with low socks, and a white blouse printed with bluebirds. She thought she should have worn something nicer. Maybe he would have thought she was successful and reported it back to the family.

Greg had already ordered a cup of coffee. He was wearing a

green fleece vest, and his sandy hair flopped over his eyes. His knuckles were thick and brown around the white ceramic mug. Farmer hands, her mother would have said.

"No problem at all. Good to see you." He stood up as if to hug her, but she took a seat on the bench opposite him instead. "Traffic wasn't too bad. I was surprised. Took just about three hours to get here."

"Huh." Del waved to the waitress.

"But I stopped for gas. Think I could have done it in under three. Just about."

The waitress appeared at the end of the booth. Her hair was short with frosted green tips, and she had perspiration stains under her arms.

"Just a cup of coffee," Del said.

Maybe she'd get fries when Greg left. She was hungry but not desperate enough to extend her conversation with him.

"How long has it been, do you think?" Greg had a dopey, friendly smile. He was the least smart of the three brothers, and the worst at sports. All three of them had played football and baseball. Greg was junior varsity every year. He had some kind of learning difficulty related to reading, and Del had sometimes seen him at the study lab at school, pecking out words with his pointer fingers. She liked him best of his brothers because he seemed the least malicious, but still she didn't like him very much.

"My mom's funeral," she told him. Greg had come with his brothers and his mom. Uncle Chuck arrived last, sat in the back row, and left before the service concluded.

"Oh yeah. Yeah. Sorry. That must have been it." He was silent for a moment, then spooned more sugar into his coffee.

"Why are you—why are you here?"

"So—it's a funny story. You haven't been home in a while, so you haven't seen it. The town, it's really building up. You remember that development my dad did in the field on the east side of town, where the old horse stable was? Well, that sold right up. So then he did a second one, and it happened the same. Eighteen houses, two cul-de-sacs, sold in a month. Now me and Mitch and Kevin are all part of the family business along with Dad. There's a new insurance company up Route 9. So there's all these families moving in. It's nice. A couple restaurants opened by the river. A pizza place, too. It's fancy: you can get a pizza with potatoes and rosemary on it. You'd like it."

Del didn't respond. It was unclear how she came across as a person who liked "fancy" pizza. Greg glanced at her, then raised his now-empty mug to the waitress. When it was refilled, he pumped it full of cream and sugar and stirred until Del was ready to pull the spoon away from his fat brown hands.

"So why I'm here to talk to you—it's about the house."

"What house?"

"Your house."

She had locked the front door after her mother's funeral, gotten a ride from her mother's friend Eleanor to the local bus station, and bought a ticket to the city where her father lived. Occasionally she remembered that she owned a house, and she was surprised by the fact.

"What about the house?" she asked.

"That side of the pond is best for development. The land is pretty flat and dry, and it's near the highway. And we own all the land around it, so we could develop the whole area. But the old house, it's a problem. No one wants to live next to an abandoned house. The lot, too—it's not how they build houses now. There's too much land; you could fit three houses on it. Efficiency's the thing. Space efficiency. And if you ever wanted to move back, you could get a brand-new house. We'd even give you a discount."

He paused, waiting for Del's reaction. She offered none, so he continued.

"That old place, you were never planning on going back there, right? Did it even have plumbing? You just had that coal stove in there. Coal!" He chuckled at the idea. "It's basically a campsite. We just need you to sign the paperwork and we can get started. You'd get a fair deal. Family and all."

Del's coffee had gone cold. Her stomach was making little noises that she was sure Greg could hear. A man as thin as a grasshopper had come into the diner and sat at the counter alone, eating a hamburger. After him a family arrived. The youngest child was holding an orange plastic toy truck and crying. It must be near dinnertime, Del thought. Her mouth felt dusty. She wanted Greg to leave immediately so that she could order some fries with a side of gravy without having to look at his stupid pink face ever again.

She tried to imagine another family living in her house. No, she couldn't—no one would want it. Maybe a single person. A weirdo like her. They'd fix the roof. Rewire the whole thing. Paint and such. They'd make it livable. Nice, even.

"You can think on it," Greg said. "We submitted the plans to the town. It's pretty straightforward, so we think it'd get approved fast. We would start building in spring when the ground thaws."

He opened his backpack and brought out a manila envelope, which he slid across the table. She opened it and glanced at the cover sheet. The offer amounted to about four times what she made in a year.

"When you sign, mail it back to the head office. We're on Elm Street now, the old Blake Building, if you remember it. You have to get it notarized, too. You can drop it off at our office if you want. We got our own notary."

He checked his watch and gazed out the window at the backup of traffic on the road outside.

She had twenty-seven dollars in her checking account, but she bought their coffees rather than let him think she needed anything from him.

Greg stood to leave. "Goodbye, then. It was nice seeing you."

Del didn't bother getting up. "Bon voyage."

Greg jingled his keys in the pocket of his fleece and then made for the door. The air in the diner was thick with the smell of fried eggs.

When she was seven, Greg's parents had invited everyone out on their new boat. As Uncle Chuck lifted her in, she saw a metal trap with four doors that flopped open when the rope was let loose. Inside dangled a hunk of rotten chicken meat. They took the boat into shallow water and dropped the trap. A few green lobsters scuttled in, and the boys fought to be the one to snap the doors closed.

It wasn't lobster season, and anyway the lobsters were too small to eat. Instead Uncle Chuck let them bring one small lobster back to the parking lot, where Greg's eldest brother, Mitch, smashed it open with a rock. Mitch fitted a stick into the cracked-open tail meat and pushed as the lobster writhed.

She washed her hands in the diner's bathroom and took the streetcar to the neighborhood where she had lived with her father. She hadn't been there in years. She sat at the bus stop and watched the door for almost an hour until a young couple with a curly-haired dog walked out. Both the couple and the dog looked expensive. The rent must have gone up.

She walked to a nearby college bar where she wouldn't know anyone. Gin and tonics were two for one.

"Can I get a sloe gin fizz?" she asked the bartender, who had a sprinkle of acne across his cheeks.

They didn't have that. They didn't have any of the other cocktails she asked about, either. Instead she ordered four gin and tonics and took a seat on a couch covered with a brown velour throw. *Frasier* was playing on the TV. It was a hot and drowsy night, and though she had tied her hair up in a knot, some strands clung to the sweat on the back of her neck and made her feel feverish and strange.

She drank the fourth cocktail, felt a wash of salt in the back of her throat, and rushed to the nearest bathroom. It was the men's room. Thankfully, it was empty. She puked into a urinal and wiped her mouth with her sleeve.

A college boy in a school sweatshirt had taken a seat on the other end of her couch. As he leaned toward her, she caught the haze of cheap beer on his breath.

"Where you from?" he slurred in an accent she couldn't place.

"Nowhere you'd know," she told him.

She grabbed her bag, waved to the bartender, and started the long walk home.

October

Chapter Four

SHE DIDN'T TELL TYM ABOUT THE OFFER ON THE HOUSE THE NEXT day, or the day after that, either. He was barely at the apartment, instead spending all his time with Marcus. It was weird for him to behave like that. Tym's pattern over the years was clear: he met someone, spent a couple of weeks enthralled by them, spoke incessantly to Del about his boyfriend's brilliance and huge cock, then gradually cooled on both subjects until the inevitable breakup weeks or days later. She always thought that Tym was comfortable being himself and that was the problem. Himself didn't leave room for Patrick's family Thanksgiving or DeVaughn's church choir or Francesco's love of galleries.

It was fine. They were happy being loners together. For Thanksgiving every year, they bought a pumpkin pie from the neighborhood bakery and split it in front of the TV while they watched *The Women*. For Christmas their friend Dave flew in, and they went to a dumpy old gay bar and ate chicken wings until their hands were orange.

During the day she went to cafés and restaurants, filling out applications until her hand ached. She called a few temp agencies. No one was calling her back, which worried her. Her savings were enough to pay rent for a couple of months, but Del was hoping that she didn't need to dip that far. The holiday season was fantastic for temp work. People wanted to go away, fly to warmer places, attend long holiday lunch parties. Someone needed to man the phones. So why wasn't anyone returning her call?

She tried Platinum Temps but found that the line was dead.

"Tym?" she called from the kitchen one afternoon just after Tym had gotten back from work. "Do you have a phone book? I need the Yellow Pages."

Tym stepped out of his room, his eyes dull from a nap. It was the only day he'd been home overnight in the last week. He wore boxer briefs printed with a banana down the front along with an oversized T-shirt with Princess Diana's face on it.

"Coffee?" he begged.

She reached for a mug.

He was strangely remote, Del thought. Maybe a late night out. Maybe coming down from something. He was always a little funny if he'd been to the club the night before. Ketamine, probably.

"So I was thinking," he began.

She heard his words but didn't react. The message was clear from the set of his face. Things were going well with Marcus, he told her. Really well. But Marcus was getting evicted from his place. Tym's apartment was the obvious answer, but Marcus didn't want a roommate. Fair enough, Tym had thought, the apartment was too small for three. It would be good for Del, anyhow. She had a steady job and money. She could move in with people closer to her own age. She might meet new friends—wasn't that how young people on TV met their friends? Through shared housing in unbelievably large apartments with floor-to-ceiling windows? His words crowded into each other. To Del, he sounded hysterical. They had had a good run, he told her. She didn't need to move immediately, anyhow. Maybe a month or two. Marcus could squat somewhere until she figured out where she was going.

"I can be out at the end of the week."

The words surprised her as she said them. She didn't have anywhere to go, a job, enough to pay the rent at a normal apartment. She didn't have first, last, and security. She didn't even have a fucking phone book.

Tym's eyes narrowed. "You sure? It's no biggie. A month is fine."

"No." She got up to pour herself a coffee with her back to him. "I've got something else lined up anyhow. I've been meaning to tell you."

She told him about the house. She made it sound like a great opportunity. All she needed was to go home and sign the paperwork, collect her cash, and go. She'd been meaning to travel anyway. If not now, when? She wasn't getting any younger, she said. She let the last statement hang in the air like a cloud of poison gas. Tym was very sensitive about his age.

Finally, she turned to him. "So that's all fine. The end of the week is better for me, really. I've been hanging around here too long. My misspent youth has not been spent."

. . .

The day before the move, Tym called in sick to work. They both woke up late and drifted to the living room in the early afternoon. For several hours they watched TV, until Del felt dopey and stunned. Somehow it was nine p.m. Tym brought out some hash and switched to the public access channel.

A woman with a blond afro was visiting a local pizzeria to find out why pizza existed. While the owner slung dough in the air, Tym speed-dialed Vito's and ordered the regular. One medium, half mushroom, half sausage and onions. One regular Coke, one Cherry Coke, small mozzarella sticks. Extra marinara.

The buzzer buzzed what seemed like a minute later, and Del went downstairs with Tym's money; he always paid instead of walking down and up the stairs. There were certain things they used to argue about but had long since resolved.

At the bottom of the stairs was Gary, the usual delivery guy. Gary was a damp man with damp hands. He was out of breath from the three-block walk from the restaurant.

"Hey, Del."

She handed him a twenty. "Hey, Gar."

"Halloween plans?"

"Nope."

"'Kay. Well, you've got time to figure it out. Guess I'll see you before then anyhow."

Del looked up from the change he had handed her. The bills were moist. "Maybe," she said curtly.

"What, you're switching favorites? I thought we were going steady?"

It was cold outside, and Gary's panting made clouds that evaporated in front of his pink face. Looking at him gave her a feeling of pity followed by resentment that reminded her of the books she had read in middle school where the plot centered on a pet dog that was inevitably killed in the second-to-last chapter.

She returned two ones to him, then added a five. "You're right. I'll see you soon, Gar."

They ate on the couch with paper towels so there would be nothing to clean up. Tym had switched the channel. Bette Davis was on a boat, crying.

Tym stopped chewing and cleared his throat. "Are you angry?"

"Nope."

"Do you think it's going to be weird?"

She didn't respond.

"Are you going to call me and tell me where you end up? How am I going to know if you're waiting tables in Vegas? What if you collect your money and blow it all on blackjack the next day? I promised your dad—"

"Stop talking." She closed the lid of the pizza box. Yet again, she had burned the roof of her mouth with cheese.

Hash always made Tym sentimental and weepy. He needed to find a new hobby, like alcohol or church, something that would make him keep his thoughts to himself like a normal person. Bette Davis brushed the lips of a married man with her fingertips. Tym started to cry. Del took the remote from him and switched to the Weather Channel. It would rain the next day and the day after that, too. Then they watched a show about tornadoes. Too many people lived in harm's way. Those people were stupid, and took stupid risks. If they wanted to live down the road from their great-great-grandmaw just because, the least they could have done was build bunkers for themselves for when the storm inevitably hit.

In the middle of the night, Del woke on the couch. Tym's mother's homemade afghan covered her, and she was clutching a crust of pizza as if it were a baby doll. She got up and threw clothes into her father's army duffel bag until it was stuffed but not too heavy to carry. The rest of her belongings she had already moved into the basement, where the landlords had locked storage areas that tenants weren't allowed to use. Already Tym had requisitioned a couple of them for his record collection. Earlier in the week, he had snapped off a padlock and helped Del carry boxes down to a closet-sized space with the number 4 painted in white on the door.

With her clothes packed, she waited on the couch for Tym to wake up at nine, which he had said he would, and call a taxi, which he had also said he would, in order to take her to the station and say goodbye. The clock ticked five, ten, and quarter past nine. Finally she slung the bag over her shoulder, walked to his door, and considered knocking. She didn't bother.

A local city bus took her to the long-distance bus depot. It was so close to the shore that even the ticket hall stank of dried seaweed. There were two choices of buses: one that took four and a half hours and a cheaper one that took seven. She paid eleven dollars for a one-way ticket on the longer route. Then she joined the line of people sitting on the pavement next to their bags alongside the parking bay where the bus would depart.

"Go this way often?" said a skinny guy in his twenties with greasy hair and a stained white undershirt.

"No," she answered, then sat on her bag with her back to him.

She was alone in the world and she wanted to be miserable by herself, not stuck sitting next to some idiot who would tell her about drum kits for five hours until his stop was called.

The bathroom on the bus was broken. Someone near the back of the bus periodically spritzed cinnamon-scented air freshener, but it barely covered the smell of raw sewage. Outside, fast-food restaurants became gas stations became a narrow highway with leafless trees bent against the wind. They stopped briefly while the driver got out and pissed against a highway sign. After a couple of hours, a lady and her baby boarded at one of the suburban stops and took the seat next to Del. The daughter was in a pink fleece jumpsuit with a cartoon tiger on the belly.

"Hello, baby," Del said to the baby.

Drool trailed down the baby's chin as she smiled. The mother bounced the baby on her lap and said nothing.

The bus rumbled over asphalt cracked by the previous winter's ice and salt. A rolled sweater cushioned the jolts as Del tried to sleep with her head against the window. The bus drew farther west, and the landscape switched between old mill towns, dead cornstalks, and withered shade tobacco. Alongside U-PICK-EM signs near the highway turnoffs, fat pumpkins shone like moons.

Her hometown didn't have a bus station, so her ticket was to the next town over. It was a gray day, and the light was failing already. Her plan—to walk—seemed stupid. She should have asked someone to pick her up, but there was no one. She planned to meet her cousins in the morning, but nothing would compel her to contact them for help. She would sleep in a ditch if it came to that.

The bus arrived at her stop at half past five. The station was small, just two bays pointed east and west, with a coin-operated snack machine and a shuttered ticket window. When the bus pulled away, she found herself alone, the only deposit. The cold air was mulchy and sweet. Looking around at the squat brick buildings and empty street, she felt a strange sense of familiarity and ownership, as if the place itself had been packed away while she lived elsewhere and reassembled for her return.

She walked along the road for a couple of blocks, passing a sewing goods store, a Polish bakery, and a thrift store, all out of business. Finally she saw the lights of a convenience store. She needed Advil and a pay phone.

The bell jingled when she opened the door. Above a rack of magazines, a television played *Wheel of Fortune* at maximum volume. The man at the counter pushed a carton of cigarettes to a silver-haired woman wearing a floor-length mink coat.

"Eleanor?" Del asked.

The woman turned and removed the unlit cigarette from her lipsticked mouth.

Del dropped her bag to the ground and smiled.

Eleanor shook her head. "Adela? I'll be damned."

They walked out to Eleanor's car, an old black Lincoln that she had left chugging puffs of exhaust into the cold air.

"I'd say this is like seeing a ghost, but ghosts are better dressed." Eleanor lit her cigarette and pulled her coat tightly around her thin frame as she leaned against the car.

"It's been a long time," Del admitted.

"Why're you back here? Did someone die? Hopefully one of those damned cousins of yours. They're real captains of industry. Built all over the pasture next to the fire station. Wouldn't be surprised if they opened a theme park next." She exhaled and glanced at Del. "You put on weight."

"I'm exactly the same."

Del was used to Eleanor. Five times divorced and now permanently single, Eleanor used to take Del and her mother to the outlet mall once a year as a girls' day out. They would try on shoes and clothes and then have lunch in the food court. Eleanor always had coffee and cigarettes. *Suck in your gut and stick out your butt.* She was obsessed with weight, her own and others'.

"Just think 'salad.' That's what I do. A can of tuna fish for lunch, and a salad for dinner. Out of the bag, they sell them at the Stop and Go now. Throw out the packet of dressing. Couldn't be easier."

"Cut it out."

Eleanor nodded approvingly. "Sparky. You need that. Now, where are you going? Tell me you're not walking like you're some kinda friendless indigent."

· · ·

The drive took only ten minutes along Route 2 before the exit into town. There was a sign announcing the town's name and population, but Del didn't get a close enough look to see it. When she had left as a teenager, the sign reported about five thousand residents. Had it doubled? Tripled? Del pretended to listen to Eleanor's stories while she stared out the window. What had been a dairy farm on the edge of town was now a cul-de-sac of two-story houses with attached garages. A sign said MURROW LANE.

The Lincoln's seats were low, and she felt as if she were sitting in the bed of a roller skate traveling down Main Street. They passed the library, the town hall, the police station, and the two rival Italian restaurants with identical red neon signs.

"So that's how that ended," Eleanor concluded. "The police said they couldn't pick out whose teeth were whose. Just slopped them all in and cremated them together. Divided the ashes equally and handed half to each widow."

"Huh," Del replied.

Eleanor glanced at her and smiled. "Are you sure you want me to drop you off back at the old place? I don't suppose you set anything up—electricity, water? My place isn't exactly the Ritz, but I do have soap."

"It doesn't matter. I'm only staying a couple days, and then they'll sell it to the next people. I think it will all be sorted out by the end of the week. I don't care."

"Either way. I hate to think of staying in there myself. Locked up so long. Wouldn't be surprised if it's haunted. Did your grandparents seem like the types to haunt?"

Del shook her head. In photos of them as middle-aged farmers, her grandmother was a fat woman with a flat nose wearing a kerchief, standing next to a thin bald man with a permanent frown.

"Old country." Eleanor shuddered. "Not my people."

They pulled onto Del's street. It was on the edge of town, only two old farmhouses surrounded by fields, and there were no streetlights. The night was black except for Eleanor's car lights and the house at the far end of the street with a SOLD sign at the end of the driveway.

"You'll call me, will you?" Eleanor asked.

"I don't have a phone."

"Dinner then. Tomorrow night."

"Of course. Duck à l'orange with soufflé and chocolate mousse?"

Eleanor's rasping laugh filled the car. "I'll pick you up at six."

Del closed the car door. The front of the house was illuminated by the Lincoln's headlights. She searched through her backpack and found a flashlight alongside a flattened peanut butter sandwich she had meant to eat on the bus. She clicked the flashlight on and waved to Eleanor.

Brushing away a small black spider, she fitted her old house key into the lock. The door wheezed open as Del stepped into the stale air. She felt as if she had opened a tomb that had been locked for a thousand years. Behind her, Eleanor's car crunched over the gravel driveway, switched gears, and sped down the road.

Del's flashlight scanned the living room: a stilled rocking chair, the potbelly stove, the brick-colored rug her mother had knotted out of dyed rags. An empty can on the coffee table. She remembered her parents' parties: scratchy, bearded faces; disco music; and spilled beer. In the kitchen, there was still a bowl and a spoon in the sink. Probably the cereal she had eaten on the day of her mother's funeral. She dropped her bag on the living room floor and went upstairs. The door was open to her parents' bedroom. A metal bed frame coated in chipped white paint. Wallpaper printed with nosegays of pansies. Her mother's bedside table was stacked with paperbacks; on her father's sat a magazine folded to the crossword puzzle page. Del blew the dust off the page and saw that it was only half complete. She took the magazine and a red Bic pen, then closed the door.

The door to her own room was closed. The hinge creaked as she pushed it open. Posters were taped to the walls, celebrities she had torn out of teen magazines. Boys with frost-tipped hair. None of the faces meant anything to her now. Green and purple plastic necklaces dangled over a mirror on top of her bureau. She contemplated her own reflection and then traced her initials in the dust over her face. It didn't feel like her room at all. It belonged to someone else, not a younger version of herself but a different person altogether, someone who might have married her high school boyfriend or bought a ticket to travel around Europe by train.

It was early, but she was tired and hungry. Downstairs, she dragged her bag across the living room, pushed the coffee table aside, and lay down on the rug with her arm across the duffel bag as if it were a person. The flashlight flickered. She switched it off and blinked, alone in the dark. She would need new batteries in the morning.

Chapter Five

DEL WOKE ON THE LIVING ROOM FLOOR AND FELT HER BREATH hanging in the air above her. Her stomach grumbled. She realized she hadn't eaten the night before. In her duffel bag she found the squashed peanut butter sandwich and peeled back the plastic.

Her watch read 7:12 a.m. It was too early to see the Murrows. She leapt up from the floor and ran in place to start her pulse moving again. Her feet were dead from the cold. She didn't know how long it would take to arrange the deal—maybe three or four days—but she wouldn't be able to stay in the house without any heat.

In her bag, she found another sweater and a pair of leggings to add under her jeans. Then she grabbed the dented bucket by the door and went outside.

The early morning light was sharp and bright. A red bird sat on the silver maple in front of the house, amid a fist of dead leaves. There were no other buildings within sight, just crumbling stone walls and fallow fields. Between her house and the neighbors', there was a low stone wall and woods that seemed enormous when she was a child but pitifully small now. Probably it would take five minutes to cross it and reach the neighbors' yard, yet as a girl she would play there for hours.

Del walked across the frosted grass to the side of the house and tried to open the lock of the wooden coal chest. It was rusted shut. She jogged down to the shed at the base of the lawn in front of the small pond. It was open. She found a spade and brought it back. Using it as a lever, she wrenched the coal chest open. There was a small pile of unused coal, dusty and mobbed with cobwebs.

In the house, by the potbelly stove, there was a packet of kindling and a box of Marlboro matches. She loaded the stove and struck the first match. Nothing. The second and third: the same. The fourth match hissed and smoked but died without a flame. There were none left.

Her back ached from sleeping on the floor, and yet she was happy not to have slept in her own bed or in that of her parents. The quiet was too eerie. All her treasured belongings, the jigsaw puzzles, the magazine posters, the gel pens, but no noise or heat.

She wanted out. She wanted to wrap up this business as soon as possible, get a bus ticket, and find somewhere else to live, like the desert. Nevada would never be as cold as this. She had never been there, but she imagined a permanent, scalding heat. Sidewalks that sizzled in August. No one would know her or know where she came from. She would say that her parents had retired to Florida and that they were too busy with their cribbage club to ever visit.

If all she had to do was sign some paperwork, surely she could collect her check and be on the bus out of here tomorrow?

She pulled on her coat and headed toward the center of town. Her road was gravel, turning into pavement past the feed and grain store, and then into a sidewalk just outside Main Street.

Walking quickly, she pulled up the hood on her jacket so it was close to her face. She didn't want to be seen or recognized. In and out. Keep it brief, keep it clean.

On Main Street, she pushed open the aluminum-clad door of Jack's Lunch and took an empty booth. It was the perfect viewing point to see when the lights switched on at her uncle's office, which sat on the corner of Main and Elm.

"What can I get you?" The waitress, who was probably in her fifties, had purple bangs.

"Coffee."

"Nothing to eat?"

"Not for now, thanks."

She would get bread and jelly at the store. At last count, she had $712.35. Who knew what the deposit would be on her new apartment or how much it would cost to get there, wherever it was.

There were two men sitting at the counter whom she didn't know. None of the other booths were taken. The waitress wasn't someone Del recognized. It was strange: she had assumed that she would know everyone and immediately be tossed into conversations that she'd rather avoid, but no one seemed to pay attention to her at all. She felt her breath steady and realized that there had been a pressure on her chest since she'd entered the center of town, as if a foot were pressing down on her heart. No one would talk to her. She was like a ghost, flitting unseen through her territory.

She had spent a lot of time in the diner when she was a teen. The place hadn't changed: the same ceramic mugs with a rust-colored double ring at the top, the same paper place mats with a connect-the-dots and an animal to color in. Other than the two bars, it was the only place on Main Street that was open past nine p.m., which basically made it a nightclub for the teen-age population of the town. She'd gone there with Frankie and Dob and Jo, eating plates of fries and chicken fingers until the neon light in the window switched off and they had to disperse at midnight.

Where were Dob and Jo now? Twenty-four. They must have jobs and apartments, or even houses, probably somewhere else. Frankie, now that was a different matter. With any luck, Frankie had been found out as the vile person that she was and flung out of town.

The door opened. Del glanced up. An old man with a folded newspaper nodded to the waitress, who palmed the kitchen bell.

"Fred's usual," the waitress called out.

The diner window had steamed up, so Del wiped it with her sleeve. Just down the road she could see the big old Victorian on the corner, formerly a lawyer's office, which now housed her uncle's development company. They had painted it cranberry red with gold and cream accents. It looked like a bordello in an old movie, a place where Jean Harlow would walk down the stairs in a black lace mantilla.

Besides the diner, Main Street had the same two bars, a fruitery, two Italian restaurants, a corner store, and a police station, as well as another couple of restaurants that she didn't recognize. The movie theater had closed.

The smell of fat and a sulfurous whiff of boiling eggs. The waitress slid Fred's usual in front of Fred—a pile of home fries, nearly burnt, with a fried egg on top.

Del had a refill of coffee, and then another. Refills were free.

The waitress returned again, but without the carafe. "You going to get something to eat?"

"No. Just the check."

The waitress frowned. "A dollar fifteen. Don't mind if I don't write it out for you."

Del fished through her coin purse and counted out dimes and nickels, which she left on the table with a fifteen percent tip. The windows had steamed up again when she walked out the door.

A woman with a stroller fed a meter on the street, which was otherwise dead.

Maybe the Murrows didn't get in this early. What day of the week was it, anyhow? Monday? Maybe they were closed on Mondays, or went to their construction sites or something. Maybe the whole thing could be organized by letter. That's it—she would write a letter, drop it in their mailbox, and wait for their reply. Of course she could find a notary anywhere. She would make it a requirement of the new town that she moved to: must have a notary. She would just need paper and a pen, which the waitress in the diner would certainly have.

"Well, lookee here."

She was pulled into an embrace before she could stop it. It wouldn't matter if she was blindfolded—she would know Uncle Chuck immediately from his smell. Chewing tobacco and Good & Plenty licorice candy.

She stepped back. His face was round and red from years of outdoor labor. He was wearing an expensive-looking gray fleece jacket and brown boater shoes. His hair was the classic Murrow sandy brown, now streaked with white.

"There's our girl, all grown up! Greg didn't say you were coming today. You should have stayed with us."

"Thanks," she said evenly, careful not to offer even a polite smile. "I stayed at the old house."

"That's just crazy. Do you even have electricity in that pit?"

"It's fine. It's just a short stay. It's like camping."

Chuck laughed as if she had made an amazing joke and clapped her on the shoulder.

"Like camping!" he roared. "Adela, you always were a funny little chicken. Let's get you inside where it's warm. We're just over the road here. We'll see if we've got any fixings for s'mores that you can take back to the house. Camping!"

He led her up the stairs of Murrow Construction, telling her about how he'd outbid the other potential owners of the building. It wasn't an interesting story, and so she didn't respond or encourage him in any way.

Inside the door was a large staircase tipped in gold leaf.

"Mitch! Kevin! Get your butts down here!" Chuck shouted up the stairs.

Her cousins appeared at the top of the stairs dressed in khakis and fleece jackets that matched their father's. For the first time she noted an eagle logo sewn over the heart, on top of the word Murrow, which was stitched in an elaborate font.

"Your cousin Adela," Chuck said, as if they might not know her.

To be fair, she wouldn't have recognized them if she had met them on the street. One is still thin and one is still fat, but otherwise, they look different than they did as teenagers. She remembered Kevin as having been a middling talent at sports and Mitch as having the looks and charm of a freshly boiled weasel.

"Hi, cuz," Kevin said, offering her a hand to shake. She held out her hand, and he shook her fingertips only.

Mitch nodded, his hands in his pockets. "How's it going?"

Chuck led her into a ground-floor office that had his name on the door on a bronze plaque. He took a seat behind a massive walnut desk that was covered in piles of manila file folders. "Greg is on-site this week. Big development happening out near the highway. Not sure if you saw it?"

She said she hadn't.

Chuck's office might have been the living room back when the building was somebody's house. It was enormous, with thick goldenrod floor-to-ceiling curtains with a fleur-de-lis pattern and an unstained cream-colored carpet. The thermostat was turned up to max, and she began to regret the leggings under her jeans.

"It's pretty straightforward," Chuck started, his smile disappearing as he pulled a manila folder from the desk drawer and flicked through the documents inside. "We already own all the land around the house. Just not the house itself. A few months ago we bought the Francis place at the end of the street. Old Man Francis died, and we put Mrs. Francis in a home. A nice one. You can see it makes sense to have all the lots within one development. More efficient that way. Unfortunately, we can't use the land on the other side of the pond. It's marshland, too expensive to do all the digging and filling we'd need to do in order for the houses not to sink into the ground. All you have to do is sign the papers, and then we get started. Of course, anything you want from the house, that's all yours. Not sure that you'd want any of it, though, probably just junk. Don't worry, we can take care of all that, clear it out for you. My treat."

He smiled at her like a person who had just remembered that he had been told to appear friendly.

She imagined a set of twelve identical houses, each with a window on either side of the door, painted in the same shades as Murrow Construction: red, yellow, cream. She wondered if they would put up new cladding over her old house to make it match the development, or if they'd leave it as it was. Maybe they'd fix it up but leave it as it was to give the development a sense of history. She pictured the entrance sign for the development: OLD FARM ESTATES. Yes, they'd probably do something like that to increase the value. She imagined the type of people who would buy in the development and thought that they weren't the kind who would want to live in a place that had been slapped up in a week. They would be people who wanted to tell their guests that their house was built in the old cow patch. Perhaps they'd even keep the dilapidated pigsty.

Her stomach made a noise again. Uncle Chuck didn't notice, or pretended not to as he continued telling her about his current enterprises, which seemed to consist of a rental storage facility in the next town over.

"There's lots of value there," he finished. "We just have to lock it in."

"How long will this take?" she asked.

"Storage facilities are quick to put up but slow to fill up, that's what they say. You have to do a lot of advertising to get people to spot you. But then once you get them, it's done. No one remembers to empty the place at the end of the contract. Automatic renewal, that's where the dollars are. It's a money-spinner."

"I mean the transaction. Once I sign, how long until I get a check?"

Chuck sat back in his chair. "Not long. There's just the legalities. You could sign and we could send your check if you're in a hurry. Do you want me to send it on somewhere? I guess you've got to get back to your job. What is it you're doing these days anyhow? Did Greg say you're a dentist?"

"I'm not a dentist."

Chuck grinned. His teeth were large, like ice blocks. "No, that didn't sound right. Didn't finish high school, did you? Funny dentist that would be. I bet this payout will be handy, then. It's basically like you won the lottery without having to buy a ticket."

"Sure," she said, picking at the dry skin on her knuckle.

He shuffled some papers on his desk, then sorted them into three piles. "Just have to spend it wisely, you see. You could invest. Make your money make some money itself. That's what I told my boys. Hard work and wise investments. That's what makes a man a success." He paused and glanced at her. "You're not a drinker like your mother, are you?"

She looked at him coldly. "No."

"Guess I won't even ask you if you share your father's pursuits." He smiled again, then unlocked a drawer at his desk and took out a thick file. From it he removed a stack of papers held together with an oversized gold paper clip. "Just sign where there are yellow flags. Auntie Jeanne put those there. She's good at those little touches."

Del picked up the papers and considered the cup of pens on his desk. She could sign now and be out of town in the afternoon. Of course, he couldn't send the check to her. Where would he send it? She had neither an address nor a post office box. Maybe she could get it sent to Tym and then Tym could forward it.

There was a knock at the door. Jeanne entered the office.

"Did I hear right? Is it true? Adela, it's been too long!" Jeanne hugged her and Del hugged her back. When Del last saw Jeanne, her aunt was in a Laura Ashley phase of long print dresses and cardigans. Since then, she had put on about ten pounds and had a fuller face. Somehow she had started to look more like a Murrow, with the same pink cheeks as her husband. She wore bootcut jeans, heeled boots, and a quilted camel-colored jacket.

"Don't you look beautiful?" Jeanne said, holding Del at arm's length. "Your face is the picture of your mom. Your hair is so dark, like your dad's. Those beautiful waves—so exotic."

Jeanne reached for a lock of hair, and her fingertip glanced Del's neck. Del backed away from her.

"Adela was just wrapping up her business here," Chuck interrupted. He pulled a branded Murrow Construction pen out of the cup and slid it across the desk toward the contract.

"Oh, Chuck. You're always in a rush. Patience is a virtue."

"Of course." Chuck practiced his smile again. "Of course you're right, Jeannie."

"What do you say, Adela, do you want to catch up? I'm just running some errands, but we could do them together?"

"Sounds good." As soon as Jeanne offered an out, Del realized she couldn't wait to escape Chuck's office. It was too warm, too damp, as if they were sitting inside a mouth. She didn't want to breathe Chuck's breaths for another second.

Her uncle packed up the paperwork along with a pen and put it inside a Murrow-branded folder and then a Murrow-branded tote bag. He told her to come by the next day to drop everything off and then they could discuss the timing of the payments.

"Don't laugh," Jeanne said as they left the office and walked across the lot to her car, which was an enormous gold Mercedes SUV with a "Murrow2" license plate.

"When did you get that?" Del asked.

"Uncle Chuck got it for me last year after some business came through. He's against buying now. New car every two years when the lease is up. Chuck says it doesn't make sense otherwise; then you're just paying to fix something that's more broken every day. I'm going to the Stop and Go; is that fine?"

Del opened the door, and a small white dog leapt at her.

"That's Elmo," Jeanne said. "He's our new little puppy. Eight months old."

Del had forgotten about Jeanne's dogs. The Murrows got a new dog every other year or so. Always a new breed. They'd had a Scottie, a Shar-Pei, a Weimaraner, and a beagle when she was a child. The dogs pissed everywhere, barked madly, and were sent away to mysterious "farms" when they grew out of the puppy phase. The problem was always the type of dog, and they fixed the problem by trying out a new breed. When she was a kid, Del loved the puppies. Now, she thought, it was strange and gruesome.

Elmo sat in Del's lap as they drove. It was a fluffy type of dog with runny brown eyes.

At the donut stand just inside the entrance of the grocery store, Jeanne bought them coffees and a bag full of glazed donut holes. Two pumps of sugar-free hazelnut syrup for Jeanne. Del took hers with half-and-half and ate most of the donuts.

"The Home Depot wasn't open when you lived here, was it?"

"Nope."

"Lot of new things opening up," Jeanne continued as she lifted a megapack of paper towels into her cart. "The developments help. Lots of new people coming in who don't mind driving an hour to their jobs. A different kinda life."

"That's good. I mean, if you have to live here. It's nice to have conveniences."

Jeanne touched her arm above the elbow and squeezed. "Adela, I can't get over how much you look like your mother. I miss Louise so much."

"Thanks."

Del couldn't remember any photos of her mother as a young woman. By the time she died, she was on the scrawny side of thin, with gray-streaked sandy hair and bags under her eyes. She mostly wore oversized tracksuits that were clean on good days. Del took after her father.

"How long do you think you'll be around? Long enough to come by for dinner?"

"I'm just wrapping things up. I'll stay tonight but then I'll probably leave tomorrow or something like that." She needed to figure out the address routing for her money, and probably check in with Tym.

Jeanne frowned. "That's too bad for us. We just see so little of you. I'm sure your cousins would have liked to spend time with you, plus all your friends from school."

Del shrugged. "Places to go, people to see. It's just a quick stop."

"That's disappointing. I won't try to convince you, but I wish you'd reconsider. You could stay with us if you wanted. I could use some female energy in the house."

Del pretended to read the nutritional information on a box of cereal.

Eventually Jeanne finished her shopping, and Del picked up a few necessities. Her aunt insisted on paying for everything. The boy who was working the checkout greeted Jeanne and asked how the cream puffs had gone down at her party the previous week.

"Oh, they were just delicious, Billy," she told him. "What an absolute *treat*."

On the ride back to Del's place, they stopped at the feed and grain store, where Del bought a small sack of coal, a box of long matches, and some candles. She also bought a gumball at the machine inside the store.

"I forgot how much you liked candy," Jeanne remarked as they stood in the parking lot.

"My dad used to buy gumballs for me every time we came here." Her father had liked to garden. This was where they'd come for fertilizer for the bulbs he ordered through a mail-order catalog every year.

Jeanne nodded. Back inside the SUV, the little dog flung himself at the window. "I can't help but wonder sometimes. What it would have been like if your mom met someone else. Someone more stable."

Del looked at her feet. The tips of her sneakers were filthy with gravel dust. "My dad was very stable."

"You know what I mean."

"He was very stable. He always had a job, had friends. No one ever had to hose down his puke off the doormat."

"I didn't mean it like that. Just a thought, how things could've been better for you both. It was good seeing you, Adela. I wish you would come by more often."

"Del."

"What's that?"

Del spat out the gum, which dropped onto the gravel. "Del. No one calls me Adela anymore. It's not my name."

"I think you're doing a good thing. Leaving past things behind. We know it wasn't easy, but now it's a chance for you to do whatever you've been wanting to do. It's not like you were going to move into that old house anyhow. It's not fit for living. It'll be a relief when they knock it down. Then when you come to visit, you'll just stay with us."

"When they what?" Del asked. Her tongue tasted of artificial grape flavoring.

"When they knock it down for the development. If I were you, I'd just leave everything inside and go. Storage is expensive, and everyone abandons their things anyhow. If you didn't need it before, you don't need it now. What you deserve is a fresh start."

Another car pulled into the lot, and Jeanne went over to say hey to the woman behind the wheel. They talked about shrubbery as Jeanne's dog continued to hurl itself against the driver's-side window.

"I'm going," Del shouted over to her. "I'll walk."

"Just a minute." Jeanne waved from the car window where she was speaking to her friend. "I'll drive you."

"It's no problem. Catch you another time."

Del took her grocery bag from the car, threw the dog back in, and began her walk home. Within minutes, her arm was sore from the bag of coal. She put down the bag for a moment and then pinched her other arm, the one that wasn't holding the coal. The best way to deal with hurt was to balance it. When everything hurt, nothing did.

So they were going to knock down her house. Of course they were. Of course there would be no point in keeping it up when they assembled the kit houses they were building for commuters who would microwave their scrambled eggs and then drive for forty-five minutes to offices where they sold insurance. How stupid she had been, how naïve.

Did it even matter? It's not like she would come back to this town anyhow, once she was settled somewhere better. She would never hear from any of these people again. She'd never tell anyone where she was going, and if any of them ever managed to locate her, she would burn their letters unread.

Opening the door to the house, she dropped all the bags to the floor. The smell hit her, something that she had missed the night before when she'd been exhausted and overwhelmed by the cold and the dark. Spearmint gum, Marlboro cigarettes, cedar, and mold. It was the scent of her parents and of her childhood. It smelled like when she came home from school, from camp, from the church basement where she learned prayers every Thursday in the late afternoon.

She lay down on the couch, closed her eyes, and breathed.

Hours later, there was a knock at the door. It was Eleanor.

"Forget about our dinner?"

She was wearing a different fur coat than the day before. This coat had little heads with polished fangs.

"I don't cook," Eleanor apologized as they got in the car.

They drove out of town, Eleanor's window open as she held a cigarette out into the cold night air, and headed to a chain restaurant off the highway. They sat in a booth in an otherwise empty section. Fake vintage Coke signs were pinned to the walls.

"I like this place," Eleanor remarked. "It doesn't have airs."

Del got a chicken potpie, and Eleanor ordered a red clam chowder off the early bird discount menu. As they ate, Del told Eleanor about her meeting with her uncle and aunt, and that the house would be knocked down.

"Of course, dummy. Rich people don't like to look at poor people's houses."

Del stared at her. "What rich people are moving to town to live on a Murrow Estate?"

Eleanor dropped her spoon to the table, leaving half her soup unfinished, and pushed aside the plastic packet of fish-shaped crackers. "Same difference. Middle-class people don't like to look at shacks. What do you want me to tell you?"

"I wouldn't move back to this pig-shit town if you paid me a million bucks. Chuck has always been a total asshole for no reason."

"Who knows why Chuck does what he does? Maybe because your mom was pretty and he thought your grandparents favored her. She was a little dolly when she was a child. Skin like it was dipped in milk. Your grandmother made all her clothes, frilly dresses. Chuck worked on the farm since he was crawling."

"They gave Chuck all the land. They gave him an empire, basically."

"From his point of view, they gave your mother the house, which was the most valuable thing they had at the time. They gave him the fields: they gave him *work*. And he goes off and marries your lovely auntie and has his lovely family and builds that empire from scratch, while your mom goes and does everything wrong and lets the house fall down around her. He took what he got and he made it better; she took what she got and she let it get worse. He was embarrassed of her, honey. He's a climber, and she reminded him of what he climbed out of. Don't get me wrong, I'm as disgusted with Chuck as you are. That's the problem with families. It's the Roman Empire on a smaller scale."

"What about your family?"

"One brother. I poisoned him for the inheritance."

Del raised her eyebrows.

"He's an accountant. Retired, beach house, too many grandchildren to count. His wife sends a newsletter every Christmas. I toss it on the fire on Christmas Eve. Just my little holiday ritual. Then I send them a fruitcake that I got from somebody else. I've been married and divorced five times, darling. I abandoned the bosom of familial contentment a long time ago. As have you."

Del sighed. "I don't know what to do about Chuck. It just, it feels wrong. Letting him knock the house down. I don't know why. I don't want to live there, but I don't want to see him destroy it, either. It's hard to explain. In the house, with all their stuff. Their cigarettes and their crossword puzzles. They're there, Eleanor. And he wants to knock it down."

"Well, you've got a choice."

Del frowned. It wasn't as obvious as that. With her fork, she levered a hunk of cold crust off the side of her ceramic dish. "I don't have any money, I don't have a job, and I don't have a place to live. How much of a choice is that?"

"I don't know what to tell you, honey. But I know what your mother would say to old Chuckie Small Balls."

"What's that?"

"She'd tell him to fuck himself."

Eleanor lifted her index finger into the air and summoned the bill.

Chapter Six

DEL LEFT THE PAPERWORK FROM THE MURROWS ON THE COFFEE table overnight.

Again, she slept on the living room floor. Again, she slept with her arm draped over the duffel bag.

In the morning, she lit the coal stove, and then peeled an orange on top of the stack of documents as the room warmed up.

After that, she opened the newspaper she had bought the previous day and unfolded it over the fruit peels. There was a rumor of a new movie theater in the county. An insurance salesman called Ken had been promoted to vice president. The mayor had come out in support of the sidewalk expansion project. A controversy had erupted over renaming the local elementary school.

Orange oil soaked through the sports section. She flipped the page to the crossword puzzle. A five-letter word meaning Monday, in French. She had taken a year of French in high school. She thought back. It was on the tip of her tongue. *Le longue? Le langue.*

The first knock was quiet enough to ignore. The second one came louder.

It was probably Jehovah's Witnesses. She opened the door only a crack and peeked through. Worse than evangelists: it was her cousin Greg.

"Didn't wake you up, did I?" He had the same dopey smile on his face as always.

"No."

"My dad sent me over here. He just wanted to know if you had signed the paperwork. Guess he thought he'd save you the walk into town."

The sheepish expression on his face told her everything she needed to know. He was aware that this was a ridiculous thing to say, but he'd said it anyhow.

"No, I haven't signed." She blinked. The cold breeze nipped at her cheeks.

Greg shifted his weight. "If you just want to sign it now, I can wait. Save you the errand. It's only a few pages."

She stared at him. Greg wore a red-and-black-checked jacket, work boots, and jeans. An immaculate black backpack sat at his feet. There wasn't a speck of dirt on him. She wondered what kind of "site" he worked on. He looked like a clerk at a construction supply shop, the guy who pointed you in the direction of the two-by-fours while he barked into a walkie-talkie.

"I haven't signed yet. You should probably head off to work. There must be somewhere more important you're supposed to be."

"They just want the land, you know. If you want anything inside, you can have it. And if it's the money—he'll negotiate. He's cheap, you know he's always been cheap, but he'll do it. It just needs to be cleaned up here so they can lay out the new development in the spring. Hell, move the whole house if you want to."

"Oh, sure!" she said, her tone poisonous. "I'll just pick it up and move it. Just like that. I don't know why you're saying 'they' anyhow. You're doing it. You're knocking down the house so you can get richer. You're part of the whole scheme and you don't care. So don't pretend you're better than any of them. You're not my friend, Greg."

"It's not me." He wrapped his arms around his chest in the cold. "I've been working on the storage facility. It's Mitch and Kevin working on the new development."

Greg had dark little eyes. The eyes were the windows to the soul, which probably meant that he had a tiny brain, too. She remembered reading that cats had a brain the size of a walnut, or maybe it was a grape. That must make Greg's the size of an M&M. Her head was pounding. She could be asleep now or at least alone with her thoughts and the crossword. *Lundi.* That was it. Why was he always the one showing up, pushing her to do something? Why was he the diplomat while his brothers, Mitch and Kevin, did the actual work? Didn't he see that his family didn't respect him?

She opened the door slightly so that he couldn't miss her expression. "Oh, I get it," she said sweetly. "It's because you're the family idiot."

He stepped backward.

"They're always sending you on the errands they don't want to do while they do the actual—I don't know—*construction*? Maybe figure out why that is."

"Fine," he said, picking up the backpack and slinging it over his shoulder. "Fine, Adela. I was just trying to help."

"That's not my name anymore. We're not pals. Don't talk to me like you know me."

She closed the door.

She felt something dark and sour in the back of her throat. It might have been pity at being so cruel to someone who was so clearly pathetic, but she decided instead that it was the headache from sleeping on a wood floor. There was no Advil in her bag, so she waited ten minutes, until she was certain she wouldn't run into Greg again, then put on her shoes and started walking.

The sunlight was nauseatingly bright. Her head clanged like a tin can being struck with a spoon. She walked quickly, her face buried in a scarf, and didn't pass anyone by foot or by car. Her watch was back at home, but she thought it must be past eight in the morning.

There was a little convenience store on the edge of town, DeVito's. They sold donuts in the morning and sandwiches in the afternoon as well as the necessary items that you didn't want to drive twenty minutes to buy: cigarettes, tampons, baking powder. Sal DeVito had gone to school with Del. As she opened the door, she hoped the place had changed hands or at least that no one would recognize her.

A woman with dyed blond hair read a magazine at the counter, which was laden with a cardboard box full of powdered jelly donuts. Del dodged down an aisle.

"What can I get you?" asked the clerk.

Del furtively approached the counter, her head down in case anyone walked through the door. "Advil."

"Packet or bottle?"

"Just a packet, please." Del fumbled with her wallet.

"It's you," the woman behind the counter said evenly. "Isn't it?"

Del looked up.

Frankie. Her closest friend from school. As a teenager, Frankie's hair had been dark, nearly black. Then as now, her skin had the same eerie translucence as a baby's, with fine veining on her eyelids.

Frankie pulled a foil packet of medicine off the display behind the counter. "Well, that's the fucking surprise of the year. What brings you back? Funeral?"

Del frowned as she pulled out some quarters. "Family business."

"Of course. The famous Murrows. What are you doing now?"

Del hadn't forgotten what Frankie did, and she wouldn't pretend things were normal. The span of years didn't matter and never would. She stared at the coin purse in her wallet as she counted out the change.

"Me, I married Sal DeVito," Frankie told her without waiting for a response to her question. "We have two kids. Remember Sal?"

There were photos of small children above the register. In elementary school Sal had run card games in the playground during recess, and Mama DeVito dropped off homemade ziti every day because he refused to eat the franks and beans they served in the cafeteria.

"What is it? Six or seven years? Eight?" Frankie shook her head. "And you don't look any different at all." The way she said it didn't sound like a compliment.

Del felt a growing awareness of her ratty jeans and the jacket she'd bought from an Army-Navy store. It wasn't that different from how she dressed in high school. Shabby un-chic.

"You look older. It's probably the hair," Del said flatly. "Anyhow, I've got to be getting back. Family meeting. Good luck with everything."

"Sayonara." Frankie waved.

Del left a stack of coins on the counter and rushed out the door. At the end of the block, she plugged her remaining quarters in the pay phone and dialed.

"Yellow, yellow, yellow," the recording said. "You've got Tym and Del. Tym is out tripping the light fantastic, and Del is an adult child who is too lazy to pick up the phone."

She heard herself laughing in the background of the message.

The recording continued: "Leave a message and we'll get back to you. Or we won't, depending on how we feel about you. Adios!"

Del cleared her throat. "I'm here. Everything's fine."

The wind picked up. Her cheeks were wet. She reached in her pocket and fished out a balled-up napkin that she used to wipe her eyes. "Everything's fine, yeah. Just wrapping some things up now, then I'll be in touch when I get where I'm going. Hope everything's good there. Hi to Marcus. Hi to the pizza boy. Have you talked to Dave? Hi to him. Hi to everyone."

She and Frankie had met in elementary school and were best friends up through high school. It had all ended the night Frankie's big brother offered to drop them off at a bar where they supposedly didn't check IDs. Frankie's brother was always stirring shit up, and it was an oddly nice thing for him to do, but given the tragic and limitless ennui of being a sixteen-year-old girl in a shitty little farm town, they didn't question it.

It was a forty-five-minute drive outside town, and they had planned the operation for weeks. Frankie's brother, Frank Junior, was going to meet a girl at a party and would drop them off on his way. He'd pick them up three hours later. If they didn't get in, tough shit—they'd have to sit in the parking lot and wait. Or walk home in the dark and get raped and murdered, their choice.

At school that day, Adela and Frankie planned their cosmopolitan personas. Frankie would be Brooke. She wanted a name that wasn't Frank based. Brooke was a twenty-six-year-old lawyer who lived in a high-rise with her boyfriend but had a Colombian lover on the side. She ordered delivery sushi every night. When it was very fresh, it didn't taste at all like fish.

Adela decided to go by Del. The name made her seem more sophisticated somehow, more difficult to place. Del was twenty-two, worked in advertising, wore blazers, and was only in this shitty part of the state because she was on her way to somewhere better, but Brooke made them stop for a drink. Brooke was a slut with poor impulse control; they got along because of their shared interests in horse racing and French cinema.

Frank Junior pulled into the lot and glanced at the girls in the rearview mirror. "Meet here at midnight. You get booted, that's not my problem. Call Mom, and the next ride I give you is to your funeral."

After Frank Junior's car sped out of the lot, chucking gravel at them, they stood under a light near the entrance.

"You look good," Frankie said to Adela.

Adela was wearing lipstick, which she never did normally, but it seemed like something Del would do. Del would have bought it someplace classy, like a department store, and put it on her charge account. Adela had stolen it from Dollar Drug.

"You, too, *Brooke*."

The bar was just off the highway, a single-story log building. No one had parked in front, but the dimly lit lot to the side had several cars. There was nothing else around, just trees and the hum of trucks on the freeway.

Frankie opened the door. Inside, there was more wood paneling, a number of neon beer signs, and an old man wiping the bar with a dirty cloth. They sat in a dark corner under a tattered rainbow flag.

"Is this what bars are like?" Frankie whispered. She liked to play at being a sophisticate, but in reality, her parents kept her and her brother under constant surveillance. Frankie wasn't allowed to go to Adela's house. They never discussed this rule.

Perhaps because of this air of familial degeneracy, Frankie assumed Adela knew more of the world than she did.

"This is quiet," Adela offered sagely. "It'll pick up later."

Two men in plaid shirts walked through the front door, nodded to the bartender, and continued through a beaded curtain that led to a back room.

"Should we go back there?" Frankie whispered. "Looks like that's where the people are."

"Let's just stay here." Who knew what was going on in

back? If they went, they'd be identified as impostors. It was a long walk home.

They spent two and a half hours sipping beers very slowly so they didn't encounter the bartender too frequently. After the alcohol hit, Frankie got chatty with the bartender. She returned with two cocktails that tasted like orange juice laced with battery acid.

"C'mon, Adela," Frankie begged, pulling her hand. "We can't go into school tomorrow and say that we sat by ourselves the whole time. This is our adventure!"

A whiff of tobacco drifted up from the back. Blue light filtered through the amber beaded curtain as someone tapped a microphone in the back room.

"Hello?" a man mumbled. "Hello, hello?"

"Forget you. I'm going." Frankie picked up her drink and walked through the curtain. Adela followed.

The back room was surprisingly large and dark, with a small stage. A spinning orb on the ceiling shot specks of multicolored light across the room. A dozen or so men sat around the stage in small groups, with a few loners drinking beer by themselves.

On a television screen, words appeared and an animated purple ball bounced from one to the next.

"Kind of a dump," Frankie remarked.

The man on the dark stage was thin, with pressed blue jeans, a checked shirt, and a too-large cowboy hat tipped over his face. His singing was quiet and unsure, but gained confidence as the song continued. Eventually he lifted his gaze and stared directly at a man who sat in the front row wearing an identical style of outfit. Why were all these guys dressed like cowboys? Was it a convention? What was this place?

> *Like a river flows, surely to the sea*
> *Darling, so it goes . . .*

Frankie choked down a laugh. "Oh my god. Is it? That's— that's your dad!"

Adela swung around and ran out of the room, through the bar, and outside. The air was choking.

Frank Junior was waiting with the engine off. When they got in the car, he looked at them with a teasing smile. "How'd you like it?"

Adela stared out the window.

Frankie punched her brother in the arm. "You asshole. You knew it was a bar for fags. I'm gonna get you for this."

Frankie fell asleep with her face against the car window, leaving a smear of makeup and mouth slime by the time they pulled into Adela's driveway.

Adela's mother was up watching *Night Court* and drinking a vodka tonic.

"Your dad's working late."

She hadn't asked Adela where she was going, so there was no need to lie. Adela threw up, washed her face, and then went to bed.

At school the next day, everyone knew what had happened. Frankie had spilled the beans.

Chapter Seven

DEL DIDN'T REALIZE UNTIL SHE WAS HALFWAY TO HER DESTINA-
tion that she'd left the packet of Advil on the counter at DeVito's.
Fuck it. She wasn't going back. The freezing air and adrenaline
had wiped away the tension in her head and replaced it with
something else. She walked quickly and with purpose until her
calf muscles felt like overstretched rubber bands.

She passed the large burial ground at the Italian church.
Most Catholics went there in the end, but when her parents
died she couldn't imagine either of them at St. Sebby's. After
her mother's death, she had called her father to ask if her
mother had ever said what she wanted. Del was seventeen and
had never planned a funeral. Her mother hadn't left a will or
ever discussed her opinions on eternal rest. Her father didn't
call her back, so Del did what she thought was right.

The smaller cemetery, the one for the Jews, atheists, and
Congregationalists, was just outside town, alongside an abandoned granite quarry. Del lifted the chain over the white gate
and let herself in. The graveyard was tall and narrow, with a

driving loop shaped like a sewing needle. Within the needle's eye was the oldest section of headstones, the settlers. There were no cars or people or sounds except for her feet crunching over the stiff frosted grass. By the caretaker's shed she found the tap, a bucket, and an old rag.

They had put up the marker after she'd left town, so she had never seen it. It wasn't hard to find. After the death, her mother's bank account was locked down and Del had only a handful of twenties from her job at the jewelry store, so she got the free headstone that was provided by the military when the dead person had been a soldier or a military spouse. Threading through the crumbling brownstone tablets with photos of dead babies and the fat granite markers that listed extended families, she spotted the small white lozenge that rose from the ground like a tongue. Her mother's name and dates were carved into the front.

After her father died, she thought of getting his name carved into the back. Although they had never discussed it—had never considered before his heart attack that he, too, would die one day, and perhaps earlier than he wanted to—she knew that he wouldn't want to return to that town, linked forever with her mother and those people, even if it was in name alone. He had loved war documentaries, country-western music, cheap noodles, cheap beer, and the sea. A car trip to a Southern battlefield did not appeal, so after his death, she, Tym, Dave, and Bruce the Moose took the ferry, and after they'd each smoked a cigarette from his last pack and clinked bottles of Bud Light, they opened the canister of cremains and let the ash and bone fall into the ocean.

Her fingers traced the mossy letters of her mother's name. She had been forty-two when she died. Del soaked the rag in the bucket of warm water and began to scour the top of the stone. Green lines of moss flaked away easily, but the rust-colored stains remained regardless of how hard she scrubbed.

She wondered what their relationship would have been like if her mother's car hadn't smashed into the tree. Maybe they would have been friends by now. She exhaled, and a puff of air appeared and evaporated in front of her. Probably not. But maybe they would have seen each other at Christmas or something. Her mother would burn the roast beef, they'd both drink too much, and at some point after the bottle of amaretto came out, her mother would lean across the table, her eyes narrow, her breath hot with almonds, and mumble, "The thing about you is . . ."

Something caught in Del's throat. She could walk to the bus station now and leave it all behind. Or even get the check from her uncle and then burn it. Never see or hear of a Murrow again. She could change her name, disappear, and send Tym an occasional postcard so that he'd think she was working as a waitress in Utah, was married to a guy called Nolan, and had four kids.

She slumped and sat on the frozen grass above her mother's body. It was no good pretending. Despite the space that she had built between her parents, despite the chip of bone from her father's body that had fallen by her feet on the ferry and that she'd gently picked up, held in her palm for a moment, and then hurled into the ocean, she knew that both of them were there with her in that town, inside the house, and that was where they'd always be.

They were in the stale tobacco smell, in the broken oven where her father had made London broil on Sunday nights, in the bathroom where her mother had taped the newspaper crossword to the door at a height visible from the toilet. They were in the stacks of her father's library books, which he could never be bothered to return. The Murrows wanted to take the land, but they would be taking all the rest of it, too. The crayon lines of the height chart in the kitchen, the jigsaw puzzle cabinet, the chink in the bricks where her father had hidden ceramic animals that came with boxes of tea so that she could find them. What they destroyed wouldn't mean anything to the Murrows, but they would think that they had won and that her family had lost. Her mother would hate that.

She stood and picked up the bucket. She placed her other hand on the cap of the damp headstone and said goodbye.

She walked slowly back toward town. The back of her coat had a damp patch where she'd sat on the grass. Cars whizzed past, but she didn't pay attention. In her mind, she was sorting piles of money and working out her plan.

She opened the heavy front door and closed it behind her. The entryway was silent except for the ticking of a clock. Two p.m. The thick carpet hushed her steps as she approached the next door and opened it.

Her uncle was sitting behind his desk, reading a newspaper. He looked up.

"I'm here to talk about the sale," she told him, her gaze steady. "But I have some conditions."

November

Chapter Eight

HE SAID HE WOULD CONSIDER HER COUNTEROFFER AND THAT IT might take him a number of days. Seven, he estimated, at least. He'd need to speak to his lawyer, and then that lawyer might need to speak to another lawyer. These sorts of things were complicated, he told her. And her suggestion was very atypical, like nothing anyone reasonable would have considered. Not being in the business, she wouldn't understand. Complications took time, and time was money, but money was also money, and he had to consider that, too.

But when she heard the knock on the door of her house that night, she knew it had been decided already. Yes or no, she thought, turning the knob. No or yes.

Of course it was Greg.

He didn't attempt any small talk. She invited him inside, and they sat in the living room. She took the couch and gave him the three-legged milking stool on the other side of the coffee table. He was too big for it, and his belly slopped over his thighs.

"This is what you agreed to," he said, laying out the documents in small piles on the ground.

She would be paid slightly less than her uncle's initial offer. In exchange, she would keep the house. None of the land was hers, though, so she would need to move any physical objects belonging to her. That included the house itself as well as the contents. She had also negotiated to transfer to her ownership a small patch of land on the other side of the pond, where it was too swampy to ever develop the next extension of Murrow Estates. Her uncle didn't seem to care about this at all, but she thought with delight on the fact that the new residents of this Murrow Estate would look down their sloping backyards to a small pond and, on the other side of that pond, a huge pile of her junk. As she scanned the page detailing the transfer of the quarter acre of land to her, she could still imagine the smirk on her uncle's face. Silly, he would have thought. Sentimental. Pathetic.

Probably he didn't think she could do it.

She could keep the dismantled parts and contents of the house on her new land, but there was a substantial caveat. The timeline was agreed upon and unchanging. Construction on the new development started in March, and whatever she left on the site would be demolished and removed on March first, when the bulldozers moved in to level the land. She would be paid then and not before.

Greg and Del didn't speak as she began to initial and sign the pages that were flagged with yellow stickers. She reached the final signature and held her pen above it, thinking.

Greg spoke quickly, the words chasing each other like fizz

spilling down a soda can. "I think this is a crazy idea. Crazy. Dumb. You didn't think it through. How are you going to do it? I've seen someone move a house, once. They lifted it off the foundations and put it on a flatbed. There must have been twenty guys there who knew what they were doing. They did it because the house was worth something. And there isn't even a road to the land you got. How're you going to move anything there? Do you even own a hammer? You're Jack and the fucking Beanstalk. You traded for a handful of beans and you think you're some genius."

She frowned, then returned to the document. She signed, in red ink, with a flourish.

"Don't worry about me," she said. "I'll get done what I've got to do."

"You're wasting your time. In March they're gonna come here with a bulldozer and knock everything down. You think they're laughing at you now? Wait till you see my dad with a backhoe knocking your house down."

The candle on the coffee table flickered.

He pointed to the potbelly stove. "How are you even going to stay here through the winter? With *that*? You're crazy. And why? Just so you can come back and look at a pile of your old trash?"

Compared to the day she arrived, Del thought it was fairly toasty with the coal fire going. She spoke to him without any heat in her words. "This isn't about my trash. It's yours. I'm just showing it to you. This is going to happen. You don't need to worry about how unless you intend to help me, which you don't. This is the end of your involvement. You can show up in

March and laugh at me, too, if you want. Bring the canapés. I'll have the Cold Duck."

Greg put a slice of grape-flavored gum in his mouth and stared at her, shaking his head. "Fine. Don't say I didn't warn you. You know jack shit about houses or construction. Or deconstruction. That's what this is. I'm not gonna be surprised if we find you dead under a pile of bricks. Write your will now."

She gathered the papers and straightened them into a neat stack. "The house has a timber frame, not brick. I'd expect you to know that, with your construction expertise. You know, Greg, you're probably my favorite cousin. I know that's not saying a lot because the other two are complete chucklefucks, but I don't actually think you're a bad guy. You're just a stooge who gets used and you never tell them to fuck off, so they treat you like shit again and again and you just take it, like you're too mentally incapacitated to understand what's going on. I guess I can feel a little sympathy for you, but honestly it isn't very much."

Greg flinched, and she continued, "Let me be totally clear: when March comes, there's not going to be a piece of wood or nail that belongs to me here. They are not going to take or destroy a single part of my parents' house. And I don't care if I have to carry it on my back to get it out of here. So don't get in my way, and don't tell me what I can't do. There are two options: you can help or you can disappear. You may be stuck listening to their bullshit for the rest of your life so that you can collect a check, but not me, amigo. I'm free. Which you'll never be."

He chomped on his gum, seized the stack of papers, and

shoved them into a folder. After she heard his truck crawl over the gravel driveway, she threw more coal in the fire and wrapped herself in a blanket while she did a crossword.

She woke in the morning with the blanket still around her, her head tilted backward, and a line of mucus across her cheek. There was a grinding noise along the side of the house. Greg's truck was in the driveway with an empty trailer behind it. She lifted the blind to look in the backyard, preparing herself for whatever the Murrows had asked him to do. Maybe they would carve their name in the dead grass, to remind her every day that the land was theirs. She didn't care. It meant nothing.

Greg was driving a backhoe along the curve of the pond. He took the long way, avoiding the small wooden bridge her dad had built over the creek that fed the pond. He arrived at the quarter acre of land that now belonged to her according to the terms of the contract. The pond was small, only fifteen strokes across, so Del had a close view as Greg's backhoe gnawed chunks of earth and dropped them, tearing out skunk cabbage, hemlock, and black ash.

She pulled the milking stool to the window and sat down, watching him clear the land. She didn't know why he was helping her, or even if he was. Could this be some kind of plot? A double cross? He finished after an hour. The land was lumpy and raw but free of trees and brush. The backhoe had made a path from her house to the cleared site.

Greg ticked the backhoe along the same path he had entered, beside the pond, along the side of the house, and then up into the trailer. When she saw him get into the driver's seat, she opened the front door of the house.

"Don't tell them it was me," he said, his cheeks pink from the cold.

She saluted him with two fingers, and he shifted the truck into reverse.

After he disappeared, she put on her coat and shoes. It was time to move.

Chapter Nine

DEL TRACKED OVER THE BACKHOE'S PATH TO VIEW THE CLEARED site. Her canvas sneakers pulled moisture from the frozen grass and turned a darker shade of gray. The earth around the pond's rim was crusted with ice, but where Greg had upturned the topsoil her feet sank into the dirt. Circling the perimeter of the site, over torn leaves and snapped tree branches, she saw that it was larger than expected. Not large enough for the house as it was, but she wouldn't be moving it whole, as Greg had pointed out. It would need to be in piles or something.

She studied the building from the water's edge. The pond was dark and still with a patchy, thin layer of ice. It would take a few more weeks for it to freeze completely. From behind, the house resembled a dollhouse made out of a cardboard box by a child. Four four-panel windows and a door. Now even in its simplicity, it looked complex. Where to begin? Pick a side of the house and attack? Was there a strategic way of doing it? She assessed the structure as if looking at it for the first time, now a project instead of a home to which she had a key. Her feet were cold and wet. Above her, branches clattered in the wind.

Different shoes. She had a pair of boots in her bag—she'd need those. Tools. Her father had been a mechanic, so she could probably find most of what she wanted in the shed. Tarps to lay on the ground. A raincoat. Coffee.

The last she needed before the others. The house had no electricity and no way to boil water. It was probably something she could solve quickly with a phone call, but she didn't have a phone. She supposed she could call from a pay phone, except she didn't have quarters and the nearest phone was outside De-Vito's. The whole operation seemed unnecessarily difficult, so instead she'd do it the easiest way, which she'd done before, for the five weeks she had stayed in her dad's apartment after he died and the utilities shut off one by one. She would camp.

Back in the house, she changed her shoes and found the candy cane wool scarf Tym's mom had made her before she died a few years earlier. Every year Del had received a home-made gift in the mail along with a Polish Christmas card with a nativity scene. There were matching gloves somewhere, but she'd dig them out later.

With the scarf wound around her neck, she pocketed her wallet and started walking toward town. First, coffee, then a visit to the feed and grain store. They'd have all the equipment she needed to be self-sufficient. With a camping stove and some gas canisters for cooking as well as her coal stove for warmth, she wouldn't need gas or electricity. She'd get some battery-operated lanterns. Water came from a well in the yard. So long as she had groceries and coal, she could go for weeks without seeing anyone. The idea filled her with a sense of satisfaction, and she walked quickly. The Murrows didn't know who they were dealing with, but they'd find out soon enough.

By the time she arrived at Jack's Lunch, her nose was streaming. She pulled a napkin from a silver dispenser on the counter, wiped her face until it was red, and took a seat. No one was at the diner, but it didn't matter anymore if anyone saw her. Once she finished her errands, she would vanish except for an occasional grocery store run, which she could do at night or at dawn when the other creeps were buying peanut butter, ice cream, and a suspicious amount of sinus medicine. Her family would hear from her in the spring when she was done.

"Coffee?" It was the same waitress as last time.

"Yes." Del's stomach rumbled. "Scrambled eggs and toast, please."

"White, wheat, or rye?"

"Rye."

Minutes later, a plate rattled against the aluminum-topped food service area. The waitress slid it in front of Del, then returned to her position near the coffee maker, where she leaned against the wall and stared out the window.

Sliding her thumbnail under the tab of a single-serve grape jelly, Del thought about her next moves. She wouldn't be paid until March, and her savings would stretch only if she was very careful. She couldn't eat out, for one. She glanced up at the waitress, who was humming to herself as she observed a car maneuvering awkwardly into a parking spot. Del quietly removed six jelly packets from the caddy and pocketed them.

"Could've asked," said the waitress, who was still looking out the window.

"Sorry?"

"You could have asked. I don't give a shit if you steal. I don't own the place. But if you steal right in front of me, you're treating me like an asshole."

"Oh. Well, I'm sorry." Del sheepishly retrieved the packets from her pocket and put them back on the counter. She didn't know if she should put them back.

"Keep them," the waitress said as if hearing her thoughts. "Like I said, I don't give a shit. Just don't act like you're getting away with something."

Del left the packets on the counter and felt her face flush with embarrassment. They were mixed fruit, she noted. The foil showed a cornucopia of fruits. The label listed apple, grape, corn syrup, and preservative as the only ingredients.

"Why are you here?" the waitress asked. "You've been here twice now, so you're not driving through town. Visiting someone?"

"No."

"Then you've moved here?"

"No."

Finally the waitress's trance was broken, and she looked away from the window. "Then what? I'm starting to feel like I'm on $25,000 Pyramid."

"Just staying. Temporarily."

"Weird place to stay. Nothing going on here."

"It's temporary," she said curtly.

"Huh." The waitress came closer and clicked her sparkly

nails on the countertop. "So you grew up here. Or you've got family here. Or both."

Her toast was cut straight up and down. She hated it that way. It seemed lazy, somehow lazier than cutting it on the diagonal, which took no more time but required a sense of aesthetics. Even for a diner, the quality wasn't acceptable. Most places cut on the diagonal so it was nicer than the pulpy sandwiches you remembered from school lunchtime, when the jelly would have swamped through the Wonder Bread, leaving a grayish-purple bruise in the center, the stench of damp bread flooding the room as paper bags crinkled open in the cafeteria. She pushed the plate away.

Nails on the counter. *Click click click.* "Where did you go when you weren't here? Big-city gal now? Why didn't you stay?"

It was like being psychoanalyzed by a child.

"None of your business."

Because people got stuck in places like this. Because some people were meant to leave. Because she had seen a documentary about a colony of ants that were caught up in a paste laid by a spider. They walked right to their doom: marriages, mortgages, retirement homes full of old people who stank of rotten fruit and medicine, their skin brittle as old paper, pulp just below the surface. Even in the best-case scenario, she would have been on the first bus out of town.

"Freedom," Del added, not catching the waitress's eye.

The waitress snorted, glancing at Del's mussed hair. "Funny kind of freedom."

Del stood and snatched her coat from the next stool. "I want the check."

The waitress tapped the register and produced a printout. The coffee wasn't on the bill. Del started to correct her.

"I told you I don't care. Take the jelly. There's never anyone interesting to talk to. The fogies just want to tell me about their colitis. Sorry I'm such a busybody. My rheumatism's kicking in today, it's probably that." She stretched out her left leg and rotated from the ankle three times.

Del unzipped her wallet and found no bills. The previous day she had taken a few twenties out and put them in a book in the house so that she could keep an eye on her spending. She had forgotten to put one back in her wallet this morning. The waitress studied her as she unsnapped the coin purse and picked at a mix of dimes and nickels.

"Forget it. Pay next time."

Del was furious with herself. "I'll—I'll go home and get the money. I can be back in an hour."

"I mean it. Don't bother. You can walk there and back six times if you want, but it's nothing to me. Pay next time."

Del stuffed the jelly packets into her coat pocket and made for the exit. Just as she pressed her hand on the door, she saw Frankie walk by outside. Frankie's eyes were on her feet; she was walking carefully over patches of ice on the sidewalk and holding a little boy's hand. Del stopped, her hand on the brass panel of the door, and waited until Frankie disappeared. Behind her she heard the hum of the dishwasher while the waitress stacked ceramic coffee cups. One, two, three, one, two, three. Another deep breath and she pushed, glanced down the side-walk, then turned toward home.

Chapter Ten

AFTER RETRIEVING SOME CASH, SHE BOUGHT SOME THINGS SHE needed from the feed and grain store, including a camp stove, gas canisters, and a bag of coal. Back at home, she read a paperback copy of *Hollywood Babylon*, which had belonged to her mother, slept on the couch for a few hours, and then when her hunger became too much to ignore but it felt late enough for the school and commuter crowd to have dissipated, she wrapped up in a coat and scarf once again, found her matching gloves, got her canvas high school backpack, and began the trek to the Stop and Go.

The supermarket was on the other side of town, but rather than take Main Street, she took backstreets that were familiar from childhood. There was the church where she'd gone to nursery school and the place where her junior high boyfriend of eight days had lived. His parents had insisted they stay on the back porch or by the pool, where they could be observed. She could see the aboveground pool, a winter cover over the top. She wondered if Nick still lived there, if he was a townie with a beer gut and a Blockbuster card, or whether he was one of the people who had gone off to college and then kept heading farther away, like arrows that once released would never return. She remembered Nick as a mama's boy, glancing at the sliding doors to the kitchen to wave at his parents before he dived into the pool. He was probably masturbating in a basement not far from here while his parents watched the news upstairs.

Some of the streets still had old farmhouses from the 1800s or prim Victorians on big tracts of land, the lawns rolling long and green behind them like unspooled carpets. Faux lanterns glowed in paneled windows. Some families had already placed wreaths on their doors. It was only early November. Probably they needed to leap from holiday to holiday because waiting to die in a town like this was so incredibly dull.

She tracked through one of the older streets and arrived at what had been a field when she still lived there. It was a Murrow Estate now. She assumed she could walk through and get to a street on the other side that would take her northeast, a straight shot to the grocery store. Instead she kept finding herself in a cul-de-sac, turning back on herself, trying another street, and finding another dead end. When did streets stop going anywhere? Wasn't that the entire point of a street: to go somewhere?

The houses were all the same, Neocolonials, two floors, five windows, in complementary shades, with a thin strip of land dividing them, close enough so that a person standing in the middle could touch both houses. She tried a street that she thought would lead back to her point of origin but found herself in another cul-de-sac. Frustrated, she stood under a lamp, bathed in blue-white light, and dug her hands into her pockets. It was fucking freezing. *Freezing her tits off,* she would have said to Tym, and Tym would have made a joke about there being not much to freeze.

What was Tym doing right now? Drugs, almost certainly. He would be off work, probably at the apartment smoking and watching old movies or listening to one of his five billion records, most of which he kept in the forbidden storage lockers beneath the building. Marcus might be cooking in the kitchen. Marcus was on the Atkins diet so there would be the smell of fish or broiled meat. She had no sense of what day it was. November, definitely. Wednesday or Thursday probably. Around nine p.m., maybe. A cough rattled in her throat. She spat on the sidewalk and inspected the mucus, which was thick and yellow. Shit. Not bronchitis again. There was no money for a doctor's appointment.

Windows flickered with light from TVs. Outside there was no noise except for the buzz of the streetlights. She studied the identical houses, picked the two that were dark, and quickly slipped between them. On her left, the lawn hadn't been seeded. She guessed that no one had moved in yet. On the right the owners had built a fence around the backyard. The light through the fence slats glowed an eerie green. She heard a splash and stopped.

"Polo," a woman's voice said. A man laughed. A hot tub rumbled alive and masked the rest of their conversation.

Who were these people? What kind of person would want to live here? She stepped gently toward the fence and peered through a gap in the slats. Clouds of steam rose from the tub. A woman with dark blond hair, damp and piled on her head. A blue bikini. The man with his back to Del splashed again, and the woman smiled as the water trickled down her face, but Del saw a flash of annoyance, recognized a brittle power shift between them. The woman opened her arms like wings and rested them on the edge of the tub. The man glided over to her, keeping his chest level with the water, and tilted his head to kiss the woman's neck. Even in the poor light, even after years of absence, she recognized him immediately. Sal DeVito. Frankie's husband. Del let out a laugh, then clapped her hand over her mouth.

The blonde peered at the fence. "Did you hear that?"

Del grabbed her backpack and ran into the dark behind the houses. Just after the property line, her feet sank into soft earth that had been overturned into little piles. Groundhogs? No, just the edge of the development. In the light cast off from the houses, she was just able to make out a mountain of dirt to her left. She turned north toward the occasional blink of head-lights. At the edge of the road, she climbed over a berm and stepped onto the asphalt. It was Route 3. Behind her, she now recognized, was the old McKintrick farm, now scraped clean in preparation for construction. Her mother used to take her there to visit the McKintricks, who had goats and cows and had been friends with her grandparents. Through the trees on the other side of the road she could see the vast, brightly lit parking lot of the Stop and Go. Sal DeVito fucking around on Frankie. She laughed until tears came to her eyes. Headlights appeared far down the lane. Del ran across the road and continued laughing, a high-pitched hysterical sound unfamiliar to her, until the supermarket's doors wheezed open for her.

· · ·

The supermarket was, as she had hoped, mostly empty except for employees. She nodded at the guy working the checkout as she entered. His drowsy lids barely registered her, but she recognized the same kid who was working the day shift when she was shopping with Jeanne.

Sal DeVito. What she wouldn't give to see the look on Frankie's face when she found out. The thrill of it all gave an electric quality to the evening.

Del clutched a red basket and drifted into the produce section, where puffs of mist landed on a pile of green and yellow peppers. She was cold to the bone, even with her scarf and gloves still on. Nothing about salad appealed to her.

She added to her basket bags of premixed oatmeal, white rice, and beans. She wanted a treat. Something for bad days, when everything hurt. In the cereal aisle, two boys were goofing off in front of the Froot Loops. College age, she thought, maybe on break from school. The shorter one wore long cotton shorts, a T-shirt, and a denim jacket. Boys never had an accurate sense of weather. You couldn't trust them with a thermostat. The taller one bent down and gently nuzzled the underdressed boy's neck. They were in a world that excluded her, the checkout clerk, the piped-in Michael Bolton ballad, and the employee pushing dirty water with a mop at the end of the aisle, where there was an empty, green-tinged lobster tank. She stood behind them, uncomfortably close, and felt for the first time in a long time that she was all alone and would rather not be. She breathed the air that they had exhaled. It smelled of cinnamon gum.

The shorter boy turned toward her. His face was speckled with acne.

"Excuse me?" he said pointedly.

"Sorry."

Darting forward, she pulled a box of Fruit Roll-Ups from the shelf, not bothering to look at the flavor. They were all the same anyhow. Cornucopia of fruit-flavored.

The checkout clerk was texting on a black flip phone as Del lined up her purchases.

"How's it going?" Del asked.

The clerk looked up, slightly dazed, and shrugged his shoulders. She knew his type. Stoner. A high school dropout, probably.

"Tired," he said. "Working doubles. You?"

"Same."

She scanned the items and let them drift to the bottom of the lane. Del paid cash, asked for some quarters, and then loaded her backpack.

Outside the store, there was an old pay phone under a floodlight in the nearly empty parking lot. She fed coins into the box and dialed.

"Hiiiiiii," the recorded voice said. "It's Tym."

"And Marcus!" a second voice said.

"And we're not sorry to have missed your call. Leave a message."

The phone beeped. She hung up and walked home in the dark.

Chapter Eleven

DEL HAD WORK BUT NO JOB. A TIMELINE BUT NO BOSS. NO PAY-check, but a payout at the end of her project. Given all this, and that her eventual move would most likely lead to another temp job in another office with frosted glass and a minifridge, she made an executive decision to operate with no regard to time.

There were only three clocks in the house: one alarm clock in each bedroom and a small antique clock that sat on the mantel in the living room. In addition, she had a semifunctioning Keith Haring Swatch that Tym had given her as a birthday present two years earlier. Time pressed in on her, and her deadline of March first felt too close.

The first day of the move, she woke late. Her watch showed that it was just past eleven a.m. She crossed out the day on the pocket calendar they'd given her free with purchase at the feed store, then fixed oatmeal on the camp stove. She sprinkled salt on top and ate it out of the pot with a wooden spoon before burying her Swatch in the deepest part of her dad's army bag and then putting on her coat and gloves.

Outside the air was chilled and growing colder. The sky was the color of a tarnished spoon, a fogged gray that looked like it could be scraped off with a fingernail. She piled tarps into her arms and carried them over to her land on the other side of the pond. Laid end to end, the blue tarps covered nearly the entire site. She pinned the corners with rocks, but despite this the tarps lifted in the wind, making a heavy rumble that reminded her of being at sea on a long journey, although she had never been at sea on a long journey. The sense of nostalgia pulled at her, and she wondered if it reminded her of a movie about the sea, or a dream in which she was at sea. She stepped on a corner and weighed it down with a larger rock. *Now, Voyager? The Poseidon Adventure?* No. *Jaws,* maybe. Did *Jaws* have any sailboats? Yes, the scene with the kids. Another corner lifted and cracked. She couldn't think of another ocean movie. Ants crawled across the tarp, storm-tossed by the wind. She moved aside so they could get where they were going. Returning to the house, she pulled the alarm clocks out of the wall sockets, then ferried them, cords dangling, to the tarp along with the wooden mantel clock. She dumped all the clocks in the furthest corner. Goodbye, time. She would work from when she woke up until there wasn't any light. She looked up. The Pleiades appeared faintly in the sky. Afternoon already? She had taken too long to get ready. She'd need to get a move on tomorrow.

She carried from the living room a pile of afghans, boxes of jigsaw puzzles, and a green music box filled with plastic jewelry. With the lid open, a ballerina in pale-blue tulle spun slowly as the box tinkled out the tune of the sugar plum fairy song from *The Nutcracker*. She closed the lid and placed the box under an afghan.

Would Tym call her? No, he couldn't. She didn't have a phone. She couldn't afford to set up service for the one in the house. If she got a cell phone, she was certain that other people would get the number, too, and then there would be something else she needed to avoid. She wanted to go through life completely unnoticed, below level, submarine. If she kept calling him, eventually Tym would pick up and tell her all the gossip. Some of Marcus's clients at the gym were minor local celebrities, like the married news anchor who offered to give the trainers blow jobs in the bathroom. Maybe Tym quit the photo-processing desk, or their landlords, the Verdiccis, were finally revealed to be a Russian crime syndicate, as they had long suspected. Had their friend Maury died? What was Tym watching on TV? She had missed his Halloween favorites, the old VHS copies of *Black Narcissus* and *The Innocents* that would one day be chewed up in the machine and need to be stolen from somewhere else. Tym called the tape of *The Innocents* his "Little Darling" and only allowed it to be played once a year, on Halloween itself, when he had, on occasion, dressed up as Deborah Kerr in a nun's habit as tribute to her role in *Black Narcissus*.

Back at the house, her childhood bedroom maintained its strange, airless quality. She sat on the bed and bounced for a minute, watching the top of her head appear and disappear in the mirror on top of the bureau. Then she pulled out the flat storage containers from under the bed. One of the containers let off the smell of mold as she began to unseal it. Inside she found a set of My Little Ponys blooming with gray spots on their soft plastic bodies.

What kind of girl had she been? There were the sporty girls, the pretty ones, the popular ones, the girls who liked horses. Girls who read, girls who danced, girls who never left the sides of their mothers, girls who went to church every weekend and sang in the choir, girls who hiked and knew every bird and rock. Girls who were good at crafts, girls who were terrible at school. The math girls, the social studies girls, the piano girls. Girls who knew how to braid hair, play cat's cradle, limbo, smile. Del was not any of those girls. She stroked a blue pony's mane and then snapped the container closed.

The other container had some of her clothes from high school. She sorted through the folded tops, found an orange puffer vest, a thermal shirt, and some socks that she set aside, and then shoved the rest of the clothes back into the container. She carried each container across the pond.

Over the course of the afternoon, she moved most of her belongings from the room, taking the shortest path to her new land, which involved walking over the small wooden bridge her father had built over the creek. At first, she carefully reviewed each object before she threw it in the pile to be moved, but eventually she grew bored and irritable. There was simply too much to do. By the time she got to her chest of drawers, she was just dumping things on the ground. The bed she clawed apart with the back of a hammer and then hauled the wooden frame, piece by piece, onto the tarp. At twilight she dragged the single mattress, printed with pink flowers, toward her land.

Every twenty steps, she stopped to rest. The base of the mattress was soaked through with mud and dirt. She didn't care. It was hers and it was going. When her arms ached and her throat became sore from wheezing in the cold air, she repeated a word under her breath. *Mine mine mine.* She imagined Chuck's big red face when he arrived in March, ready for his triumph, and found the land bare. It was enough to bring a smile to her face.

When she reached the tarp, she pulled the mattress up on its side and then let it fall with a thud. Her knees sore, her hands raw with cold and splinters, she crawled on top of it and stared at the sky. Her breath formed an atmosphere above her.

The Pleiades were sharp and bright through the thin clouds. For her eighth birthday, her father had bought a used telescope kit and showed her the stars. He was into that sort of thing: little kits and projects, wooden boats, battlefield re-creations with tiny hand-painted tin men. He had a skittish energy and was always trying to learn how things worked or what they meant. She used the telescope a few times, then never again, so he donated it to the Goodwill. The Big Dipper, Venus, and the Pleiades were all that she could still identify. For a brief period he had been interested in mythology: his books from the mail subscription service were still on a shelf in the living room. All she remembered of the Pleiades was that they were sisters, turned into stars to escape someone who was chasing them. She could see her father's finger, stained with motor oil, pointing to a page in one of his books. Then as now, she couldn't muster any enthusiasm for it. The basic story seemed to be that families were messy, which she did not need to learn. She preferred her grandmother's books about saints, whose lives were eccentric, brief, bloody, and much more interesting than anything she ever read at school.

She crossed her arms over her chest and hugged herself against the cold. She was doing it, despite what they'd said. It was not only possible, it was happening. Tomorrow she'd do the box spring and finish the rest of the room. Then she'd start on the living room, followed by the kitchen and the bathroom. Finally her parents' bedroom. A single snowflake drifted down from the sky and fell to rest on her cheek. She removed her glove and touched the spot where it melted against her skin.

Chapter Twelve

SHE LEFT THE CURTAINS DRAWN ON THE BACK WINDOW IN THE hope that when the sun rose it would wake her. When her eyes fluttered open, it was bright and still. She decided it was probably midmorning.

After brushing her teeth, she pissed, then as she lifted her shirt over her head to change her clothes, she caught a whiff of herself. The tap on the bath rattled when she turned it on and spat rust-colored water into the tub. She opened the drain, waited, and tried again. There remained a pinkish hue to the water, which was cold and ran out quickly. The tank must be empty. She boiled a pot on her camp stove, brought it into the bathroom, and removed a folded peach-colored washcloth from the pile under the sink. Working quickly, she took off her clothes, wiped herself down with the wet washcloth, used another washcloth to lather an old bar of soap from the tub, and wiped herself down again. The soap smelled of candied violets. She had left the bathroom door open while she bathed. Why did it matter?

Wrapped in a towel, she explored her reflection in the oval

mirror above the sink and thought about her hair. It had been a while since she had combed it. It was dark, wavy, and thick, like her father's, and fell just to her shoulders. She removed her hair tie and touched the back, feeling the cloud of knots from where her head rested on the pillow at night. In the top drawer of the cabinet below the sink, she found the pair of scissors her mother had used to cut the family's hair. Del pulled her bangs taut and snipped across. The line was straight enough, ending just north of her eyebrows. She twisted the hair by her left ear and sliced again. The longest piece ended by her chin. She raised the scissors to cut another piece, when she sensed motion from the living room. She held her breath and peeped through the crack in the door. What could have gotten into the house? A raccoon? In the daytime? No, it was her imagination. She saw nothing at all. She opened the door wider, returned to the mirror, brought the scissors to her face again, and began to snip, when the mirror reflected a flash of motion behind the couch.

"Who is it? Who's there?" She ran into the living room, holding the knotted towel against her chest. Someone dashed out the back door. She followed but tripped over her backpack and fell to the ground. When she recovered from the fall and ran out the door, she saw someone being absorbed into the thicket of trees between her house and the old Francis farm down the street.

"Hey! You! Stop!" Del shouted. She got to the low stone wall at the edge of the property and stopped. She was barefoot, shivering, and dressed only in a towel. The person was gone.

"I saw you!" she continued. "I don't know who you are, but if you think you're going to fuck with me, think again!"

There was no movement in the trees. The person could still

be there, hiding, or could have cut through to the old Francis property, or gotten to the road. Was it her cousins? Mitch or Kevin? It would be just like them to try to spook her, throw her off. Well, fuck them. She was unspookable. Psychological warfare only worked on the malleable.

She paced for a while on her side of the wall, watching for any twitch of branches, and then turned back to the house. She latched both the back door and the front, then put on her clothes in the bathroom with the door closed. In the living room, she inspected the items she expected to find there. What was missing? A bag of oatmeal was upset but unopened. The bag of kidney beans had spilled on the ground. Was the person looking through her stuff?

Returning to the bathroom mirror, she lifted the scissors and snipped. Her hair was fairly even, or even enough. She dressed, went out to the living room, and stood by the back door, where she could see the blue rectangle of overlaid tarps that delineated her land. Only the area furthest to the back of the plot was covered with the house interiors—she had plenty of space to go. She was pleased with her progress. She turned to make some breakfast when her bare foot landed on something. She looked down. A kidney bean.

Chapter Thirteen

OVER THE NEXT THREE DAYS, SHE COMPLETED HER ROOM, FIRST
dragging the box spring through the trench she'd created the
day before with the mattress. On the final day, she lifted two
boxes out of her closet, carried them to the back door, felt the
ache of her arms, and left one behind. Each time she walked out
the back door, she locked it and glanced over to the stone wall
before carrying her things to the other side of the pond.

Empty, the room appeared smaller than she had expected.
She walked around the perimeter, letting her finger catch in
the bumps and divots in the walls. At child height, the paint
was marked with pencil. Most of the figures she couldn't make
out. They were just lines. She went into the living room to rest.

She chucked some coal into the stove and was disappointed
to see that the bag was two-thirds empty. She would need to use
less coal or go to the feed and grain store every other week. It
was only mid-November; certainly it would get much colder as
the season moved on and the snow began. She clapped her hands
to shake off the soot, then sat back on her heels and looked

around. Her father's army backpack had vomited over the floor. She could fold her clothes and put them in piles, but why? There was enough to do without keeping up appearances for no one's sake. She thought of herself as an animal hibernating for winter. This was her cave, or her woodpecker hole. Why not live like an animal? She fingered a knot in her uncombed hair.

"Why not?" she said out loud.

No one answered.

The pyramid of hot coal in the stove collapsed and sent up a drift of heat. It wasn't so bad here, anyway. She'd appreciate the niceties of modern life when she had them. Central heating. Lights. Water that wasn't pink from whatever sediment had seeped into the well or the pipes.

The gravel driveway crackled with the weight of a car. Del turned to see the flash of headlights come through the window. Footsteps approached, followed by a light tap on the door. She hadn't bothered with any candles, so the only light inside was from the coal stove. Could she pretend she was out? She remained motionless.

A knock came again, louder this time, followed by the rattle of the doorknob.

"I know you're in there!" Eleanor's voice said. "Are you going to leave an old lady outside in the cold?"

Del sighed, pushed herself up from the ground, and opened the door.

"Jesus, it stinks in here," Eleanor said. "And why's it so *dark*? What are you, a *bat*?"

Eleanor handed two bags to Del, who brought them to the couch.

"Voilà: chow," Eleanor said. "All easy things. Low cal. You can just put them in the fridge and have them later."

"There's no electricity."

Eleanor radiated dismay.

"I heard about you. That old piss-cup Chuck has told people all about your wild plan. It sounds insane."

"I know."

"It *is* insane."

"Fine."

Eleanor studied Del and finally laughed. "You know, you're just like your mother. Stubborn. Stubbornness will kill you. It killed her."

"Vodka and black ice and the tree in the Spiveys' front yard killed her."

Eleanor shook her head and laid out the contents of her bags. Two clamshells of iceberg lettuce salad with anemic tomato wedges. Three tins of sardines. Carrot soup in a tall glass jar. Weird-looking bread. A tall plastic cup of hard-boiled eggs with packets of salt and pepper taped to the side.

"Thanks, I appreciate it."

"You look like hell. You looked bad when I found you at the gas station that day. But somehow you look worse now."

Del smiled. "You don't like the haircut?"

"You look like Louise Brooks at a mental institution. In fact, I think Louise Brooks went to a mental institution. Or was she the prostitute?"

"Thanks. I'm flattered."

"Kid, I told your mother I'd look after you. I haven't done an amazing job. I'm not great with the phone. Or the train, or the bus. But now you're here, and I can make good on my promise. Why stay? You're sitting in a house with no heat or electricity. There's a camp stove on the floor. I can't even begin to tell you how grim this all looks. Lepers have it better. At least they live in colonies."

"It's temporary."

"It can be even more temporary. Leave tomorrow. Just get out of town."

"Nah." Del popped open a salad container with her thumbs.

"Why? For this?" Eleanor gestured to the shabby room.

"Maybe. Maybe for revenge. Or something. I don't know. I guess I am stubborn. But that's fine. Sometimes stubbornness gets you what you want."

"You're a mystery wrapped in an enigma wrapped in a terrible haircut."

Del shrugged. "It'll grow out."

Eleanor shrugged off her mink coat and sat back on the couch. "Can a girl get a drink around here?"

Del opened her mother's liquor cabinet, which had originally belonged to her grandparents and was still stocked with very old liqueurs. There were ancient glass bottles with pebbled textures and green or blue liquid inside. The colors of the liquid reminded her of advertisements for panty liners. Anything halfway decent was long gone.

She held up a bottle of curaçao. "Any interest?"

"Looks disgusting. I'll try it."

Del found two glasses in the kitchen while Eleanor tore open a can of sardines and used a plastic fork to smear them on a piece of low-calorie unleavened bread. The room smelled of fish and smoke. Del lit two candles and shook out a five-hundred-piece jigsaw puzzle onto the coffee table. It was a balloon in midflight. The bands of color on the balloon made it easy to match pieces, so they started there first instead of the edges, which, Del's father had told her, was always the logical beginning point.

Eleanor was adept at finding matches, while Del found herself frustrated when the pieces she chose didn't click into place.

"Not there." Eleanor gestured to the other side of the orange band in the center of the balloon. "Other side. You just look at the shapes."

The curaçao, while blue, tasted surprisingly of oranges. Eleanor's teeth took on a grayish tinge at the second glass.

"This is disgusting," Eleanor said.

"I agree," Del said, and poured herself another.

When there was nothing to do but the sky, Eleanor put her coat on again and pressed the sleeve against her cheek.

"I feel that this is all a terrible mistake," she said, her voice too loud for a room that was silent except for the occasional crackle from the coal stove. "Now I've said my piece. I will not support you in your self-destruction. There are too many bodies buried around here. We don't need another, please and thank you."

"That's OK." Del picked up the central part of the puzzle, the part they'd finished, and watched as it folded and crumbled to pieces, which she swept into the box. She was never going to finish it on her own.

"You should pack up and go. That's my take."

"Thank you, Eleanor."

"Call me when you want a ride to the bus station. Or don't call. Send a pigeon. Don't leave without saying goodbye. You know where I live."

"Thank you, Eleanor."

They got to the door. Eleanor examined the room again, and Del saw her assessing the open liquor cabinet, the dying coal fire, the broken-up puzzle.

"I mean it. Get out of here."

"Thank you, Eleanor."

"Can I give you some advice?"

"No."

"Too bad. There's a difference between being sad about the things that have happened and deciding to dig your claws into it. I'm seventy-four years old. I have several failed marriages and no children. I have plenty to be sad about. But I don't organize my whole life around it, and neither should you."

Eleanor clasped her coat shut and walked out into the unlit driveway. Del held the door open until Eleanor's car door closed and the headlights flooded the face of the house.

Chapter Fourteen

DEL KNEW HOW SHE APPEARED IN ELEANOR'S EYES—LIKE SOME kind of burrowing animal, small and frantic in its den. That was how she saw herself, too. If she emptied the living room, brought it down to just the bare necessities, it would be simpler and less depressing to be alone all the time.

She hunted through the liquor cabinet, set aside a couple of bottles that didn't look like they belonged in a tiki lounge in 1955, and carried the cabinet itself to the other side of the pond. The grass was frosted, and the ground crunched at each step. The tarp wasn't even twenty-five percent covered, and yet she felt as if she'd been working for months. The cabinet scraped her arms until they were red and sore. Her shoulders ached. Muscles in her neck that she hadn't been aware of weeks before now burned each time she turned her head.

Next she took the couch cushions across. She wouldn't be having visitors anymore, so it didn't matter. The couch itself she couldn't carry on her own. Maybe a job for an ax. She left it to think about later.

She rolled up the rug, piled up boxes of jigsaw puzzles and board games, and pulled down the various metal plaques with cute sayings that had been on the wall since her grandparents were alive. *Behind every strong man is a strong woman telling him that he's wrong,* one said in a cheery white script wreathed with pink flowers. She could barely remember her grandmother. Her grandfather had died before she was born. Was this something they had bought or something that was given to them as a gift? She threw the plaque in the pond. It cracked the thin layer of ice with a satisfying sound and disappeared forever.

The next two weeks passed in total silence. There was no sign of the person who had entered her house, though frequently she glanced at the woods between her house and the neighbors', trying to spy any kind of unusual movement. She disassembled most of the kitchen. According to the wall calendar, it was Thanksgiving by the time she packed up the half-empty bottles of Avon bubble bath under the bathroom sink. The smell reminded her of urinary tract infections. She felt a slight pain in the side of her head, like a needle was pricking her, as she carried her father's beard trimmer and shaving accoutrements to the other side of the pond. The pricking became deeper and more profound as she walked back home, and by the time she packed up the last box of her mother's light ash blond hair dye, she decided that she needed to lie down.

She carefully reclined on the bare couch and wished she hadn't moved the cushions already. The fabric had a grainy texture that made her think of being on the beach. Her hand touched a cold penny. It felt colder than a coin should or could be. She wondered if it had been in the couch since her grand-parents' time and whether it was worth any money. She was running out of money. What's the most a penny could be worth? How could she redeem its value? She imagined herself at the bank, sliding a penny across the counter, and having a nickel returned to her.

She woke the next day damp and shivering. Her clothes had an animal stench and her breath had a smoky flavor, as if she herself was burning from the inside out. The light from outside was thin and gray. Was it daybreak or sunset? She closed her eyes and fell back asleep.

She woke again in the dark. What day was it? Was something moving outside the window? It didn't matter. Her mouth was dry and sore. She crawled to the bathroom sink, pulled herself upright, and put her lips to the tap. The water pulsed irregularly and splashed over her cheeks. She gulped until she began choking, then eased the tap shut again. She lowered herself to the floor and looked out to the living room. The couch seemed very far away. Breathing set off a catastrophic chain of events: lungs prickling, throat fenced with glass, mouth cracked and bleeding. She pulled herself up to the lip of the bathtub and heaved her weight over the side. The enamel was cool against her cheek. She closed her eyes and slept again.

It was morning when she next woke. Del swam in the mint shade of the tub and surrounding tiles. Above the bath a small window was cracked open, and a stream of cold air flowed across her face. She tipped her head back and inhaled. After a few minutes, she lifted her head, then let it drop again. She was tired and dehydrated, sore to her bones, but whatever illness had happened to her had gone. She pulled herself up to her knees, came to sitting on the side of the tub, then brought herself upright. She ran her tongue over her papery lips and then moved carefully toward the kitchen.

After drinking a glass of water, she looked out the kitchen window toward the pond. Some of it had gone clear and dark; other pockets were still white and frosted. The ground was covered in a few inches of snow. She poured another glass of water and moved to the couch. The coal stove hadn't been lit in days, and the room was freezing, but the rankness of her clothes was so overwhelming that she stripped to her bra and underwear before she sat down on the floor. What day was it? How much time had she lost? A couple of days? A week?

On the ground in front of her, where the coffee table had once been, were three small battered boxes. The first had a bottle of cough medicine with a pink crust along the rim of the cap. The other two boxes had pills in foil packets, one of blue tablets and the other with green and white capsules. Del had moved all the medicine out of the bathroom when she cleared out that room. She hadn't seen any of these. Where had they come from? She turned over the box of green capsules. On the back was a sticker from the pharmacy. The label read KENNETH FRANCIS in block letters. The next-door neighbor, long dead. The house that the Murrows had bought and that would be knocked down along with hers.

She checked the door to the backyard and realized that she hadn't locked it the last time she had entered. She leapt up and ran to the bathroom, where she wrapped a towel around her-self. Her head swam from hunger and dehydration. She locked the back door and then went to her store of food. Nothing was missing, but there was something new. An outdated, half-eaten bag of garlic pretzels. Who was this person? Was this someone's idea of psychological torture?

She cooked a big bowl of oatmeal and ate it out of the pot with a wooden spoon. Still hungry, she hunted through her bag of groceries and found that it was mostly empty. A quarter cup of dried beans, one granola bar, and the pretzels. Someone was entering her house, watching her, doing things to help her, or at least wanting her to think they were helping her. And she needed to figure out who exactly it was and what they wanted.

December

Chapter Fifteen

IT COULDN'T BE HELPED.

She'd spent the morning and most of the afternoon on the couch, hungry and weak, trying to convince herself that she didn't need to do what she knew she must. She'd considered every alternative. Death was one alternative, just giving up and lying on the couch until she expired, but, on balance, it scored fewer points than the leading option.

She dressed warmly and put on a pair of her mother's snow boots. In front of the door was a drift that had accumulated over several days. Shoving the door only packed the snow tighter. Putting her shoulder against the door, she gave a final shove with all her weight. It opened enough for her to slip through. As the lock scraped against her hip bone and retracted, she realized that she might have lost a good deal of weight.

It was slow going, though the snow was only halfway up her calf. It would get worse. Tym complained about this characteristic in her—he said she was too negative. But if she knew something that was bad would certainly get worse, what was the trouble in saying so? She wished Tym were around so she could argue with him. He would be wearing shorts despite the weather and would have sweat stains under his arms as he always did. He would gesture with the wooden spoon in his hand, flinging so much pasta sauce that the walls would look like they were papered with red polka dots. She loved Tym. Had she ever told him? Probably not. It was too late now. Was that being negative or being realistic?

Five minutes later, she was at the end of her driveway, and fifteen minutes after that, she passed the Francis house near the end of the street. No signs of life. She stuck her middle finger up just in case anyone was watching and continued on.

By the time she reached the edge of town, her clothes were soaked with sweat. DeVito's was open, as it always was. Because the family lived in an apartment on top of the store, it was the only reliably open shop during the snow days of her youth. Her mother might send her out with a ten-dollar bill and instructions to get bologna, hot chocolate, and a loaf of Wonder Bread.

Count the change, her mother would say. *You never know with those Italians.*

The bells tinkled above the door.

"You again?" Frankie said.

Her hair was even lighter than the last time Del saw her. The highlights were so blond they bordered on white.

"Me again."

On the counter there was a rectangular pan of pizza with a puffy tall dough and a sprinkle of Parmesan. The smell of salted tomatoes felt like an anesthetic. She could eat the whole pan. Carefully she ran her fingertips over the coins in her pocket.

"How long are you planning on hanging around?"

"Not much longer. How's Sal, by the way?" She smiled. "Is he doing well?"

Frankie relaxed back in her chair and stared at Del as if surprised by the pleasantry. "Yeah, fine. He's here on weekends sometimes, helping out. He's with Public Works. Does some jobs with your cousins, actually."

"Oh, Sal gets around, does he?" Del was liking this more than she should. "Good to have a spoon in every pot, I guess."

"Guess you could say that."

"The profit motive," Del added cryptically.

"Uh-huh. So what exactly are you doing here?"

"Right now I'm just buying some food. Gonna have someone over later. Nice to have a cozy snow day. Could I get two slices of pizza, three donuts, and I'll grab a bottle of soda? Two-liter."

Frankie snorted. "Sounds like my kids' ideal lunch."

"Maybe so, maybe so," Del said lightly. "So Sal, he does something with the sewers or something? Laying pipe?"

Tym would absolutely love this. Tym would be hiding behind the rack of chips, cackling so hard the bags crackled under the weight of his pure joy.

"I don't really ask what he gets up to at work. I just cash the checks. That's what it's like, being married. I guess you wouldn't know."

"You'd be surprised what I know."

Frankie gave her a withering glance, then punched the keys on the register. "How's your dad, anyhow? Doing well? He dating anyone interesting?"

"No," Del said shortly.

"No to which question?" Frankie asked.

"All of them."

"Aha. Well, that settles it. Eleven forty-two, please."

Del handed over two bills and counted out the change.

"Don't worry about the two cents. I'll cover you. Take good care," Frankie said.

"Your hair looks like shit. Have a nice day!" Del said with a smile as she walked under the bells above the door.

Over at the pay phone, when she was certain that Frankie couldn't see her, Del shoved the chocolate ring donut into her face. Frankie was such an asshole. There was probably icing on her face, but fuck it. She dug into the bag and pulled out a raspberry jelly donut. Ripped in half, it looked like an artery had burst.

That was an emergency visit, and no such emergency would happen again. Fuck Frankie and her pathetic life. It was all lies anyhow. One day Sal would fuck the wrong girl, a lunatic who would come running to Frankie. Rumors and gossip were the rivers that ran underneath small towns like this one. People's lives were so pathetic and boring they lived to say the wrong thing to the right person. Del just wished she could drop in for the moment when Frankie found out what being a total fucking bitch all her life had gotten her.

There was a bigger problem Del needed to think about: cash flow. She had seventeen dollars left. Sixteen fifty once she dropped the coins into the pay phone slot.

"Hello?"

"Tym?"

"Del?"

Frozen wind whipped across her face. She wasn't sure if the damp she felt around her eyes was a reaction to this.

"You jerk," Tym said. "I've been trying to get in touch with you for weeks. Well, not trying too hard, honestly—I don't have an address or a phone number—but I've been vaguely considering where you are on odd occasions. What's up? Are you somewhere warm? Miami? Tell me if it's as good as everyone says."

There was a noise she was making, and when she made it her whole body shuddered and folded into itself.

"Are you crying?" Tym asked.

She rubbed her glove across her face. It pulled away with a trail of slime leading to her nose.

"No," she gulped.

"Sure. Where are you?"

"I'm still at home."

Tym paused. "Why the fuck did you do something like that?"

"Long story."

"Listen: I'm actually getting out of town tomorrow. You remember Barry?"

"Gollum?" she asked.

Barry was someone Tym had dated briefly several years ago. He referred to his own dick as "Precious."

"Exactly. Anyhow, Barry's hooked me up with a gig out in the sticks. Maybe an hour from you. I'm running a Christmas tree farm for a week. The guy who was doing it had some medical emergency. His wife died, or his mistress died, or someone in Guatemala is on life support or something. I can't remember everyone's shit, frankly. Anyhow, Barry needed someone to live on-site for a week and run the place before the guy comes back. It's just a trailer out in the middle of fucking—"

"I'll come," Del interrupted. "I can do a week. Could use the money, actually."

"I was going to suggest a visit," Tym said. "But sure, if you want."

"Yeah, yeah. It would be good to see you."

"No problem. Give me your address. I'll pick you up sometime tomorrow. Not sure what time. My license expired, makes it kinda hard to rent a car."

Del gave him all the details and then hung up.

The light was failing as she walked home. After ten minutes, there were no more streetlights, and she continued in the dark. She stumbled forward in the snow, finding her own tracks. Her bones clicked inside their joints, reminding her of the sound of bare tree limbs on a windy autumn day.

"Tym is coming," she said to herself. "Tym a-comin'. Tym a-comin'."

She smiled to herself and repeated the phrase, a chant, a summons, a train coming down the tracks, until she got home.

Chapter Sixteen

TYM WAS NOT A MORNING PERSON, SO SHE KNEW WHEN SHE GOT up that there was no chance he would arrive anytime soon. For years he had been threatened for arriving late to work at various photo labs across the city but still couldn't rise before ten a.m., so she expected him in the afternoon at the earliest. Still, she wrote a note to him and taped it on the door.

Out running an errand. Back in 5.

In the house, she put one piece of cold pizza aside in case he arrived hungry and she had nothing to offer other than slightly pink well water. After eating everything else that remained from her trip to DeVito's and finishing the bottle of orange soda, she suited up and walked out the front door. A dusting had fallen the night before and layered over her footprints, which still left visible indentations in the snow.

The element of surprise was important. It couldn't continue

like this. She came through the woods and approached the
house quickly from the side, where she hoped no one would be
able to spot her advance. Every Sunday of her childhood was
spent watching public television documentaries about Antie-
tam and Shiloh and Gettysburg with her father. She tried to
remember any of the ambush tactics, but could only recall the
piles and piles of corpses in silver gelatin prints.

The front door of the Francis place was an awful color, like
dehydrated piss. She knocked so hard the door rattled in its
frame.

"Who's in there? Open up!"

Silence.

She banged again, even harder. "Open the fucking door,
coward. I know you're in there."

Again, nothing. She tried the handle. It twisted smoothly
and gave way.

In the dim front hallway was a wooden staircase with a white
banister. Attached to the banister was a metal rail supporting a
chair, a seat belt dangling limply from the side. Mr. Francis had
had his leg amputated. Diabetes, was it? It was boiling hot inside
the house—someone had turned the furnace on.

"Hey, asshole," she called up the stairs. "You'd better come
out. I've got a gun. You wouldn't want to catch me by surprise."

There was the sound of a piece of tape coming unstuck. She
stepped quietly toward the room to the right of the staircase.
On the other side of the dark wooden doorframe she saw a
brick fireplace with a mantel heavy with framed photos of the
Francis clan. She stepped farther into the room, onto a red Ori-
ental rug.

Greg sat on a plastic-covered couch wearing a pair of board shorts. He seemed confused and embarrassed.

"What the fuck are you doing here? Are you spying on me? Is this part of some big plot?"

He shook his head. "N-no. Nothing like that."

"Then why are you here? Did you drop that medicine off at my house?"

He stood up, his bare calves peeling away from the couch protector.

"Yeah, I did. You hadn't moved anything for a couple days. I thought you maybe quit and left, which would have been smart. I looked in the sliding door and saw you on the couch. Thought you were dead at first. I was going to call 911."

Del scanned the room. There was a pile of neatly stacked cups and a coffeepot on a small table at the rear of the room, below a faux oil painting of a man on horseback chasing a fox. On the glass-topped coffee table in front of the couch where Greg had been sitting, a stack of textbooks sat in a pile.

"Are you . . . studying?"

He shrugged, avoiding eye contact.

"Why?"

"Well. I'm not actually sure I want to be doing what I'm doing. Thought I might go to college. But I never took the SATs, so I have to do that to get in. I don't remember geometry. That's all."

"And you're doing that here—why?"

He stared at the carpet like a child being punished. "Because if my dad found out, he wouldn't understand. Murrow Construction—that's the family business. He's proud that all of us are in on it. Right now he's got me on a project of my own. Nothing too complex. I just come here when I'm studying, as a break from work."

Del sat in a high-backed rocking chair next to the sofa. It creaked under her weight.

"What a stupid fucking plan."

He snorted. "You're one to talk."

"At least I have an end point. What's your plan? You're going to be an accountant or something? Weren't you bad at school?"

He lifted his chin. "Just reading. I was always good at algebra and chemistry."

"A mad scientist? What?"

"Sales."

"Right. Selling what?"

"Doesn't matter. You just have to be pretty good at math. A relationship person. It'll be a business degree. I just don't want to work in construction my whole life. Here. A Murrow. My brothers are better than me at it. I'm always going to be the one they shit on, just like you said."

Del rocked the chair as she scanned the room. "I haven't been in this house in twenty years probably."

"Yeah. It was sad. Mr. Francis died a long time ago. Mrs. Francis was alone. She never left the house much after he died. Had a full-time nurse who came every day. I stopped by sometimes to say hi. She was always nice to me when we were kids. Do you remember their Halloween candy?"

Del closed her eyes. "Legendary. Full-size bars."

"Exactly. None of that homemade shit. Apples. Or snack-size. Or anything with coconut.

"Her hands were so gnarled. Arthritis. They used to cane chairs, remember? She stopped doing that a long time ago, but it didn't matter. They were like claws."

She rubbed her eyes. Mr. and Mrs. Francis had always been lovely to her. When she was very little, she would go to their house when she returned on the school bus and no one was home. They had Lorna Doones and pineapple juice on TV trays while watching Phil Donahue. She hated to think of Mrs. Francis on her own, curled up in bed like a withered shrimp.

"Then Uncle Chuck got the house?" she asked Greg.

"Yeah. He offered Mrs. Francis's niece enough money for Mrs. Francis to go to a retirement home, so she got power of attorney and sold the house. She was at Sunset Estates, the one out by Route 4, but she died a few months ago. I used to go to see her. She had stopped talking. Didn't last long once she got to the home. Never saw the niece again, but I guess she had cashed her check." Greg peeled the skin around his thumb. "Dad always knew he wanted to build up around here. He already owned all the land around it, except for your house and this one. And the new on-ramp to the highway is being built in the spring, so that'll be a five-minute drive. Businesswise, it made sense."

"How practical."

They sat in silence until Greg rose abruptly and poured himself a coffee.

"Want one?" he asked, his back to her.

"No."

She was thinking of his great escape. How Uncle Chuck would react when he knew one of his little weasels was digging out of the burrow. Mitch and Kevin would be furious. Greg was turning out to be, if not a good guy per se, at least less of an asshole than the others. Mitch and Kevin had seemed, in their greed and their meanness and their desire to capitulate to their father's wishes, interchangeable. Maybe Greg was indeed different after all.

"Have you gone down to the basement?" she asked.

He smiled. "It's still there."

Del flicked on the light at the top of the stairs. The basement floor was coated in a high gloss on which had settled a thin layer of dust. She remembered exactly where everything was. The key sat inside the lock of the games cabinet. She took off her coat, opened the cabinet, and pulled the wooden box of shuffleboard accessories out from a stack that included Twister, Monopoly, and Chinese checkers.

Greg pushed a broom over the painted part of the floor to knock off the dust and then handed Del a cue. She gave him four discs from the box. Oldest went first: it was Mr. Francis's house rules because it gave Mrs. Francis the first try. Greg overshot, his disc landing against Del's toe. Her shot landed early, just before the tip of the scoring pyramid. Greg's second shot was better, shouldering Del's off the board and dropping into the eight zone. They didn't speak, though Del winced dramatically when Greg's shots got the better of her. She had always been terrible at losing.

At the final shot, Del had two in scoring position and Greg had three. She positioned her cue for a center shot and shoved. One of Greg's discs spun off the board, but she knocked one of her own discs out of the scoring zone as well. Final score: seventeen to sixteen, Del.

"Good game," he said, offering a handshake as if they were in an elementary school lineup after a soccer match.

She took his hand.

"You can come back sometime, if you're around. Play again."

"Thanks," she said. "I'm actually going out of town for a week. I've got some business to take care of. Then I've got to catch up on moving."

"Maybe after that?"

"Maybe. Once I'm caught up. Hard deadline, you know."

He grinned.

She put her coat back on and went up the stairs. Greg stayed in the basement, pulling board games out of the cabinet and looking through the boxes of pieces.

"Good luck with geometry," she shouted down from the top of the stairs.

"Thanks," he yelled back. "Good luck with whatever you're doing. Come by if you want to play again. Or want electricity."

Chapter Seventeen

HE WAS SITTING ON THE COUCH EATING THE REMAINING SLICE OF cold tomato pie when she got home.

"Tym!" she said.

"The sign on the door said five minutes," he replied. "I've been here twenty. Jesus, this place is depressing."

"Want the tour?"

He grimaced. "I think I've seen enough. Get in the car— we've got to be at the tree lot by one p.m. or Barry's sending some guys out to kneecap me. I borrowed the car from Oscar's mother. You remember Oscar? Used to work at the photo lab. Beautiful jaw, Oscar. Anyhow, his mother had a stroke and is confined to her home, so I could borrow it if I took it before she woke up and returned it in a week after she's gone to sleep. The garage door is creaky."

"Very kind of Oscar's mother."

"Isn't it? I need about seven coffees, so your bags had better be packed."

He surveyed the room again, the bare walls, low ceiling, and general air of mole-ness. "I can see why Stan got out of here."

"Oh, shut up," she said, shoving T-shirts into her bag. She hadn't been able to do laundry, so she was on to the oversized T-shirts from her youth that had other girls' names printed in sparkly puff paint. Her mom had bought them ten for a dollar at the Goodwill.

He lifted one from the pile and waltzed around the room with the shirt. "Tammy, Tammy, Tammy's in love."

She took the puff-paint Tammy shirt back from him, added it to the bag, and zipped the top.

At the drive-through coffee shop they got a box of cider donut holes and two megalarge coffees with half-and-half and sugar.

"I'm going on a diet after this," Tym said. "But I need to have energy for all the manual labor you're going to do."

"Me?"

"You're young and supple. Life hasn't destroyed you yet. You're going to saw down the trees and carry them to the customers' cars."

"What are you going to do?"

"Supervise. Cook the books. Take the cash. Get paid."

"Uh-huh."

He glanced at her as they entered the highway on-ramp.

"Feeling OK?" he asked.

"Fine."

"Just wondering. You're very thin. Low carb, no carb, or low fat?"

She shook her head. "Manual labor. Also, I was sick. I had the flu or something."

"Eat another donut. Eat ten. I don't need my half, actually. Just forty percent. Save that fat one down at the bottom of the box for me. I like when there's a big air pocket inside. It makes the dough kinda gummy and stretchy."

She wrinkled her nose. "How's Marcus?"

He released the signal light and eased between two cars.

"Marcus is fine," he said finally.

"Just fine?"

"Word of the day, I suppose."

"Do you . . . like living with someone? Romantically speaking, of course. I assume I will always be your favorite roommate."

"Oh," he said, focused on the license plate of the car in front of them. "That didn't work out."

"What!"

"Yeah. It lasted about a month, or six weeks maybe. It turns out he had all these annoying habits. Like he liked to be in the same room as me all the time. And he didn't like pasta—who doesn't like pasta? He wanted to eat a high-protein diet and nothing else. Fried steaks every night. You can't imagine the odor. So I told him we'd compromise, and I would cook on days ending in 'y.' He didn't like that plan. And did you realize that he had absolutely terrible taste in TV? No kidding—he wanted to watch Ken Burns documentaries. You should really tell people you have a character flaw like that up front so no one is forced to invest any time in you."

"My dad liked all those shows."

"Yeah, but I never had to live with your dad, so I didn't care about his shit taste. All of his taste was shit, actually. Food, music, movies. God rest his soul, may he rest forever in the palm of our Lord." Tym did the sign of the cross. "So anyhow, I said to myself, Self, you're a fifty-five-year-old gay man with the body of a pudgy Polish-Greek Adonis and the mind of an artist. You didn't labor for ten years at the photo-processing counter of various drugstores just so that you could come home to the stink of fried meat and watch a nine-part series on the Civil War. Life is short, bitter, and cruel. I want to watch *Cat-Women of the Moon*, smoke dope, eat spaghetti, and not have to share the covers with someone who has been mainlining beef fat."

"What did he say?"

"He moved out."

His face showed no emotion. Del wondered how he really felt, but she knew not to press him.

"And that's that?"

"I'm happy," he said, finally looking at her. "Happiest I've been in years."

Del bit into a donut. This was very interesting news indeed.

"How's everyone else?" she asked him.

He filled her in on the news of everyone else in the neighborhood—the pizza delivery guy had disappeared; the bodega owner had been caught for credit card fraud; various people in their circle were either sick or recovering; Stan's old friend Cal, a schoolteacher, had AIDS, and the cocktail, once promising, had stopped working. How many was that now, who had died? Too many. One of Tym's friends who had a col-

lection of 45s to rival his own had also died, and Tym bought
the collection off the dead man's boyfriend. He had now taken
up all the forbidden spaces beneath the Verdiccis' building and
had moved a recliner and a record player into one of the storage
areas to use as his listening crib.

She listened with interest but, in the back of her mind, was
calculating. Her room at Tym's was free again. Would he let
her move back in? Did she want to? What if all the horrible
mechanics that had set her into motion and led her here could
be reversed? She would be back on the couch with Tym, a couch
with cushions. They'd get to know the new delivery guy. She'd
find a job picking up phones somewhere. She imagined lying in
her old bed, under the red and blue patchwork comforter, and
her heart beat hard at the thought.

"We're here," Tym said. "Exit 28."

They took the off-ramp and followed the signs to the tree
farm, which was just another couple of minutes down the road.
They pulled into the empty lot at one minute before one.

"Plenty of time to spare," Tym said, cutting the engine.

They grabbed their bags and walked over the crackling
gravel to the trailer parked at the mouth of the farm. There was
a flutter of the curtain inside, then a skinny blond man walked
out the door.

"You're late," he said, pressing a key into Tym's hand.

"Barry said one," Tym responded icily.

"Barry said yesterday," the blond guy said as he walked toward the road.

"Where's our orientation?" Tym shouted. "How does it work?"

The guy raised his hands in the air in surrender, but didn't bother looking back at them before he disappeared down the road.

Tym climbed the aluminum steps into the trailer. It smelled of beer and weed. There was a small table with a lockbox of cash as well as a ream of paper tree tags and three black permanent markers.

"What are the hours, do you think?" Del asked.

He opened a cupboard and shuffled through the papers. "There's nothing here. So whatever we make them. I propose that we open at noon. No, two p.m. Maybe noon on weekends."

"Seconded."

"I propose further that we work until we're tired or until someone is so much of an asshole we can't take it anymore."

"Further seconded."

Tym raised the latch on the door near the back of the trailer and peeped in. "Bunk beds. I'm on the bottom. No cheese or onions for you."

"Do you think we can get delivery out here?"

"Doubtful. But we'll try. We can always run out for fast food. By which I mean I'll run out, you stay here selling trees. I hate cold fries."

"Fine."

He lifted his eyes toward her. "And then there's the matter of pay."

"Indeed." She was prepared to argue.

"Barry's giving me fifty percent of the proceeds over the week. I'll cut you in for half of that."

"Half? Really?"

"I am expecting you to do basically all of the work. Also, you look like you're about to keel over. You need to go back with enough bread for your bread."

She accepted his proposal.

They spent the afternoon going through all the documents left in the trailer. They found a bunch of receipts for Chinese delivery and learned that the blond guy was a fan of chow mein, so that was what they called him. Chow Mein didn't leave any sense of what trees cost, whether or not they needed to advertise, or what any part of the process might be. In the locked cashbox, there was a twenty, two tens, two fives, twenty ones, and a sleeve of quarters. They were both surprised that Chow Mein hadn't made away with all the cash, but perhaps it was good news, and there was so much earning potential that eighty dollars meant nothing to him.

"Bonanza," Tym said, fanning himself with the dollar bills.

"Better get ready for work," Del told him.

She put on a red-and-white-striped apron that said McTavish's Tree Farm and stood by the entrance to the road for an hour. A few cars passed but none slowed or stopped. Returning to the trailer, she found Tym poking his straw at the bottom of his coffee.

"When is it?" she asked him.

"Huh?" he asked.

"What day is it? When are we? In the history of time, what's today's day, month, and year?"

"Tuesday, December second, 1997. Who is the president? Are you feeling woozy? Head injury?"

She shrugged. "Who cares? When do people start shopping for Christmas trees?"

Tym considered the question. "Probably around now, but mostly on weekends. Weekdays before Christmas, probably, but not some random Tuesday at three p.m."

Just as he finished speaking, a car crackled across the gravel lot. Del leapt up from her seat and went out to meet them.

The driver rolled down the window of his Suburban.

"Know the way to the Weapons World?" he asked.

She didn't.

"Want a Christmas tree?" she asked him.

"No way. It'd be dead by Christmas." He pressed a button, and the window drew closed again.

She returned to the trailer, where Tym had plugged in a kitchen-sized TV that he had found in a cabinet. *The Oprah Winfrey Show* was on. He handed her a pipe.

"He's cheating on you," he jeered at the TV. "Move on! Get over it! Have some self-respect."

They watched the rest of the episode, followed by the local news. Heavy snow expected in some parts of the state. Man with gun. Priests accused.

"I'd favor a glass of water," she said.

"What an extraordinary turn of phrase," he replied, his eyes on the television.

She poured a glass of Poland Spring into an amber-colored plastic cup. They had agreed to work at the tree farm until Monday, when someone else would come to relieve them. If the weekend ended up being the only days that they made money, they were in trouble. In normal circumstances, she would gladly have embraced five days of smoking weed and watching TV on the fold-down couch in a camper. They would have eaten salted fries hot out of the paper bag and smoked until even Sally Jessy Raphael seemed interesting. But there was something in the back of her mind—some deep, horrible, uncomfortable itch that felt like a conscience, or adulthood, or simply a desire not to be found dead in her house with an empty bag of dried pinto beans next to her, that made her speak up.

"We've got to market ourselves," she said quietly.

"What?" Tym asked, clicking through the ten channels again and again.

"Cash flow. We've got to get some coming in. We can't rely on only Saturday and Sunday, or else why are we here? We might as well just stay at the Days Inn, where at least someone cleans your room, and then show up on Saturday morning to work."

"Not the worst idea in the world. They probably have Turner Classic Movies."

"But we're not there, we're here. We might as well make the best of it."

She convinced Tym to get back in the car. Although, like Tym's, her license had expired, she took the wheel. They drove very slowly to the local craft shop, where she paid the guy at the printer counter twenty bucks from the kitty to make some signs.

While Tym took a nap, she walked out to the highway in the fading daylight and used thin pieces of rope to lash their signs over the fast-food exit markers.

McTavish's Xmas Trees. Half Off Early Birdz.
Prices ⬆ Next Wknd.
Exit NOW!!!

She returned to the trailer and waited.

A little past seven, the gravel crunched, and she peeked out the trailer's narrow rectangular window. It wasn't one car, but two. Couldn't be asking for directions to the gun shop unless it was a caravan of idiots racing to shoot each other.

She put her coat and hat on and stood in front of the trailer.

"Hi there!" she greeted them. "Here for some trees?"

They were. One car was a couple who hopped out and went walking through the lanes of firs on their own. The other car was a mother with two children of indeterminate ages.

"Ho ho ho," Del said to them with forced enthusiasm. She was wearing a long woolen elf cap that she had found in the trailer. The children blinked and ignored her.

"Can you tell us where to find one where the things won't fall off? The leaves?"

"We've got high-quality trees here," Del told her confidently. "All needles do fall eventually, but ours are the hardiest. You won't find better ones anywhere."

The mother nodded. "And how much?"

"Normally thirty dollars for a six-footer or above, twenty for anything shorter. But this week, you're in luck. Weekdays only, we're talking half off."

"Not bad," she said. "Freddie. Mikey. Go find a tree. Not too big."

The boys raced off into the lanes.

They sold three trees that night. She took payment back in the trailer, where Tym was watching *Timecop* with a bowl of sour cream and onion chips on his lap.

He was dismissive when she returned from shutting off the floodlights and locking the gate. "I could've earned more at the photo lab."

"Just the beginning," she said as she pulled on a sweater over her pajamas and climbed into the top bunk. "You'll see."

Tym stayed up late watching TV in the main room while she lay in the bedroom with the door open. The TV cast a weird blue light that made it hard to sleep, so she didn't. She thought of their little apartment in the city, the pan of frying onions, and the comfort of knowing that someone else was nearly always there. Her breathing slowed. Tym chuckled at something. The lighter clicked again. Did Tym want her to move back? She was sure he would bring it up with her. Or maybe he thought she preferred to go it alone, and she should say something? It would just need to be the right time. She didn't want to make him feel bad about the Marcus thing not working out.

Tym switched to a midnight movie, and she turned to face the wall, the wiry bed squeaking under her.

Chapter Eighteen

THEY GOT DRIVE-THROUGH HASH BROWNS AND COFFEE FOR breakfast, then returned to work. The aroma of the tree farm reminded her of bathroom air freshener. Tym unfolded two aluminum lawn chairs with lime-green vinyl webbing, and they sat in the sun in front of the trailer while drinking their coffees. He was wearing reflective, aviator-style sunglasses, with a lilac handmade scarf knitted by his mother wound around his throat.

"What's the scene out here?" he asked.

"There is no scene."

"I've been to a gay bar in *Boise*, for god's sake. If Idaho has a gay bar, there must be one here."

"There is one. The Rusty Spike. Just not sure you'd call it a scene."

"Oh, the Rusty Spike. Of course. Stan's place. A real honky-tonk."

She sipped. "I went there once, in high school."

"Right, right, right. You told me about that. Jesus Christ. And that girl who told everyone at your school and then your mom found out and they broke up. Jessica or whatever her name was."

"Frankie."

He chuckled. "What an asshole. She's probably a dyke now."

"Married with two kids."

"Even worse. Suburban living death. At least you and your dad both escaped."

A thing that bothered Del, had always bothered her, was the way that Stan's friends, some of whom were her friends as well, had talked about his escape. He escaped. His life was bad, and then it got better until he died of a heart attack, age fifty-one, and was turned into ash and then tossed into the ocean, where he drifted, like snow, onto the backs of sharks and crabs.

He did escape. And then he was happy in the city with his friends, though Del would argue that even before that he was pretty happy, too, because he had wanted to be a family man. When she arrived on his doorstep after her mother's funeral, she knew two things were true: that her father loved her very much, and that she was angry at him for leaving them behind.

But Del escaped, too, or at least had escaped. But her mother had not, had lived all her life and then died in a town she always seemed to dislike. Del thought of her final year of high school, after her father had left and she was alone with her mother. Their social circle tightening like a noose. Her mother no longer pretending to go to work. The leased car being taken away and her mother buying a tin-can replacement. The lights off. The spoiled Yoplait in the fridge. Her mother's problem wasn't her father; Del knew enough to know that. Her mother's problems were her family, her drinking, being broke, being angry, being stubborn, being stuck. Louise had never been a resourceful person. She couldn't pull herself up the way Stan had: moving to a new city; reconnecting with Tym, a friend from childhood; getting a new job, new friends, and a new place to live. And yet still Del hated to think of it: her father's escape, her own, their brilliant lives laughing at Buster Keaton movies from the back of the ninety-nine-cent theater, and her mother left behind, even if she was somewhere where no one could bother her ever again.

"Think I'll check it out." Tym tossed his empty foam cup, which made a hollow noise as it bounced along the gravel.

"Mmm, not sure. Not much of a scene, like I said. There's a bowling alley and a bunch of old diners on the turnpike. Fifties retro vibe—you might like it. We could get some dinner."

"I ride alone, Tonto. I'm going to see if there's any talent worth being pursued for a weeklong infatuation."

The first car rolled in just after noon, and a steady trickle continued throughout the day. Even Tym rose from his chair at one point and pointed in the direction of some trees.

By the time she turned on the floodlights at nearly five p.m., they had already earned more than a hundred dollars.

"Not bad," Tym said, counting the bills into the partitioned lockbox inside the trailer. "Good takings for you. Sixty-forty."

"Not so fast. We agreed fifty-fifty."

"I realized I'm lazier than I had imagined. That's sixty-forty you. Unless we wreck Oscar's mother's car, in which case it's one hundred percent to pay off whoever sees us sinking the wreck into the nearest pond and doesn't report us to the police for murder and racketeering."

"Thanks. Money's been tight."

Tym removed from a cabinet a large vinyl bag with a nozzle attached to it.

"Solar-heated camp shower," he read doubtfully as he inspected the label. He flicked the small rubber nozzle with his thumb and then put the bag back in the cabinet and spritzed himself with a cedar-scented cologne that momentarily obscured the mildew and smoke odor of the trailer. "I'll try to hook up with someone who works at a motel so we can use the shower. I've been meaning to tell you: you smell horrible."

"Thanks. Better yet, maybe you'll meet a property owner. A captain of industry."

Tym wrinkled his nose. "Around here? I'll take my chances with a motel employee. At least I'll know the place was bleached recently."

He snatched his keys and coat and departed.

Del turned on the TV. Wavy gray lines rolled horizontally down the screen and obscured the picture. She switched it off and explored the cabinets. There was a completed book of crossword puzzles, several nudie magazines with dog-eared pages, and a game of Boggle that appeared to be missing many of the letter cubes. She shook the plastic box and tipped the cubes into slots.

DOG. CONES. WENT.

She stroked the back of her hand, which felt soft and plump, as if it had been injected with warm butter. Tym's society, and three square meals a day, had led to an improvement in her general health. She could still make out the bones of her rib cage, like a sheet laid over a rake.

DOES. SENT. NEST.

It felt awkward, Tym still not saying anything about the empty room in his apartment. Maybe he was afraid of hurting her feelings, if it came across like he was letting her move back in because he didn't think she was up to the challenge of defeating the Murrows. Tym was a tenderhearted person. He hated for people to know it, but she did.

Every year, on the anniversary of his mother's death, he pulled out taped copies of *The Judy Garland Show* that had belonged to her and watched them on the couch of the apartment. When Beata had come to America, the first movie she had seen was *Meet Me in St. Louis* at a dime theater in Brooklyn, and it had sparked in her a lifelong love of Judy. Tym wasn't a Judy gay or a theater gay, as he would tell anyone. He was a Vincent Price gay, a hallucinogens gay, a *Motorpsycho* gay. But to remember his mother, Tym watched episode nine, with Judy and Barbra's duet. He could recite by heart their awkward scripted banter before they started singing a blend of "Get Happy" and "Happy Days Are Here Again." Soon enough, Del learned it, too, but when the cue came and the women began singing, Tym grew quiet and turned to face the window, and that was when Del knew that he was crying. She never said anything.

It was up to her, then, to be bold now. She just needed to decide how she wanted the conversation to go. She ran her fingertips across the back of her hand, circling the cracked knuckles, then moving down the plane toward her wrist. It would be so much easier if she just went home with Tym and started fresh in a place where she knew the rules, and where she'd never have to see her rat-faced family again.

She put the game away and turned on the TV again. Suzanne Sugarbaker was giving a speech on *Designing Women*. Del rested her head on her arms on top of the Formica table and soon fell asleep.

Chapter Nineteen

TYM KICKED THE TRAILER'S DOOR SEVERAL TIMES UNTIL DEL WAS roused and got up. Still wearing the clothes he had on the previous night, he held a steaming coffee in each hand and nodded in the direction of the lawn chairs, where there was a breakfast platter on each seat. A couple of inches of snow coated the ground, but Tym had swept it from the chairs. Del put on her coat, sat next to him, and ripped into the grape jelly packet.

"How did it go?" she asked.

"Meh. Not a lot of talent."

"Successful enough, though? You didn't come back."

"I drank too much and fell asleep in the car outside the bar. I woke up this morning because there was an officer of the law tapping on my window. And do you know what? I think he might have been homophobic!"

"Is that so?" Del asked, gnawing off a chunk of hash brown.

"He called me a fag. While accurate, I can't say I liked the tone of his voice. At least he didn't look up the plates. I don't know how I would have explained that one."

"Close call."

"I'm going again tonight. The bartender's a nice guy, actually. He gave me two for one, for being cute. Then he gave another guy three for one and I was momentarily furious, but I got over it soon enough, or I guess I wouldn't have had to sleep in the car."

Del imagined another night of one-player Boggle. It was Thursday. Perhaps a popular night to buy a Christmas tree? Most likely she'd work late and fall asleep immediately thereafter. Either way, she would need to use the car to pick up something to eat before Tym ran off to meet his bartender again.

Tym reached into the plastic bag at his feet and pulled out a copy of *People* magazine. Some woman in Iowa with questionable hair had given birth to seven children.

"Nightmare," Tym said, skipping past the septuplets to find a story about dead Michael Hutchence. "Absolute fucking nightmare."

"Did you ever think of having kids?" she asked him.

"Not ever. I wanted to live in a high-rise condominium with a liveried driver and a cocktail cart."

She laughed. "You wanted to be Poirot?"

"Who wouldn't, darling?"

After a two-page spread on a hospital TV show was a story about a young woman who had gotten AIDS after a root canal. The dentist was suspected.

"Another youthful innocent struck down," Tym mused before turning the page.

"Tragedy," Del concurred. She had read that magazine

sometimes when she cleaned offices. The people dying of the disease were always children or white women who had been cruelly infected because of blood transfusions or evil dentists.

"Now that I'm slightly awake but also trying desperately to avoid getting involved with any actual work, tell me what you're doing with the house."

She told him about Chuck and Greg. About her run-in with Frankie. About visiting her mother's grave and about finding out that Chuck intended to demolish the house. About the deal she had made and the March deadline. Occasionally he interjected, calling Frankie a bitch and her family morons.

"So I decided to keep it," she concluded. "The house."

"Oof."

"You're the first person not to ask me why."

"Because I know you."

"Oh yeah?"

"You're stubborn and incomprehensible. A lot like Stan, actually. Family trait, I guess. I think it's a dumb plan. It sounds impossible. Even if it were possible, it's pointless. You'll probably do it anyway."

"Thanks." It was below freezing, and she felt ice glazing her bones. Tym, of course, was still wearing shorts. Leaping to her feet, she ran in place to shake off the cold. "So anyhow, I was thinking."

"What's that?" Tym asked.

She kicked the snow, and a piece of gravel stuttered across the lot. "With Marcus out. I was thinking that maybe . . . maybe you want a roommate again?"

His face turned serious. A little sad, even. He rested his

hands in his lap and looked out over the lot, the trees dusted with a fine layer of clean powder.

"I don't want kids, Del. Never did. I thought you were going to move out after a few months. You didn't and that was OK. I got used to it. We had a good time. I'm getting to be an old man now. I just want to watch *Maury* with my nuts out. You can't just sit in my apartment waiting to take over the lease when I die."

"Oh." She felt her face flush with embarrassment. Of course Tym didn't want her. Of course he didn't. How pathetic she must have seemed.

"Do I think you should stay around here and do your house thing? No. Do I think you should come back? Also no. It's time for you to try something new. What're you going to be on your birthday? Twenty-three?"

"Twenty-five."

He whistled. "Shit. Time flies when you're smoking dope and earning minimum wage at Walgreens."

She smiled at him. They didn't speak for a couple of minutes. Tym peeled the thin, soggy crust away from his toast and ate the white part. Then a black SUV pulled into the lot, and a woman climbed out.

"Can I get some help?" she asked, not removing the enormous sunglasses that obscured her face. "I need a tree. A big one. But I just had my nails done. I'm not touching *anything*."

Del hauled the tree to the black SUV, and then after that there was almost no break between cars. Some families trotted out to the lanes by themselves and spent an hour selecting a tree. Others told Del their specifications and wanted to be led to the exact right option. Seven-foot Douglas fir. Twin six-foot Fraser firs for the front of a department store. A tiny but full two-foot spruce for an elderly woman who paid seven dollars in change from a flower-printed crushed-velvet coin purse.

Del was occupied all day and barely spoke to Tym. In the late afternoon they turned on the floodlights. The pace dwindled and dropped off. When she climbed into the trailer near eight p.m., Tym was watching the end of *Wheel of Fortune* and putting on a new shirt.

"I'm going to the bar. You can come, if you want."

"Mmm. Dunno. Might just hang back here. Catch something on TV later."

"Don't be a moron. It's cold as a witch's tit in here. We can get some dinner and a drink beforehand. We've only got a little while left, anyhow, then we're both back to the grind. Let's tie one on."

On occasion, Del had gone to bars with Tym and whoever he was dating at the time. There were all sorts of places in the city, ones that showed porn on dozens of screens in tiny, dark-painted rooms, and clubs with sound systems that vibrated the floor and drinks that tasted like electrified candy. Tym liked an old-man bar. He wanted no-label gin and a bartender who had worked there for thirty years and didn't give a shit about anybody.

She put on her coat and got in Oscar's mother's car. On the turnpike, they stopped at a fifties-style steak restaurant, where they paid too much for gristly, butter-soaked sirloins and plate-sized baked potatoes with little silver boats of sour cream sprinkled with chives. The waitress and the bartender both appeared to be in their seventies. Tym was in his element. He made a joke to the waitress about Herbert Hoover at which Del smiled politely. The bartender sent over two gin gimlets.

"I hope your daughter is of legal drinking age?" the waitress asked with a teasing smile.

Tym raised his eyebrows to Del when the waitress left. "Jesus, I'm old. One favor, before you send me to the retirement home: shoot me right here, between the eyes. And get your aim right the first time."

Del took the wheel when they drove to the bar. Tym had already had four drinks. The road was slick with black ice. She didn't remember the route or even the exit. In her memory of the time she went with Frankie, she got in Frankie's brother's car, and suddenly they had arrived at a place that looked like a log cabin.

His head tipped backward into the neck rest, Tym told her the way. After an exit off the turnpike, the street became dark and quiet, hedged with tall pines on each side.

"Not far now," Tym mumbled drowsily.

She parked at the rear of the lot and scurried around to open Tym's door for him. "My apologies for the lack of uniform, sir."

"That's fine, Miss Lemon, but ensure this is addressed tomorrow."

The interior of the bar wasn't at all what she remembered. The walls were now blue, with poorly drawn tropical-themed murals. Tym and Del dropped their coats in a corner booth that looked over the street and had an enormous parrot painted on the adjoining wall.

"Wally," Tym said, approaching the bartender. "Wall-Man. Wallerino."

As the man stood up from loading the dishwasher, his back cracked. "Pleased to see you again. And a date?"

"This is the lovely Adela, daughter of my good friend Stanley. You may remember him as a native of these parts."

"Don't remember a Stanley," the bartender said.

"Oh well. As is my understanding, he frequented this drinkery. And frequently, he explored parts previously unknown."

"Already had a few drinks, I see?"

"It's fine," Del said. "I'm driving."

"Good girl. What can I get you?"

They sat at their booth with a gin fizz for Tym and a Coke for Del. Tym checked out the guys who came through the door but didn't approach any of them.

"You're a bit of a heavy breather, you know," he said to her.

"Ah, are we at that part of the night?"

"What part's that?"

"The tell-me-everything-that's-annoying-about-me part of the night."

"So funny you should say that. Marcus said something like that, too. But his arms *did* smell like old cheese. I think it was something to do with the bodybuilding drugs he was taking."

"I liked Marcus," she said.

He looked out the window into the darkened lot. "Marcus moved out."

"Yeah. You told him to."

He circled his hands around his cocktail. Foam capped the melting ice cubes at the bottom of the glass. "I didn't want him to go."

"Then why'd you tell him to?"

"I didn't. I just said could he stop watching bad TV. Could he cook better food? Could he emit an aroma other than cheese? Could he stop training the guy from Action News who was always offering him blow jobs because I had to see that guy on TV every night at six? A little discretion goes a long way."

"And he didn't like that."

"I'm tired of losing people, Adela. It's exhausting."

Headlights illuminated the black pavement. Car after car, people going somewhere to somebody.

"Have you heard from him?" she asked.

"No. Maybe I'm just gonna be alone. Maybe I like it. I don't know. Do you know how many people I know who died?"

She thought back, just to the ones she knew. Bruce the Moose. Brent. Adam. Phil the Pill.

"Fifty?"

"I don't even know. A hundred? Maybe more. Some, I forget their names. The first was this beautiful boy I met at a club. I was forty. Had just broken up with someone, and I went out by myself to tie one on. His name was Andre. He was wearing a mesh shirt with blue lightning bolts on it. Oh, Del, if you could have seen him. A body for the Greeks, and the most amazing dancer. He was *elegant*. I saw a mark on his hip, right above the bone, like a bruise. We knew people were dying, but I didn't think of it. I went back to the same club a month later, but he wasn't there. Later I met someone who knew him. They said he had died, not long after I'd met him. But here I am. Everyone is dead."

"Yeah," she said with sympathy. "I know."

"No. It's not the same. It's something you're never gonna understand. You're the kid. You were always supposed to live longer than the people around you. My friends, my boyfriends, even the young ones, they're all dead. Why me?"

"Why not you?"

"I've never done anything for anyone."

"You did something for me."

"Did I?"

"Sure. Of course you did. Where would I have gone, without you?"

"Maybe." Tym signaled to the bartender for another round. "If I could see that boy again, Andre, you know what I would tell him? I would tell him that he was the most beautiful thing I had ever seen and will ever see. I'd tell him that when I close my eyes, I see that mesh shirt and the two blue lightning bolts. Even now, there's never been anything like him. I think he knew it, but I would have told it to him all the same."

"I had no idea."

"That's your luck. It's just your luck. You'll never have any idea."

She didn't know what to say. A melancholy song came on the jukebox, one she didn't recognize, and she wished she could reach the plug and rip it out of the wall.

Tym closed his eyes. "Maybe you and me were meant to be alone, Del. Maybe this is it for us."

Del got their drinks from the bar counter and handed Tym's to him. Then she went to the jukebox and thumbed through the pages of songs. Tym was just tired, she knew. He had slept in the car the previous night and on the uncomfortable bunk bed the night before. Lack of sleep made him nervy, but he would feel better tomorrow.

Jimmy Buffett. John Mellencamp. Who had bought the songs for this thing? And were they formally or only informally in league with Satan?

She thought about Nick, the first boy she had a crush on, the mama's boy with the pool. And about Brian, the guy she'd dated for a few months in high school before she and Frankie decided he was unbearably boring. Brian had played drums in a Grateful Dead cover band. He had thin hands and an Afro.

Then there were the guys she had met in bars in the city, some college boys, some workers, some in-betweeners who had no idea what they were doing. Some she had gone home with, some not. What if they were all dead? What if after she had met each one, they had simply disappeared, like Andre with the lightning bolt shirt? She thought of Bruce the Moose in his hospital bed, bare and collapsed, crying for his mother, who refused to visit him. Her father, still alive then, had ushered Del out of the room and told her to go back home and wait for him there. He didn't like her to see things like that. *You're just a kid*, he told her.

She returned to the table and dropped her stack of quarters on the table.

"The music is killing my brain cells," she announced. "Let's go home."

Tym crawled into his bunk and was snoring within minutes. From the top bunk, Del watched him sleeping, then dropped on top of him the blanket she had stolen the previous night. His yellow socks poked out the end. She read a couple of chapters of a terrible sci-fi novel that she had found in the cabinet, then clicked off the light and dreamed of robots shooting laser guns.

Tym's whistle cut into her dream.

"Morning, sunshine." He handed her a bag of donuts. "Freezing again. Want to hear something terrifying? They recognize me at the donut place now, and I'm getting free bags. I like to think it's my adorable face."

She dropped down from her bunk, put on an oversized sweatshirt, and joined him in the living area.

"Feeling alright?" she asked.

"Peachy. Think you'll break yesterday's record?"

She shrugged. "What're our takings now? We must be over three hundred."

"Minus steaks, minus cocktails, minus breakfast. Oh, and I bought a pack of cigarettes and a joint from a guy at the bar. Still above one, one fifty, I reckon."

Her toes tingled with cold. She broke open four packets of fake sugar and poured them into her coffee. "Any particular plans for today?"

"Just a nap, I think. When do you suppose the busiest time is? I think I'll take a nap around then. Just to make sure you get your exercise and some experience. What if your next job is some kind of similar enterprise? You'll want this on your résumé. 'Business manager at tree farm.'"

"Thanks." She grimaced. "So thoughtful of you. I'll be sure to use you as a reference."

"Never missed a day of work," he said with the intonation of an old-timey radio commercial. "Dependable as adult diapers."

She threw a powdered donut hole at his face. "You creep. Drink your coffee. We've got to go tag some trees. Let's say they're all six-footers."

Tym swatted and missed the donut, which landed squarely on his nose.

Del laughed and thought she wanted him never, ever to leave her again.

Chapter Twenty

AS IT TURNED OUT, THE WEEKEND WAS A POPULAR TIME TO BUY A tree. Saturday's takings were an all-time record, and they celebrated that night with a pancake dinner at the twenty-four-hour diner. Tym claimed that he wouldn't have dessert, then ordered a slice of cheesecake with canned cherries slopped over the top. He revealed his intention to go on a diet, but ate the entire thing anyhow.

"I'm just big-boned," he complained on Sunday morning at the drive-through when their extra-large vanilla lattes were handed through the car window. "It's the eastern European genes."

Del was already missing him. They had agreed that on Monday morning they'd get breakfast after the handover with the tree farm manager, then he would drop her back at home and head back to the city by himself. It was a long drive, and he hoped to be on the road by noon, which probably meant more like two p.m.

When they arrived back at the farm with their coffees, the

lot was already half full and several families were milling through the lanes, brushing the branches to assess the needle droppage and judging which was the weak side of the tree that should be pointed into the corner of the room.

"Thought you were open at noon," growled an old man in a checked hunting hat who stood by the door of the trailer.

"We were handling an emergency," Tym said curtly.

"What kinda emergency?"

"An arboreal emergency. You wouldn't understand. Expert-level stuff. We're on call twenty-four seven."

The old man grunted and shook his head, then followed Tym inside to pay for his tree.

Del wandered through the lanes, answering questions about price and bullshitting when she was asked about tree species, longevity, or history.

"Yeah, this is the classic German style," she told one family. "This is the kind that Queen Victoria herself had. Bit of pedigree for you there."

The parents looked vaguely interested, their four children bored to the point of despair.

By the time the afternoon rolled in, her hands were rough with dried sap, and she smelled of sweat and grape hard candy. She lay on her side under a tree, which she was cutting down with a flimsy saw. The family who had chosen it had joined Tym in the warmth of the trailer. The timer for the floodlights kicked in, and the tree lanes, strewn with fallen needles and clumps of frozen mud, were bathed in a bluish artificial light. She let go of the saw for a moment and closed her eyes, breathing in the scent of the tree her body was curled under.

"What about that one?" a woman's voice said.

"Not crazy about it," a man responded.

"OK, well, how about that one over there?"

"Nah."

"What kind do you want?"

"You know what, Francesca? I'll know it when I see it. Don't get on me like that. You know I don't like it. The nagging."

Del shifted her weight back and scanned the line of firs. The family was one lane over, on the other side of the five-foot Nordmanns. She saw the man's boots and heard children laughing.

"Behave," the man warned, his voice gruff.

"Jesus, Sal, loosen up. It's supposed to be a nice time."

Del quieted her breathing and held still, her back against a rock that wedged into her lower spine. Frankie and Sal. If she moved very strategically, she could get out before they saw her.

The sound of their footsteps faded and disappeared. Del waited another moment, then pushed herself away from the base of the tree and stood up, pulling the tree toward her. The last fibers of the base snapped, and she lifted the pine into her arms. Carrying it down the lane with a deliberate pace, she brushed the trees to either side and made a swishing noise. Scarlett O'Hara coming down the staircase at the ball. There was no one in front of her. Maybe they had left, or turned back down another lane. Del could see the family waiting impatiently by their pickup truck. Then Sal and Frankie appeared at the head of her lane.

"This place is overrun," Sal complained.

Del held the tree higher, so that it obscured most of her face. Had anyone recognized her?

"Let's go to the next section," Frankie said. "Six-footers. I want a real fat guy. Not like the one last year."

Peering through the branches, Del watched Frankie and Sal walk away, followed by two little kids in knit hats. She moved forward quickly, her shoe tips catching in the swells of frozen mud, and joined the family who had bought the tree in her arms.

"Sorry for the delay. It was a tough one."

They took the tree and didn't thank her.

Turning back toward the farm, she saw several groups of people in the tree lanes, which had been depleted by about a quarter since she and Tym had arrived. There were flashes of cardinal football coats, puffy yellow vests, children in every shade of pink, green, and blue.

A man approached her with a tree he had already sawed. "What's the price of this one?"

"It's marked on the tag. Six-foot-tall tree."

He guffawed. "This ain't a six-foot tree. I'm exactly six foot. The tree's smaller than me. Should be priced as a five-footer."

"One of you exaggerates, then. It's priced as marked."

His mouth screwed up with anger. He stared at her as if waiting for a retreat. Finally he shoved the tree, watching as it glanced off her elbow and fell with a whoosh to her feet.

"I'll take my money where it's wanted."

"Fuck off, then. Get out of here before I call the cops."

He stepped closer to her. "Think I'm not related to every cop around here? Think they're gonna take the side of, what, a tree carny, over me?"

His breath stank of old beer. She knew exactly the type, had seen him before and would see him again. The limp dick at the bar who tried to buy her a drink she didn't want, the guy who showed up without an appointment at the doctor's and wanted to barge ahead of the line. He was certain a mistake had been made by someone else, and angry if his errors couldn't be accommodated.

Del didn't break eye contact. "Hold up while I dial the phone. We'll get Officer Elroy down here pronto. Is he your cousin, your brother . . . or both?"

"Customer service! Customer service, please." Tym appeared in the door of the trailer. "We need you to answer a call on line three."

Del went to Tym. She felt the man staring her down and heard the crunch of snow behind her as he finally walked away.

"I fucking hate this town," Tym said, looking over her shoulder as the man disappeared. "Can't get away from the boonies soon enough."

In the morning, they found spray paint on the trailer. FAGGS, it said in blocky green letters.

"And you say you chose not to complete high school here?" Tym marveled. "I'm astounded. There must be some sort of direct route from this area to all the Ivy League schools."

They closed out their week with two hundred and seventy dollars. Tym gave her more than half and said that he would be happy to be a reference on her résumé if his own job title could be listed as senior director of arboreal science.

They left the interior of the trailer as they had found it,

mussed but not a disaster, and handed the next manager the lockbox with a roll of quarters, a ten-dollar bill, and ten ones.

"I need a shower like you wouldn't believe," Tym said as they paged through the menu at the diner.

"I believe," she told him, waving a hand by her nose.

"You'd hardly be the one to talk. Actually, let me give you an early birthday present." He slid a twenty-dollar bill across the table. "This is specifically for the sole purpose of a visit to a salon. Do they have those where you live? Or what are they called . . . let me translate. Hair-cuttin' shops?"

"Yes, they have those."

"Go to one. Try to drag a rake through your mop first. But go to one and get them to fix what you've done."

She ordered a hot chocolate, chocolate chip pancakes, a side of scrambled eggs, and hash browns. Tym got a Greek omelet and wheat toast with a thin coating of margarine.

After they had finished eating, he lifted his backpack onto the table.

"Got a couple of other things for you. Let's consider this your Christmas present for the next five years."

From out of the bag he pulled a pink boom box, a set of DD batteries, two CD jewel cases, and a small white box.

"What's this?"

"Adela Louise Ellis, I think you're awfully lonely. So you have here some of my favorite musical interludes, which I lovingly and illegally copied onto compact disc for you, despite my hatred of compact discs, of which you are well aware."

She flipped through the cases, looking at Tym's terrible scrawl on the white paper inserts. He had done this all for her.

"You haven't even seen the best part." He nodded toward the white box.

Inside, she found a small bronze device. She flipped it open and pressed the tiny black buttons printed with white numbers.

"Hot off the black market. Your very own cellular telephone. I got it from my drug dealer's brother's ex-cellmate, Kenny. Now you can call me. Or 911, whichever one you need first. You need to plug it in, though. It's on my family plan through next December, so don't call any phone sex hotlines, or if you do, send me a check in the mail."

She pressed a button that made the screen light up blue, shut it off, and turned it on again so that she didn't have to look at Tym. If she did, she thought that she might cry.

"This is amazing. Thank you."

"Pish posh."

Del's chest felt dull and heavy, and she was suddenly very aware of her breathing. Tym wouldn't want to see her cry. It would upset him. She watched cars trawl down the turnpike. The thick tinted windows of the diner hummed faintly with the vibration of traffic. Tym called for the check.

On the drive back to her place, Tym put one of the CDs he had burned for her into the boom box. It was Tym's version of Judy's greatest hits.

"I don't even really like Judy," he claimed. "It's just sentimental."

"Bullshit. Hey, what was that stew your mom used to make?"

"Bigos."

"That was good."

He tapped the beat of a song into the steering wheel with his thumbs. "Yeah. When I was a kid, she told me it was made out of old shoes. She left during the bad times, so she may have had some shoe stew, actually."

They were both silent through the Carnegie Hall recordings. "When You're Smiling" had a skip, and she thought he had probably recorded from a record to a tape to a CD. As they pulled into town, *The Judy Garland Show* recordings came on. From watching Tym's VHS tape collection, Del remembered what Judy looked like when she was singing the songs they listened to. Near the end of her road, yellow construction vehicles were parked and silent.

At the top of Del's driveway, Judy and Barbra started their banter. Judy was in her forties and would be dead within a handful of years. Barbra wore a silky sailor outfit like a giant toddler. Del and Tym must have watched the tape of the duet a dozen times before.

"You're so good that I hate you, I really hate you," Judy told Barbra.

Del took Barbra's part: "You're so great that I've been hating you for years."

"I love it," Tym mouthed along with Judy, fanning his face coquettishly. "Say more."

"Don't stop hating me. I need the confidence."

He put the car in park. "If you ever get a little feeling, a lack of security, call me on the phone and sing a couple notes to me. I'll give you hatred like you've never gotten before."

Del turned up the volume until the speakers trembled and then placed the boom box on the pavement so she could unload her stuff. When she went into the house and dropped her bag, Tym had already reversed out of the driveway. She hoped he could still hear the music all the way down the street.

Chapter Twenty-One

WHILE IN THE BATHROOM, SHE REALIZED THAT SHE SHOULD HAVE asked Tym to take her to the grocery store in another town. He wouldn't have thought of it: he was used to living in the city, where avoiding all the people you hated was as simple as taking a different subway line. She had fuck all to eat at home, and as she went to the sink to wash her hands, she thought she would need to make a midnight run to the Stop and Go.

A flash of yellow attracted her eye. She peered through the bathroom window, which faced the backyard. There was a backhoe by the pond, blocking her view of the bridge and the creek.

"What the fuck?" Hands still dripping, she ran out the back door.

Chuck and his sons Greg and Mitch were chatting to each other on top of a mound of newly upturned dirt.

"What the fuck!"

Chuck greeted her with a smile. "Hello, Adela. Wasn't expecting you back so soon. Greg said you were out of town on some business?"

Greg stared at his feet, embarrassed. He should have been running for his life. As usual, Mitch looked like he'd just released a poisonous fart.

"What the fuck do you think you're doing?" she asked them. "You said you weren't coming until March."

"That's right," Chuck conceded. "Fair is square, as they say. I said we're not developing *your* part of the property until March, but we do need to, uh, get established here. We're preparing the land. The cold snap really drove us to it. We can't wait till everything is completely froze up. It's efficiency. If you were in the business, you would understand."

She looked over Greg's shoulder and saw what they had done. "No. No, you didn't."

Chuck glanced back. "Oh, that. We had to take down the bridge. The whole structure was inadequate. Surprised it didn't fall down of its own accord. I'm not sure who put that one up, actually. Stan, was it? Doubt he got the permits. That's home DIY for you. Everyone thinks he's an expert."

The bridge was a pile of broken wood on either side of the creek. They had cut off the access to her site unless she walked the long way around the pond, which would easily add fifteen minutes to the journey. Fifteen minutes was nothing when it was a wait for a bus or for a frozen pizza. Fifteen extra minutes of single-handedly dragging a couch frame was impossible. Chuck had ruined everything.

It probably wasn't even purposeful. He just hadn't considered her position at all. He needed the land clear, and so he had cleared it, without any thought about how smashing the bridge would make her work unmanageable.

She felt within her a deep and horrible hatred and, without thinking, reached down and snatched a clump of frozen mud. She threw it at Chuck's face. It landed in the center of his chest, where it crumbled.

He brushed the filth from his jacket. "Now, Adela."

"Don't call me that. What is wrong with you? Why are you such an asshole? Why can't you just leave me alone?"

"Adela, don't be like that. Anger isn't a nice quality in a girl."

She seized another hunk of frozen mud and threw it at Mitch's head. He turned just as it skimmed his cheek.

"Jesus," he said, holding his jaw. "Quit it, you lunatic!"

"And you!" she said, gesturing wildly at Greg. "Pretending! You're pathetic. Leave me the fuck alone."

Greg appeared guilty or ashamed or some combination of the two, but she didn't care. He had sold her out. He was a prick, and she should never have felt any sympathy for him or his little rat face. They were all the same: greedy, conniving, rotten to their core. Chuck had been given almost everything, but he resented the crumbs that had been left to her mother. He would never have given Del a fair deal because anything that he touched turned foul and rotten.

Chuck opened his mouth like he had something else to say, but she was done listening.

Back in the house, Del found leftover green liqueur in a tall, blue, knobbly bottle. She drank it until the sun disappeared and she fell asleep.

· · ·

In the morning, she woke with a headache. It was over. She should walk to her uncle's office and tell him she was giving up. She hadn't cleared the land, as they had agreed in the contract, which probably meant a renegotiation. Knowing Chuck, he would make her take a smaller sum than they had first agreed on. He had probably known it would end this way from the beginning. It was a crazy plan, and he would have predicted that she would fail. Failure always came at a price.

If she had to admit defeat, there was no rush to do it. Instead, she put on her coat and gloves and went out into the back. A couple of inches of snow had fallen overnight. She pored over the pieces of crushed bridge on the near side of the creek and ran a gloved finger over a piece of splintered wood. There was a piece of wood from the top of the arc that she had never noticed before: it must have faced out. Set into the cedar was a small scratched heart and inside it seven characters: S L A 1982. Stanley Louise Adela.

The snow started falling again. It whipped around in gusts like great breaths, swirling, settling, seeming to fall up and down all at once.

She stared over the frozen pond for a good long time, then went to the diner to get some food and organize her thoughts.

"Back again?" the waitress said.

"I owe you some cash from last time. Need to get some breakfast, too."

"No need for the payback. The owner's actually got a fund to pay for coffee for indigents. Strangely, we don't have many indigents around here, so I've never used it before. I guess we're not on the tramp map. You were my first dip into the fund."

"Nice owner."

"Not really. He lost too many games of poker with the minister of the Second Congregational. This is the repayment plan they agreed to."

"Nice minister."

"Guess you could say that, except for the gambling problem."

She poured Del a cup of coffee and took her order. A few minutes later, a disembodied hand delivered a plate to the serving window. A couple of old men came in and took a booth behind Del. As the waitress took their order, Del scratched at the plate with her fork as she thought through her thoughts.

"Got any big plans for the day?" the waitress asked when she brought a refill of coffee.

"Actually, yes. I'm thinking of doing something stupid."

"Not drugs, I hope. My cousin's kid got hooked on meth. Went from state kindergarten teacher of the year to Skeletor in two months flat. Speaking of indigents. I guess the coffee in jail is technically free, so there's that, if you want to look on the sunny side."

"Cousins are terrible people, I guess. No, not that. Just something crazy."

The waitress inspected her and nodded gently. "So are you the Murrow cousin? Little lost lamb?"

"Yeah. You heard?"

"It's too small a town to miss the gossip. I heard what you're doing. Can't stand those cousins of yours, if you don't mind me saying. They stopped coming here a while back, though. Think they must have got a coffee machine for the office. And someone to run it for them, I'd bet. Terrible tippers."

"Terrible people."

"Seems to go hand in hand, in my many years of observation."

Del felt pleasantly warm and steady, as if the coffee were burning the hangover out of her.

"I think I'm going to do it," Del said.

To her own ears, there was a sound of desperation in her words, as if she very much wanted this stranger, whom she did not know and could choose never to see again if she liked, to tell her no, that her idea was terrible, to cut out of town that very moment. If the waitress had looked askance or even flinched, Del might well have listened and left forever for no reason other than that it was the sense of direction that she desperately wanted and, once sought, must be followed.

The waitress gently regarded Del, observing the set of her face, the bruised knuckles and faint sunburn from her week outside at the tree farm. An invisible coin flew in the air, spun forward, and landed faceup. "You know what? I think you should do whatever it is. So long as it's not drugs, like I said."

"Thank you."

With breakfast eaten and the future decided, Del got the bill, left a very large tip, and put on her coat.

. . .

There was a skateboard in the toolshed as well as a few plastic milk crates from Donaldson's, the local dairy. Del lifted her father's collection of dumbbells down from the shelf. She lashed two crates to the skateboard, then carried the dumbbells down to the pond in three trips. At the edge of the frozen water she placed the skateboard, loaded with weights inside the milk crates, and pushed. It moved a few inches and then caught on a bump in the ice. Del lay flat on her belly to reach the back of the board and shoved. The weighted board spun forward, rolling slowly to the middle of the pond, where it stopped.

She walked back to the top of the yard, where she could see the pond in its entirety. The water had frozen white, though there was a clear section of thin ice where it joined the creek. Around the skateboard she couldn't see any sign of faults or weakness caused by the weight. She went back to the shed and pulled down from the wall a set of snowshoes that must have belonged to one of her grandparents. They were large and old-fashioned, made of wood and with webbing that might have been from an animal's intestines. She strapped them to her feet and placed one foot on the ice. There was no sound. She shifted her weight forward. Nothing. She brought her second foot forward and landed it, with some hesitation, on the ice.

It occurred to her, in this moment, that she could easily split the ice, slip through, and not be found until her decomposed corpse bobbed up in the spring melt. There was no one to see her or save her. When they found the body, with snowshoes like frayed tennis rackets strapped to her feet, what would they think? What an idiotic plan, what a child. It would probably make the evening news. She snorted at the thought. It wouldn't matter to her by that point. She would be food for snapping turtles. And she had heard that death by drowning was quick and numbing, so of all the ways she had considered going—neglect, suicide, car accident, the explosion of the Iron Age–era boiler in the basement of the Verdiccis' apartment building—this might be the most favorable arrangement.

She took another step. The ice held steady. Her lips formed into something like a smile.

Having clomped back toward the shed and removed the snowshoes, she picked up an old metal instrument that looked like a claw and approached the side of the house. The pine clapboards were warped and gray from years of rain. She positioned the hook under a loose clapboard and yanked. It popped like a sore tooth.

Underneath was more wood, the texture smooth. She held the loose piece in front of her like a triumphal offering and carried it to the skateboard cart, to which she tied a lead. Slowly, slowly, she stepped back onto the ice and dragged the cart behind her. She glanced at the phone Tym had given her when both of her feet left land and then again when she reached the other side. Four minutes. Eleven less than the fifteen she expected it would take to walk around the pond. How much time could she save per day, per week, per month? It would take a mathematician to perform an expert-level calculation like that.

The exact numbers didn't matter; what mattered was the feeling of possibility.

Efficiency, she thought.

She spent the rest of the afternoon daylight piling the remaining objects from the kitchen and bathroom by the back door. There were small things, used and personal. A frayed toothbrush, a plastic cartridge of mint floss, a dissolved bar of soap that curled like a green tongue. The bathroom cabinet, attached to the wall, came down with five yanks of the metal claw. Into the milk crates she loaded the kitchen drawers, still full of utensils. Four trips later, the two rooms were bare except for the few belongings she needed. When the sun started to set, she boiled water on the camp stove and made a hot cocoa. The phone made a horrible trill.

U OK? blinked a message in thick black type. There was a number she didn't recognize. It must be Tym.

YES I AM, she wrote. Apparently everything was written in capital letters.

WHAT R U DOING, came the reply.

NOT MUCH.

For a couple of minutes no response came through. It wasn't dinnertime yet. She imagined Tym was coming home from work, or maybe at the gym. She wondered if he spoke to Marcus when he saw him, or if they just ignored each other. Tym was friends with most of his exes, but he seemed to have left those relationships with no hard feelings on either side.

The phone buzzed again.

GOOD.

She stared at the message for a while, then responded.

BYE.

Chapter Twenty-Two

HER PLAN WAS AS FOLLOWS: SHE WOULD DECONSTRUCT IN SUCH a way that the core of the house, the living room, remained intact for most of the winter, because it was too cold to be exposed to the elements for long.

To begin with, she would attack her bedroom. Already she had removed the furniture, and it was bare, waiting to be taken apart. Inside the shed were more tarps that she could use to cover holes in the roof or patch open walls. Also, there was a tent for when it really came down to it, but for the bulk of the winter, she needed heat and water, so she would attempt to deconstruct so as to leave a warm cocoon at the center of the house.

Inside out made the most sense: taking down the walls, plaster, and electricals to reveal the frame, and then disassembling the frame down to the basement level. It was the latter part of the operation that was, of course, the worry. "Disassembling the frame" sounded like such a tidy operation when it was one step of many, but the reality of it, the lifting and moving of joists, rafters, beams, and studs, was hardly simple. She had no idea how to do it, so she decided to think about it later, when she must.

Her parents' room remained exactly as it was the day she had entered the house. The door stayed closed. She would think about that later, too. There were plenty of things to do before she addressed it. The kitchen wasn't needed at all. The bathroom could survive without a roof. In fact, she liked the idea of shitting under an open sky.

To practice disassembling and ensure she was selecting the right tools for the job, she walked out to the old pigpen, which sat under the protection of a sugar maple by a collapsed barn in a field to the west of the house. The pigpen had a corrugated tin roof, pine walls, and a dirt floor. She carried several tools from the shed to try out. Her claw popped the planks off the wall and revealed the building frame, which was sunk into the dirt. A child could do it. The corrugated roof was a different story. The nails, rusted from fifty years of weather, would not yield. She pushed up on an overhang to no effect. The clouds knitted together like felt, and soon snow drifted down, first slowly and then in haste, blanketing over the discolored layer of the previous snowfall, now pocked with pheasant tracks and deer shit.

Taking hold of a low branch, she monkeyed herself onto the pigpen roof, where she tried to strip away a section of tin with the hook. No give. Finally she went back to the toolshed, selected a few more tools, and returned. There was a smaller claw that fit around the nailheads and snapped them off with a quick, firm yank. After breaking most of the nailheads in one corner of the roof, she used the larger hook as a lever. The metal yawned open.

The process took a couple of hours, and at the end she had stripped away the roof and one wall, leaving exposed a rotten frame that she knocked down with a few solid kicks. She was pink faced, soaked in sweat, triumphant.

The tools that proved most useful weren't the tools she recognized—screwdrivers, wrenches, and ratchets. They were older and heavier, and probably had belonged to her grandparents. What use they were intended for wasn't clear, so she thought of them as big claw, little claw, snapper, stripper. There was a pickax, too. There were hammers and saws still attached to the pegboard wall of the shed if she needed them later, as well as a chain saw, which seemed like it might be an enjoyable addition to her arsenal as long as she could get gas for it.

If her house was as easy as this, with the small complications of piping, electricity, a stone and mortar foundation, and a roof that was high enough to cause her death if she fell, she would probably be done far earlier than expected. A month at most. Why had the Murrows doubted her? Just to get under her skin, to make her give up. Or because they hadn't done it themselves, so they thought it was more complex an operation. Of course they had underestimated her because they thought she was impractical or stupid. Anyone could build a house. There were a thousand training programs for that. But unbuilding a house, that took some ingenuity and creativity, some grit, and that was where the Murrows fell short.

Tym didn't need to know in the meantime, especially about

walking over the frozen pond. No one did. People would tell her she couldn't do it or that it was crazy. As if that was news. She couldn't explain it, but she didn't need to. She must and so she would. Uncle Chuck was probably waiting for her in his office at that very moment. Staring at the door, waiting for the moment she would walk through with a penitent smile, a request for a favor. Could they call off the deal, and would he consider a new financial arrangement? Of course, less money would be understandable. Half? A quarter? So generous of him. Where did she need to sign?

Well, that bastard could keep on waiting.

She carried her tools to the house and attacked the inside of her bedroom wall. It must have been just below zero. Outside, the snow was beginning to cling to the ground, and she hadn't lit the coal stove, yet she barely felt the cold. She struck the wall with a pickax. This had been her grandmother's room when she and her parents had first moved into the house. She remembered her grandmother's final year, spent in the rest home, where she sat in a wipe-clean hospital chair and stared out a window that faced the parking lot, waiting to die. There were rooms in the rest home that faced a duck pond out back. Her mother had complained that Chuck wouldn't go for the extra seventeen dollars per day in fees to get a pond-facing room. Of course her mom couldn't pay it—they were barely getting by. Del turned the volume to high on Tym's boom box and put in the first CD. The Supremes. She wished Tym liked contemporary music. This was the kind of work that called for Mary J. Blige.

She hummed along to "Love Child" as she stripped the wall and watched as the chunks of plaster bound with horsehair crumbled to the carpet.

The next morning she woke at dawn and started again. She held a mug of coffee in her gloved hands and surveyed the work she had done in her bedroom the previous day. Pretty good progress. Two walls were stripped clean down to the joists, with the exterior wall within view. She swallowed the coffee, now cold, and got to work.

By the middle of the morning, she was beginning the fourth wall. That was when she heard the growl of machinery. At first, she ignored it. Nothing to do with her. Clearly something was happening at the Francis place. Her work had a rhythm, and she would not be distracted.

By noon, she was distracted. She crossed her lawn, crept over the stone wall, and walked through the woods between the two properties. On the far side, she peered through the thicket. A half dozen men in the shadow of an excavator drank out of foam cups. Of the Francis place, there was now a single standing wall and a mass of smashed bricks, broken wood, and pipes. Even the pignut tree in front of the house had been knocked over, its roots limp in the air.

One of the men tossed his cup onto the ground and climbed back into the operator's seat of the excavator.

He started the engine and swung the excavator's bucket at the standing wall. The crown of bricks fell. The excavator struck again. The chimney's throat and the surrounding wall buckled like a man taking a blow to his chest. The other workers stood together in a knot, observing the progress in silence. Within minutes, the wall was down, and the Francis house was no longer a house.

She checked her phone. It wasn't even twelve thirty. They had completely demolished the place in the space of an hour or more. The heavy machine chugged onto the road, and the remaining men drove away in their pickups.

Back at her house, she eyed her own work. It was puny, insignificant. How many hours of daylight were left? How many days, minutes, seconds? By her best guess, she had about two and a half months left to finish, assuming that she worked every day, even after the roof was gone and the gales ripped through the house while she slept.

She thought of Chuck, of his horrible face, pink and smooth, like a ham soaking in its juices. She picked up the little claw and started swinging.

Chapter Twenty-Three

HOW R U

She wondered if Tym paid per character. As long as he was paying her bill, she should be respectful of the costs involved so he wouldn't think twice about the expense and cut her off.

GD, she typed.

GREED? GOLD? GOD?

N. GOOD.

OK. GOOD.

For several minutes, there was nothing.

WHY R WE TYPING IN BIG LETTERS, he wrote.

NO IDEA.

DO SMALL LETTERS.

    HOW.

DUNNO.

    FIGURE IT OUT.

OK.

    OK.

Another pause. Tym pissing, Tym opening a beer, Tym yelling out the window to someone in the street. Someone interesting, someone boring. A new friend, an old friend, a lover, a potential. Plans for coffee. Plans for dinner. The Italian place where people wrote their names on bricks that were painted over every six months. Tym and a new flame, eating plates of hot lasagna and toasted garlic rolls. The windows fogged with their breath. Heat and comfort and love.

The phone buzzed again.

Talk tomorrow, he wrote.

    OK.

Chapter Twenty-Four

SHE WENT TO THE STOP AND GO IN THE DEAD OF NIGHT TO GET more Fruit Roll-Ups and to commit a crime. Again, she took the back way, across the disused farmland, the empty paddocks, the haunted, wheezing barns with no doors, through the new developments and their silent, creepy cul-de-sacs. By now, she had learned the direct path.

It was nearly two a.m. when she walked past a raccoon pulling garbage from a trash can outside the motion-sensing doors of the supermarket. Inside, the cashier was slumped over with his head resting on his arms. His deep, rattling cough vibrated through his back. She said hi as she passed him. It was the same guy who always seemed to be working. He was probably a few years younger than she was.

Del picked up a basket and dropped her groceries inside. Raspberry roll-ups. More oatmeal and coffee. Pinto beans. Rice. A brick of cheap chocolate.

The lobster tank was fired up and bubbling. Lobsters stood

on the backs of other lobsters and stretched their claws toward the water level of the tank. She wondered if it was a coordinated effort that had been agreed on in advance by whatever way lobsters communicated or if the lobsters on the bottom of the pile feared being left behind. An orange sticker shaped like an explosion advertised buy one lobster, get one twenty-five percent off for Christmas. Had Christmas passed already, or was it still to come? She had forgotten to mark her calendar since she got back from the tree farm with Tym.

In the refrigerated case next to the lobsters were platters of cold boiled shrimp, curled around a pool of sauce in their pink suits like swimmers in an Esther Williams movie. Holiday party time. Strands of lights, punch bowls of sherbet and bourbon-soaked cherries, four people on a couch meant for three, waiting for the sound of the doorbell. She wondered if Tym would be going to their usual place, the old Irish bar that opened at noon on Christmas Day. Was Dave flying in from Los Angeles, as usual?

"That it?" the cashier asked.

"Yeah."

"We're closed Christmas Day and New Year's Day, just so you know."

"Cool, thanks."

"By 'day' I mean we will be closed at nine p.m. on Christmas Eve and open at six a.m. on the day after Christmas. Same goes for New Year's. I know you have this night-owl vibe happening, so I wouldn't want you to show up at midnight and be disappointed." His message delivered, he hacked into his hand, his whole body shaking with him. He looked like a woodcut of a plague victim.

"Jesus. Should you see a doctor?"

"You think Stop and Go offers health insurance?"

"Point taken. Maybe if you collapse and have to go to the ER, the hospital will write off the debt. I tried that once, when I thought I had appendicitis."

"Did it work?"

"No. I had a urinary tract infection. They told me to go to Planned Parenthood and sent me a bill for five hundred dollars anyhow. But you look a lot worse than I did."

He considered her offer. "Let's keep that as a back-pocket option. Thanks for thinking of me. Who are you?"

"Del." She put out her hand to shake.

He waved her away. "You don't want this, trust me. I'm Billy."

While Del wondered if she knew any Billys related to anyone she had known as a kid, Billy carefully positioned his body and then pulled two Rolos off the shelf and slid them down the chute to meet the rest of Del's groceries.

"Camera behind us," he told her quietly. "Act normal."

She made a show of packing up her purchases in her backpack in a perfectly normal and noncriminal way. She put the Rolos in the small zippered pocket at the bottom.

"That's nice of you," she told Billy. "But why help me out?"

"You pay in change sometimes. I'm just keeping you off the streets, if it's coming to that."

She snorted. "I appreciate the thought."

"It's pretty easy to get to know the regulars when you work

overnights. There's one guy who comes in and just buys water chestnuts. Huge cans of them. What's a water chestnut? I've worked here two years, and I still don't know. Me, I'm more of a pastry man. We used to get a free donut and coffee every day, but the new owners cut that off. Deep discounts, though. And after five p.m. the donuts are fifty percent off anyhow, so with my employee discount, that's basically free. Or that's what I tell myself when I just take them and don't pay."

"The math checks out. Anyhow, thanks again for the candy."

"See you around. Happy Hanukkah. Festive Kwanzaa." He collapsed into a fit of coughing.

The parking lot was empty except for three cars. Cameras: now, that she hadn't considered. She took a look around, identified a suspicious gray metal box under the southeast awning, and then retrieved a shopping cart from the opposite side of the awning, where her actions were partly concealed by an out-of-service 7UP machine. She threw her backpack in the cart, peeled the foil back on one of the Rolos, and rolled the stolen shopping cart out of the exit and into the street.

In the morning, Del turned off the circuit breaker, then started to strip away the old electric wiring in her bedroom. The light switch, still in its original ivory ceramic casing, dangled from a stud, where it was wound around a rusted nail. Some of the electrics were cloth-covered wires and ceramic knobs that had been put in when the old house first got electricity and plumbing. Other sections she and her dad had rewired through the years when there was a fault in the system. She loved the satisfying noise of the clipper snapping through the wires. Removing the wiring was a quick job: it reminded her of summers spent in the backyard, peeling the veins out from dried oak leaves.

Outside the house, she then spent an hour shoveling broken plaster into a pile that she intended to leave for the Murrows. They hadn't agreed on waste disposal, so she would simply pretend that they had agreed for the Murrows to dispose of the waste. They had machinery, as she had seen—it was nothing to them, although she reveled in the thought of their annoyance when they found an enormous pile of trash that they would need to clean up after she was gone.

Into the shopping cart she put the wires, switches, and knobs, as well as the assorted items she had missed and left in the room: empty vials of nail polish, a dog-eared compendium of short stories from high school, and a small crystal rabbit. She wheeled the cart down the slope behind the house and onto the pond.

The snow from the previous evening left a coating as thick as a shag rug on top of the ice. The shopping cart's wheels crunched over the snow until she got to the opposite side, where she had to shove it repeatedly to get up onto the pond's edge. She dumped the cart's contents onto the tarp and looked back at the trail of footsteps alongside the ribbon of wheel tracks.

When she was a child, she skated on the pond each winter. She used her grandmother's tiny white skates until she grew out of them when she was twelve, by which point skating had lost its appeal and she preferred sitting in her room alone watching old movies on the repurposed kitchen TV. Skating was easiest early in the season, when the ice was smooth as a plate. As the winter wore on, with melting and refreezing as well as cuts from her own blades, it became a trickier operation, and she would be covered in cuts and bruises from falling. For the three days in the hospital after the crash, when they thought it was possible that her mother might not die, Del had thought about skating a lot. It was the winter of her seventeenth year, and she was alone in a chair by her mother's bed. She had called her father and her mother's old high school friend, but no one came. Minutes spun into hours, hours into days, just the two of them, alone, interrupted on rare occasions by clinical workers and the omnipresent sound of her mother's breathing. The breaths, first as faultless as early season ice, smooth and regular, then, a catch: rasping, ragged, wobbling like a blade on uneven ground. Soon the machines beeped, engaged, inhaled for her.

After unloading, Del pushed the cart back down the bank and stepped onto the ice again. Empty, the cart was loose in its joints and harder to control. She corrected it back into its tracks, but it quickly spun left and had to be dragged straight again. Two-thirds of the way across the pond, the wheel caught on packed snow and wouldn't budge. Del tried to move backward, but there was no give. She pushed the cart once, twice, a third time. Finally the snow dislodged and the cart flew out from under her. Her weight lurched forward, then back, and she fell hard, her hip striking the ice first.

She blinked in pain, her cheek against the ice. She ran a gloved hand over the snow to clear it and inspected the area around her. Fine, shallow lines spidered out from her torso. She pushed her left arm and sat up. The cart was nose down in the snow against the edge of the pond closest to the house. Carefully, very carefully, she stood and stepped forward. The ice held. She took a step, and then another. Finally she reached the edge and crawled up the bank, where she lowered herself gingerly onto the snow and sat until her head cleared.

She left the cart on the ice and walked back into the house. For five minutes, or ten, or a week she needed a break. She sat on the living room floor.

But then a knock sounded on the door.

Fuck. Now? Who? Why?

"Fuck off," she said.

"Sweetheart? Are you in there?"

Del limped to the door.

Jeanne stood on the doorstep, carrying two bags.

"You know, you should really keep this locked," Jeanne said with a concerned tone. "A family over in the next town had their entire house robbed, down to the forks and knives."

"I don't have any forks or knives."

"You could be murdered or something."

Jeanne pushed past Del and walked into the living room. All the furniture was gone except for the couch frame. Del's bed was a rumpled sleeping bag alongside the couch. There were a few plastic skins from Fruit Roll-Ups drifting across the wooden floor. Del knew it wasn't far from an insane person's hovel, but her only concern was getting Jeanne out and then finding some ibuprofen.

"Why are you here?" Del asked.

"Just making sure you're safe."

"If someone broke in, I'd put my money on me."

Jeanne frowned.

"I brought you some things. It's our big Christmas party tonight. Remember going to that? We had such a good time when you were all kids. I've got a couple tins of cookies. The peanut butter ones you like, the ones with the chocolate center. I've got some smoked salmon, too. I was worried you didn't have a fridge, but it's freezing in here." She wrapped her arms around herself as if to make a point.

Del hadn't lit the coal stove in a few days. The work warmed her, and by the time she was done working, it was time to go to bed. Plus, she couldn't be taking a break every week to go to the feed store and buy more coal. There was too much to do and too little time.

"Thanks," Del said. Cookies weren't going to solve their problems. Also, she loathed Jeanne's terrible, dry cookies. She had had to smile and eat one at Jeanne's party every year because her mother had told her that to do so was polite. That time was over. Politeness had served no purpose. They were clearly enemies. Why was Jeanne really here? Was she spying on Del's progress? Reporting back to Mission Control, same as Greg? What did Uncle Chuck want to know? Probably he was surprised when she hadn't simply given in when he had destroyed her path to the site. Most likely he was trying to understand her new tactics. They'd get nothing out of her.

"I would love it if you would come tonight. People are coming by at seven. Family might come by earlier, if you don't want to deal with all the business acquaintances. Construction talk. It bores me to death!" She chuckled and looked to Del for commiseration. Del offered nothing. "I know things haven't been great, Adela, but we're still family and it's still Christmas. Won't you think about stopping by?"

Del took in Jeanne's presence, l'eau de Jeanne. Her blond bob was newly frosted, the edges sharp as if she had been pruned that very morning. Probably she had been: Jeanne seemed like the type of person who would go to the salon to prepare for a holiday party. The skin around her lips was lightly lined, and Del knew, because her mother had told her, that Jeanne used to have a pack-a-day habit that she had hidden from her husband and children but not from Del's mother, who was also a smoker. They had smoked together on the hospital balcony when Del was born.

Jeanne probably thought that she was a nice person. And maybe she even was nice, to some people, or in certain circumstances. But Del thought, perhaps, that people should be held to a higher standard than nice, and that Jeanne fell far short of that. Del's was the sort of standard that made you cut worthless people out of your life and avoid frauds, assholes, and cowards. Jeanne would never do that because if she did, who would go to her holiday party? She would be all dolled up in her velvet dress, the tree groaning under the weight of its ornaments, piles of finger foods on inherited plates, and no one would be there to appreciate any of it, because Jeanne had been discerning for once, and it meant that her entire social pyramid had collapsed.

"I'll try to stop by."

"Are you just saying that to get me to leave?"

Del raised her eyebrows. "Guess we'll find out. Hope Santa brings you everything you deserve."

Jeanne seemed as if she might press further, but she didn't. She left the bags and then walked herself to the door.

"Merry Christmas, Adela. I'm hoping we'll see you tonight."

Del limped to the back door with the tin of peanut butter cookies. She hurled each one into the snow and watched as a crow descended to pick them apart, then she went back into the house to find some pills.

At quarter to seven, she wrapped up and began walking toward the Murrow house, which normally would be about a twenty-minute walk but took thirty with her sore hip. She still hadn't gotten any ibuprofen, but she found some of her mother's painkillers, which gave her an effervescent feeling, as if bubbles might run out of the top of her skull.

Their house was a Greek Revival of painted white bricks fronted with solid pillars on either side of the door. Electric candles flickered in each window, and there was an enormous holly wreath nailed to the front door, where a couple stood and pressed the bell. Del stood back, next to the line of parked cars alongside the driveway. Del noted Greg's truck as well as a few more Murrow corporate vehicles that could be either Greg's brothers' or some other employees'. After looking over her shoulder to see if anyone was observing her, she pushed one of the driver's-side mirrors on a Murrow vehicle until it snapped and rolled back like the eyes of a dead man.

The sound of a tinkling piano escaped as the front door shut behind the couple entering the house. Had the Murrows become the type of people who bought a piano? And if so, who played it? Probably someone they hired for parties. A paid piano man, maybe the local high school music teacher, whom they would smile at during the party and ignore if they saw him asking for donations outside the supermarket.

She waited a minute for the couple to blend into the party and then tested the door. The knob was solid brass and turned quietly. Inside, thick honey-colored carpet spilled down the massive central staircase, which ended with black-and-white-checked tiles on the floor. To the left was Chuck's TV room, which he called the den. Kids were not allowed inside the den. Back when Del was a small child, and when the parties were casual family affairs, Chuck used to sit inside the den alone with the door closed once he got bored or irritated by Jeanne's frequent social gatherings. Now the door was open, and the maroon leather couch was piled high with guest coats. There was a silver platter of keys on a polished wooden table. Del knew that the party would be at the back of the house, in a large, windowed room that the original owners had used for their indoor pool. The Murrows had filled in the pool when they bought the place. Originally the windows overlooked a field of pumpkins that Del's grandparents had planted. But why have pumpkins when you could make money? Now, Del suspected it bordered a cul-de-sac, or maybe a nuclear power plant.

There was a quick, quiet knock at the front door. It didn't carry over the sound of the piano. Del approached the door cautiously and opened it. A man in a navy wool coat held a bottle of wine. She thought he seemed like someone who worked in construction, or construction-adjacent. It was obvious that he counted something for a living. It was something about the collar of his button-down shirt: he seemed like he might have twenty of them in the same color, each one hanging in his closet in its plastic bag from the dry cleaner's.

"Sorry I'm late." He smiled. "Are you a Murrow?"

"Nope. Hired help. The party's in the back. You can leave your stuff up here if you want."

His grin disappeared as he walked past her. "Toss this on the pile?"

She took his coat, waited until he disappeared, and then went back to the den. A quick sweep of all the unattended coat pockets revealed very little of interest: crumpled receipts, more keys, packets of Kleenex, a few dollar bills, which she kept. "Asset transfer" was a phrase she had learned from her week-long temp job at a finance company.

There was a sound of voices approaching from the hall. Del stood on the other side of the door.

"Must be nice," said an unknown woman's voice. "To be born into a family like this."

"I guess." It was Greg. "I've never really known anything different. It was nice of you to come. See you in January?"

The woman apologized for not being able to stay longer but didn't sound too sorry about it. She left, and Greg retreated back to the party.

In the silver tray Del picked out four sets of keys with Murrow Construction key rings. Perfect. She moved quickly outside and tried the keys in the trucks that had the Murrow logo on their doors. Finally she found the key that unlocked Greg's truck.

She had only driven a handful of times since getting her license, but driving came naturally to her. She didn't head straight to her destination but went, instead, to the highway. With the window rolled down, the cold breeze felt like a slap, but she liked it. At the fast-food window, she ordered three fried apple pies, a large soda, and two extra-large fries. She still had change from the money she'd stolen from the Murrows' party.

By the time she got home, the cab of the truck stank of fried food. In retrospect, she should have ordered a fried fish sandwich and hid chunks of it under the floor mats. She threw the paper bag into the footwell and kept the truck running and the headlights pointed at the house as she went inside to get the rope and the ladder. With the ladder against the house, she tied a bowline knot and started up the side of the house with the rope in her teeth. It was dark near the roofline, despite the headlights. She ran her fingers across the bricks and then threw the looped rope. It fell slack against the pitched roof and dropped to the ground. She dragged it back up and threw it a second time, again missing her mark. Four more attempts later, she watched as the rope landed atop the cap and slid down the chimney. She dropped the length to the ground and climbed down.

Back at the truck, she tied the rope to a tow hook and got back in the driver's seat. With the truck in reverse, she slammed her foot on the gas pedal and watched as the top of the chimney resisted for a moment and then buckled, toppling over onto the ground below. Chunks of chimney and mortar held together in short segments on the snow. The entire operation was so smooth and beautiful she wished there was someone else to admire it.

Instead she drove in silence into a Murrow cul-de-sac, where she parked, tossed the keys into a sewer grate, and walked home.

Chapter Twenty-Five

SHE WAS STRIPPING THE KITCHEN WHEN THE DOOR BANGED open. It was nearly noon; she had expected him earlier.

"Where's my truck?" Greg shouted from the front door.

She stuck her head out of the kitchen. "You don't knock? Rude."

"I said, where's my truck, Del?"

She brushed the plaster off her forehead. "Do you see a truck?"

"No, that's why I'm asking what you did with it."

"I don't have your truck. If you lost it, I suggest you think back on everything you did yesterday and where you might have left it. That's what works for me when I've lost something."

He was frustrated now. His mistake—you can't show your weakness so early in an argument. "I drove it to a party at my family's house. You were invited. It went missing. So did a bunch of things from people's pockets."

She shrugged and picked up the small claw. "No idea. I'm

too busy for parties. I've got quite a lot of work to do, as you can see, so I'd appreciate it if you took your mystery elsewhere. Hire a detective, if you need to."

"Just because things are difficult for you doesn't mean you have to be an asshole to me." He was heating up. Like all Murrows, he gestured wildly with his hands when he was angry or frustrated.

"Oh, really?" Del said coolly. "A funny thing, then, you telling your dad that I'd be out of town so that you could destroy my path to the new site."

"It wasn't like that."

"Huh." She dug into a low cabinet that was bolted to the wall. "Because that's what it looked like."

"He was going to prep the site anyhow. He had to. It was always part of the plan. I mentioned that I'd seen you and you were headed out for a while. Actually, I thought you weren't coming back. I thought you might have left for good. You never know, with you. And by the way? Not everyone gets to be a hermit, like you. Some of us need to get on with it. Actually talk to people and see our families. Bet it never occurred to you that it's actually easy, your way."

"I completely agree. Having nothing to do with the rest of you was a very easy decision."

The bolt loosened, and the cabinet came free from the wall, landing on the linoleum floor with a crash. She lifted it and placed it in the shopping cart. That was half the cabinets done. The bare wall showed the layers of wallpaper since the house had been built: green with white sprigs, brown and cream cubes, peach and white stripes.

"So are you going to tell me where it is?" he asked.

"No idea. You were probably drunk and left it somewhere. Just go through your last steps. That's what I always did when I lost my keys."

"I tried to help you. I did. But you're a selfish asshole."

"Maybe. But I'm also very busy, so I'd appreciate it if you left. Quite a lot to do, as you know."

Greg turned to leave. She followed him to the door to make sure he drove away in his borrowed car, a lime-green two-door. Good. He deserved all that and more.

After he departed, a flock of wild turkeys nudged out of the scrubby woods across the road and gathered on her driveway. There were four of them, plump and brown, with knobbled heads like dripping wax. Del stood at the door until the birds heard a thunderclap and rushed into the woods dividing her property from the Francis place. Then she returned to the kitchen and wheeled the cabinets down to the pond.

January

Chapter Twenty-Six

THE KITCHEN TOOK A WEEK TO DISMANTLE, BECAUSE OF VARIOUS complications. Plumbing being one. She had done minor electrical work in the house with her father, but for plumbing they had called her dad's friend Reggie, who did the work in exchange for having his car fixed. There were various valves in the basement that she turned to a position that might be off or, equally, might result in a flood.

She lifted the aluminum sink from its supports and then placed it on the floor. Did Greg ever find his truck? At some point, someone must have called in the mysterious truck parked on their street. Nothing went unnoticed in small, shitty towns like this. That was probably especially the case on cul-de-sacs, with all the houses staring at each other. There would have been glances the first morning the truck was noticed, frowns and whispers the next day, then a call to 911 on the third day. Maybe officers swarmed the truck, guns drawn, to see if there was a body inside.

Either way, Greg certainly knew she had done it, and her

point had been made. The Murrows should leave her alone. She didn't want their invitations, their parties, their inquiries, or their friendly visits. She wanted to be left alone. Their little plots would have no effect.

After unscrewing the plastic pipe connectors that attached the sink to the wall, she examined the network of metal that had been revealed when she tore down the plaster. It would have been an easy job if she had power and was able to plug in the reciprocating saw in the shed. She didn't, so she used a normal saw. It took nearly ten minutes to break through the top of one metal segment, then the same amount of time to nearly saw through the bottom. She grasped the pipe and pulled. It bent but didn't give. She held it again, closer to the top, and pulled harder. The pipe bent, twisted, and finally snapped free. She watched a red drop roll down the tarnished copper. The soft part of her palm had dragged against the rough edge of cut metal and opened. She watched as the blood pulsed out of the cut. More, more. It soaked into the cuff of her sweatshirt. She was too surprised to notice the pain, so she wrapped her hand in a clean sock and continued working.

The bleeding didn't stop. It was below zero and past midnight when she got to the supermarket. They would have bandages or whatever was beyond bandages for more serious cuts. Bandages stage two. Bandages the sequel. The Bandaging.

"Hello," Billy said. "Survived the holiday season, I see?"

She blinked at him. The hip that she had smacked against the ice remained sore and stiff. It was difficult to walk to the store, and if she had been sensible, she would have gone earlier and taken the regional bus that came once an hour and hit the hot spots, such as the supermarket and the movie theater in the next town. But then she might have seen someone. Someone who recognized her or knew the Murrows or her parents. Anyone who would have wanted to talk to her. So this was better, the long, slow walk in the night, protected by the quiet.

"Can I ask what's going on?" Billy gestured to her sleeve, a queer look on his face. The blood had soaked through the sock and then through her glove. She held the arm close to her body. "Blood actually makes me want to vomit. I had to stay home from school when the Red Cross came to do their drives."

"It's just a little cut," she explained. "Do you have gauze or something?"

"Aisle seven."

She shuffled to the medications aisle. There were silver boxes of painkillers, every type of syrup, sinus medicine, pills to make you skinny, pills to wake you up, pills to put you to sleep again. At the end of the aisle she found ankle and wrist protectors for stress injuries and, beneath that, rolled gauze and tape. She got some cotton balls and antiseptic spray as well. Turning, she saw Billy at the end of the aisle.

"Are you OK?" he called out while remaining a safe distance away.

"Yeah," she mumbled. "Fine."

"Your skin is gray. Maybe you should go to the doctor."

"Unemployment doesn't come with health insurance."

"What are you going to do with that stuff? Do you even have running water at your house?"

She was flustered. "What about my house? What do you know about it?"

"Half of the people in this town are related. Everybody knows everything. I'm surprised you haven't had your photo in the paper."

When she was twelve, she very briefly had puffy, curly hair that grew around her head like a cartoon of a rain cloud. It was only for a year or so, then it became a dark, loose wave like her father's hair. But while it was curly, strangers liked to approach her in the mall or at the diner and remark on it. Old people mostly. Some of them touched it. Shirley Temple, they said. *Tell them not to look at me*, she hissed at her mother. *Tell them that I'm invisible.*

She brushed past him. "I just need to buy this stuff."

"But don't you need water? What are you going to do? Run it through a creek or something?"

"I'll figure it out."

"There's a bathroom in back for employees. It's hygienic. Or at least clean. I know because I have to clean it at the beginning of my shift. I'll give you the key—just go in there and wash up. Do me a favor and don't leave any blood behind."

She looked at him. Why was he being nice to her? What did he want?

"I'll be fine."

"You ever seen gangrene?" he asked her. "If you can't afford to eat better than rice and beans, you definitely can't afford for your fucking hand to rot off. That's surgery. You can't even imagine how much that costs."

"OK, fine," she said, exasperated. "Give me the key."

"Wipe up after! There's a spray bottle of cleaner on the floor. Use it."

In the bathroom, she gingerly removed her glove and then the sock. Both were stiff with frozen blood. With her teeth, she wrenched the plastic wrapping off the antiseptic spray and turned on the tap until it flooded the sink. She caught a glimpse of herself in the mirror above the sink as she plunged her wounded hand into the water. The fat was gone from her cheeks. Her hair had grown since she cut it. She brushed her bangs away from her eyes with her unwounded hand. She was strange to herself: thin, ropy, with a tan across her nose and cheeks from working outside. At the edge of her vision, she saw the pink water in the sink. Without looking at the cut, she pressed paper towels against it while she inspected the calendar nailed above the wastebasket.

She flew through the bathroom door and found Billy, who was rearranging the magazines at the checkout so that *Gun & Reel* was in back and *Princess Pony's WonderWorld* was in front.

"What day is it?" she asked him.

He checked his calculator watch. "January twelfth. Monday. One oh nine a.m. Capricorn, I think?"

"Fuck."

Where had the time gone? It was just six weeks or so until Chuck would come knocking. Except for her parents' room, which remained untouched, she had gutted the house's interior, but there was still so much left to do. Such as removing an entire suspended floor. And a roof.

"Could you see to that?" Billy asked her.

"What?"

Billy queasily pointed to the floor. Drops of blood. His face had gone dead white.

"I'll clean it up."

He edged away from her toward the far end of the checkout counter. "There's a mop behind the pick-a-mix. A kid threw up there this afternoon. Also, never buy from a pick-a-mix."

She went back to the bathroom to dry her hand, spray it with antiseptic, and wrap it tightly in gauze. Then, as Billy had asked, she found the mop and bucket by the pick-a-mix, which reeked of vomit, and wheeled it over to the blood. It was about two drips of blood, really. She should have made Billy do it himself. Wasn't arachnophobia cured by making people interact with spiders? Blood was undoubtedly the same. She looked up to find him. He remained on the far side of the checkout area, observing her with an air of caution.

"You should really be doing this."

"No, thanks. I'm good."

"It's your job."

"I'm a cashier, not a crime scene investigator."

She pulled the mop through the wringer. "You cleaned up the vomit."

He restraightened the already straight magazine display. "I didn't, actually. The janitor did. His shift ends at midnight."

"I've got work to do. I've got deadlines. I can't be unpaid labor."

"Get over yourself. You're cleaning up a mess you made."

She sighed. Her hand was throbbing. She needed to be in good shape to work tomorrow. Maybe she should take a pain-killer.

"OK, I've cleaned up the exactly two drops of blood that I dropped. It was like a sparrow with consumption flew through here for a quarter of a millisecond. I don't know why you're acting like a cholera victim shat himself to death in here."

He waved her away. "I'm here to conduct financial transactions on behalf of Stop and Go Enterprises, a subsidiary of GroGo National."

"I'm leaving the bucket here."

"Fine."

"I'm taking my groceries, too. I'm leaving now. And I'm not paying."

"Adios."

"I'm about to walk through the door. You'd have to come over here and see the blood if you wanted to stop me. It's actually getting quite gruesome again. The blood is getting kinda thick. Syrupy, I think you'd call it."

"Shut up," he said, plugging his ears. "Come back when you're healed."

She stepped through the automatic doors, dangling the basket of groceries in front of her in case he wanted to come and stop her. He remained on the far side of the checkout. She shrugged, loaded the stuff into her backpack, and went home.

Chapter Twenty-Seven

IT WAS DIFFICULT TO DISASSEMBLE A HOUSE AT ALL, AND BORDER-line comical to do so with a wounded hand and sore hip. She did it anyhow, because she had to. When the pain got bad, she took half of one of her mother's old painkillers until the routine of the day went dull and slippery, and then suddenly it was time to go to sleep for the night.

Six and a half weeks. It wasn't enough time. It couldn't be.

She sawed the remainder of the kitchen piping system, more carefully now than before. Loading the segments of pipe into the cart, she wheeled them down and across the frozen pond with a steady grip on the cart handles. The cold burn of the air felt good in her lungs.

Back at the house, she shook out her sleeping bag and scrubbed the oatmeal bowl from that morning. Looking around, she tried to find other things to do. She could rip the curtain hangers off the wall in the living room. She could remove the rest of the interior doors from the house. She could drag more trash to the heap. She wanted to find something to do. But she knew that she couldn't wait any longer. Reluctantly, she gathered her tools, went upstairs, and opened the door.

There was a faint aroma of mold and cigarettes. The window frame that faced the backyard was swollen with rainwater and had split. A drip rolled from the split frame to a black patch in the peach-colored carpet.

Del sat on her mother's side of the bed and flipped through the pile of books she had flung onto the comforter. Romances. A few thrillers. Her mother had loved to be scared. She opened the drawer of the bedside table and upended it onto the comforter. There were thin gold chains, a half-empty tube of hand cream, a pack of cigarettes, four jewel-toned plastic lighters, and a medal of St. Christopher, the patron saint of travelers. Del put the medal in her pocket.

She had never gotten to know her mother as an adult, and maybe that was the problem. If Del had had a chance to come back home as an adult, get in the regular sort of fights with her mother, have the regular sort of rapprochements, things would have been different. Instead she had known her mother only to the point of realizing that she'd shaped her childhood around her mother's shortcomings, had cared for herself in what little ways were possible because her mother's complications didn't leave Louise enough slack to care for her daughter, and that sense of Del's resentment, that chill, draped over the memories of her mother and wouldn't shift.

The wallpaper in the bedroom was the color of whipped butter, with a vertical repeating pattern of pansies wrapped with a purple bow. It didn't seem like either of her parents' taste. She wondered if her grandparents had chosen it, or if they had inherited it, too, and woke up every day looking at something they disliked because it just happened to be there and was too annoying to fix. That's how you end up dying after living for decades in a room you hate. She thought about her father moving into the house with her and her mother when her grandmother was at the end of her life. Did he think he would make improvements? Did they think they would sell it and move on?

Her dad had never gotten along with the Murrows. She wondered if they had known he was gay all along, or if it was because his mother was Puerto Rican. She was aware of the tension even when she was very young: her father would never go to parties at the Murrows' place. Whatever their problem with him, Del and her dad had never talked about it when she moved in with him.

The day she showed up at his door, after her mother's funeral, he seemed surprised to see her but didn't ask questions. His apartment in the city had a small spare room, so they bought an air mattress for her until he got paid the next month and bought her a real bed. For weeks after that, he went off to work at the auto body shop in the morning, and she took his house keys and walked around the city alone. Some nights he came home very late; other nights, he didn't return at all. It was a strange time. She was seventeen, her mother was dead, her father a mystery, and she was living in a new place with no friends and no cash. About a month after her arrival, a discount clothing shop hired her to fold shirts in the men's department. When her first paycheck arrived three weeks later, she came home with a large pizza and a six-pack of beer. He glanced at the beer, but then they had dinner and watched a show about Sherman's march to the sea. Something changed. Later that week, he invited her out with him and a group of friends. Gay men in their forties, like him. They were funny and welcoming, and at the end of the night, a slightly paunchy guy in shorts arrived and sat next to her.

"Hi, I'm Tym," he said.

Her parents would laugh if they could see her. Her mother would take the cigarette out of her lips and shake her head in disbelief, the same way she did when something bizarre came on the news, like a garage piled high with diapers for a family with quintuplets. Those poor idiots. Who was the idiot now?

Her father, though. Del regarded the room, from the flower-printed wallpaper to the pink crocheted throw on the foot of the bed. This space was never for him. If he were here now, he would inspect her work, notice how she was beginning to saw the pipes more efficiently or how quickly she had removed the wiring. He wouldn't tell her that she had done a good job because he wasn't one to give or take compliments, but she would know that he was impressed by how he ran his finger along the smooth cuts she had made.

She emptied the drawer from his side of the bed onto the comforter. There was a pack of cigarettes, a book of matches with a picture of a cowboy printed on the front, a box of condoms, several ballpoint pens, and a stack of business cards. She wanted a clue, something that pointed to an explanation of her parents' relationship, their personalities, how they felt about being her parents. It was just old junk.

She uncapped a pen and tried to scribble on one of the business cards. The ink had run dry.

Del wondered if it was better to have interesting parents or boring ones. Boring ones at least might have lasted longer.

They had a lot of good times, watching midnight movies on the couch or going to the county fair in the fall. It was the same every year: the slow spin of the Ferris wheel; the sly, skinny barkers; the hum of monster trucks revving in the open-air ring. Del and her father loved to fly down the superslide on burlap sacks. Her mother picked at an enormous yeasted donut rolled in hot sugar and gave Del a handful of quarters to play games in the midway. Her mother was the crack shot: when she was a kid, Louise had used a twelve-gauge to pick off the groundhogs that were harassing the crops and then stuffed their bodies down into their burrows again. Every year at the fair, Del pointed to an enormous stuffed toy, and then her mother won it for her at one of the shooting games.

It was at a shoot that they had met, Del now remembered. One of the turkey shoots in the fall, where the contestants line up against a barn and shoot at targets outlined with a fat bird. Winner takes home a frozen turkey. Her father had been in-fantry and fancied himself a shoo-in when one of his buddies invited him to a target shoot in the middle of nowhere as a funny thing to do on a weekend. Her mother had laughed when telling the story. The little Murrow girl had won every year. Her father's telling of the story didn't have any whiff of that confidence. She was just a little thing in blue jeans and a red peasant top she had sewn herself.

In both sides of the story she walked up to the strangers and stuck out her hand. *Hey,* she said. *I'm Louise Murrow, and I'm going to win this thing.* And then she did. She was seventeen. They got married the next year.

Del swung the pickax, aiming it at a nosegay in the center of the wall. Under the wallpaper, the plaster split and flaked. She struck again and again, watching the paper shred and the plaster tumble down in chunks. She fitted a shovel under a bulge in the wall and pulled the handle toward her. Nearly a quarter of the wall pulled forward and cascaded to the ground, breaking into pieces as it hit the carpet. Del coughed on the plaster dust, wiped her mouth, and continued working.

"Knock knock."

Her parents' bedroom door swung open. It was Auntie Jeanne. Del ignored her, took up the pickax again, and swung.

"Hello!" Jeanne said brightly. "Can we have a chat?"

Again Del fixed the shovel under a gap in the plaster and pulled.

"Del? Del? I am right here. You can't ignore me forever."

Behind the wallpaper was an older pattern, cornflower blue with small golden wreaths.

"I'm actually here because I need a favor. I need to stay with you for a little while. Here."

Finally, Del relented and turned to her aunt. A small duffel bag sat by Jeanne's feet.

Without saying anything, Del moved past her and took the steps two at a time to get downstairs. There was a toolbox by the back door. She removed a hammer and a few nails. From the wreckage on the kitchen floor she chose a piece of wood of about six inches in length, then went to the front door.

Jeanne came up behind her as she was working.

"What are you doing?" Jeanne asked.

Del mumbled through the three nails she held in her lips.

"What?" Jeanne asked.

Del took a nail out, positioned it over the piece of wood against the door, and swung the hammer. "I'm locking the door."

"That's an odd way of doing it."

"It's an effective way. And since none of you seem to be able to leave me alone, it's essential, apparently."

"It's just for a few days."

"No."

"It's an emergency."

"I don't care."

"You'd be doing me a favor."

"I don't owe you a favor."

"It'll make Uncle Chuck really mad."

Del paused at this. The statement had the air of truth, and yet still she wasn't sold.

"Why are you here? This isn't a vacation spot. Go to Florida if you want."

"Del, I wouldn't ask you if it weren't necessary. But it is. I've always helped you out when I could. This is me asking you for something, just one time."

"Why?"

"I had an argument with Uncle Chuck. I just need some time to breathe, clear the air. Think about my next move."

"There are motels all up and down the turnpike."

Del wasn't the least bit curious about Jeanne or her next move, whatever that might be. They had probably had a stupid argument about what kind of canapés to serve at the next Murrow company party.

"He might look there. I need to be alone. He won't think to come here. Why would anyone stay in a place like this? And I don't want anyone else to see me and to ask questions. I just need—I need a little peace."

A filthy curtain twitched in the subzero breeze. Del hadn't lit the stove in days. Lingering in the air was the stink of the rice and beans she had left to burn the previous evening.

"I'm busy. I don't have time to help you out of whatever your problem is."

"I don't need help. I just need a place to stay. Just for a few days. Please. I'll be completely out of your way."

Del smacked the remaining nails into place. She was unmoved.

"I can help you," Jeanne offered.

"How?"

"I've got the keys."

"What keys?"

"The keys to everything. The office. The equipment. All of it. Think how much time you would save if you had the right tools for the job. Even the heavy equipment you could take. So long as no one notices, you can borrow whatever you need. Murrow's a big operation now. Thirty employees."

Del avoided eye contact with Jeanne. She didn't want to encourage her. But this offer was worth considering. She hadn't taken down the lath yet. The frame of the house would take weeks, maybe more time than she had available.

"Fine. You can stay a couple days, if you are completely out of my way. Just give me the keys."

Jeanne shook her head. "No way. You'll burn the place down. I said you could borrow things, and that's what I meant. We'll go tonight, after everyone's gone home."

Del dropped the hammer in the toolbox. "I've got to go to work."

"What do you want me to do?" Jeanne asked.

"If you want to stay, you had better be invisible."

Del put down the hammer and went back upstairs to rip the carpet out of her parents' room.

By the late afternoon the sun had set, and Del could no longer make out the details well enough to continue work in the room. She had ripped out the carpet, taken the wallpaper and plaster off all four walls, and gathered everything she wanted to keep onto the mattress.

Normally at this time, she would go downstairs, light the battery-operated lanterns she had bought at the grain store, and fix dinner before an early bedtime and early rising. The plan was shot with Jeanne there. She didn't want to exchange pleasantries with her aunt. She could hear Jeanne downstairs doing god knows what, but she hoped if she remained still and quiet, her aunt might realize what a huge mistake it was staying with her and disappear.

Del sat on the edge of her parents' bed and looked out the back window, down the snow-covered lawn and across the frozen pond. In the fading twilight, she could just make out the blue tarps overlaid on her site and the strange hulking shapes of her piled belongings. It was beautiful, almost, if you didn't know that the piles were made up of cracked lamps, plastic storage containers, coats spotted with mildew, and mostly empty canisters of powdered bathroom scrub. Del felt a quiet thrill. She had done all of it herself. Hobbled, sore, thin and tired, and yet still.

There was a quiet knock on the door behind her. Del turned.

"Yoo-hoo. I organized your supplies downstairs. Gosh, if there was an apocalypse, you'd be all set."

Her aunt smiled. This was an offering. Del faced the window again. The light had gone.

"Listen," Jeanne continued. "I'm going to go get a bite. Then after that I was thinking we could stop by to pick up the stuff you need. The guys start early. Everyone will have cleared out by four p.m."

"What time is it?"

"Just after six."

Del heaved herself up from the bed and strode out the door.

"Is this going to be the extent of our interaction?" asked Jeanne, who was following her down the stairs.

"I didn't invite you over for a dinner party, Jeanne. I don't care what your problem is. I don't want to talk about it. Hire a therapist."

Jeanne smoothed her hair into place and then put on an insulated jacket with a fur-lined hood. "I know I'm asking you for the favor here. I'm in your debt. But there's no reason not to be polite, at least."

"There is every reason not to be polite. In fact, there's no reason to be polite. We can remain politely in silence, if you prefer."

Jeanne rolled her eyes dramatically and shrugged. "Fine. I give up. Let's go."

They drove at high speed down the highway to a chain restaurant three towns over, which Del guessed was so that there was no chance they would run into Uncle Chuck, but she didn't bother confirming because she didn't care.

Jeanne got grilled chicken on a bed of wilted, ranch-coated lettuce, while Del requested two orders of mozzarella sticks, the sizzlin' fajita platter, a fudge sundae with brownie bites and extra cherries, and four large Cokes. They ate in what Del hoped was a prickly silence.

Jeanne slurped the last bit of iced tea from her glass. A fake Tiffany-style lamp swung overhead.

"So," Jeanne said finally. "I've been seeing someone."

Del worked very hard to show absolutely no interest on her face. She thought about taxes, weather reports, the channel on TV that showed politicians debating over farm subsidies.

Jeanne blinked into the light bulb dangling above them. Del turned to look at the bar in such a way that she could see Jeanne without looking at her directly.

"It's a whole mess," Jeanne continued, her voice quavering. "It started off innocent. Just someone I know from a committee. We were co-leaders of the central business district holiday lights show. You remember, that's a big deal. Months of planning. We were together every day for six weeks in advance. Finding the best deal on lights. Stringing 'em up."

Could something be so scandalous yet so boring? The display, as Del remembered it, consisted of a half dozen wire-framed reindeer strung with white lights and suspended from the lampposts on Main Street. There was a committee for that?

"And he just . . ." Jeanne balled up her napkin and touched it to her nose. "He listened to me. He was interested in things I had to say. He didn't bark at me. He didn't take me for granted."

The waitress arrived to pour water into their cups. "Anything else I can get you?"

Jeanne quickly dabbed her eyes and smiled sweetly. "We're good. Just the check, please."

Del downed the last of her soda, letting the ice cubes tumble against her lips. She couldn't wait to text Tym about this. It had been more than a week since she had heard from him. She had little to say when they corresponded, so their text exchanges ended quickly, but this was something else. This might even be worth their first phone call.

Jeanne had put on her coat and was looking at her face in the mirror of a green marbled compact. "You ready?"

Del swung her legs over the fake leather bench seat and stood up. "Let's go."

Chapter Twenty-Eight

WHEN DEL WAS SMALL AND THE MURROW EMPIRE WAS NEW, THE Murrows kept their heavy equipment in a lot to the side of their old place, which was a small seventies-style ranch house on the edge of town.

Del was surprised to find Jeanne driving back toward the old house.

"Everything's still here?" Del asked.

"The land was worth more than the house. We knocked it down, put up some storage. It could have been difficult, actually, to get the land zoned for commercial, but I think Uncle Chuck made a deal with the commissioner."

"What kind of deal?"

"The commissioner's daughter got a deep discount on a house in a Murrow Estate. Cranberry Hills. She had just gotten married and nearly drove them bankrupt for the wedding. Jillian Fogarty, remember her?"

The Fogartys were a big family. Del had gone to school with one of Jillian's little sisters.

Jeanne turned into the driveway. "Dead now. Breast cancer. The commissioner's wife had it, too. Bad genes. The original Mrs. Fogarty made really good deviled eggs. Reminds me I've got to ask his new wife if she ever found the recipe."

The single-level house had been knocked down and replaced with a large corrugated steel storage shed illuminated with floodlights. Several heavy vehicles hulked in the dark to the side and the back of the shed. Jeanne fitted the key to the door of the storage shed and clicked on the light inside. Pegboard walls were hung with every type of tool. To the back were metal drawers and motorized equipment. A few heavy-duty lawn mowers sat silently on the cement floor.

Del considered her options. "So I've got one day of using whatever I choose, at best."

"Why one day?" Jeanne asked.

"When they come in in the morning, they're going to see things are missing. Greg will think it's me."

"Who do you think does the inventory around here? Mitch and Kevin?" she scoffed.

"Well, it's going to be obvious if I take ten things."

"Then don't take ten things. Think of it like a library. What's the amount of books you can take? Three? Four? They're not going to notice. It's always me on top of stuff like that. I actually caught one of our landscapers stealing. We can come back and do another exchange next week."

Del turned to look at Jeanne. "Exactly how long do you think you're staying with me?"

"Just another day or two," Jeanne assured her. "Just until things cool down a little bit and I can talk to Uncle Chuck sensibly. He gets so hot under the collar. But I can pick you up next week and do another run over here. We can get dinner, too. Just a little girl time."

Del ran her fingertips over the pegboard wall, which had outlines of the tools drawn in black marker.

Jeanne sat on a wheeled chair upholstered in a faded orange fabric and pulled out her phone. The volume was turned up, and every time she pressed a button, the phone chirped.

Some of the tools were unfamiliar to Del, but she could work out their purpose and their usefulness to her. She claimed a battery-powered box that would allow her to plug tools in despite her lack of electricity, a couple of motorized saws of different lengths, and a toolbox of assorted items. She left Jeanne inside, entranced by her phone, while she went out to look at the vehicles. There were two bulldozers, a backhoe, an excavator, a dump truck, and two machines she had never seen before. One looked like it sliced into the earth; the other looked like it flattened dirt. She didn't need either one for now. Perhaps later.

She peered through a small venting window into the shed and saw Jeanne still in her chair, texting. Pathetic. She was like a teenager. What was Uncle Chuck going to do about it? Was he madly hunting through the town, red-faced and angry, trying to find her? She wondered if he was more furious or more embarrassed. Either way, it was hilarious and exactly what he deserved. She was only too happy to do her small part to stir up the drama.

Del put the equipment she had chosen into the back of Jeanne's SUV and got into the passenger seat, which she reclined. There was no rush to get home. It was warm in the truck, and Jeanne had left the keys in the ignition, so Del turned the heat on.

Eleanor had been right. Everyone had their own Roman imperial family, with backstabbers and poisoners and liars among your nearest and dearest. It simply proved again that going it alone was best. Del turned on the radio to a classical music station and closed her eyes.

Wearing a pair of pajamas printed with tiny toasters, Jeanne walked into Del's old bedroom in the morning.

"What are you doing?" she asked Del over the racket of the saw.

"Working."

"It's six in the morning." Jeanne's hair was matted on the left side of her head. She had slept in Del's parents' room, the only place where there was still a mattress and a pillow.

"Is that so?" Del turned back to the wall and continued to saw through the horizontal strips of wood between studs. The laths fell to the floor in a dusty pile.

"Can't you get started a little later? Eight or something? A normal time?"

"No."

"Seven thirty?"

"Nope."

Jeanne yawned. "Fine. I'll go make the coffee."

Jeanne used to come to the house to have sleepovers with Del and her mom, Louise, every once in a while. They would get a movie from the video store and a megapack of candy. Jeanne liked chewy pink licorice, which Del and her mom thought was miscategorized as a variety of candy. Del and her mom sat on the couch eating one package of sour hard candy after another. Jeanne was not a morning person and would have to be roused from the couch at ten. Sometimes she had stayed for multiple days, and Del could tell her mother was pretty tired of having a guest over by the end.

Removing the lath was quick: the electrified saw whizzed through the entire room in a couple of hours. She came downstairs to get a drink and found Jeanne, mug in hand, looking out the sliding glass door to the backyard.

"This view reminds me of your mom," Jeanne said. "Remember when the ducks would come in the fall and she had stored up a whole freezer's worth of stale bread for them?"

Del went into the bathroom, which had the only remaining working sink, and poured water into the pot, then returned to the living room to boil it on the camp stove for some cocoa.

"Might go to the mall today," Jeanne continued, still looking out over the yard. "We're looking for a new fleece supplier for the company, and there's some place in the mall where they print company logos on clothes, so I'm going to check that out."

The flame on the camp stove was a thin flicker against the cheap aluminum pot. Del willed it to boil quickly so that she could go back upstairs.

"Do you need anything?" Jeanne asked, turning to her.

Del didn't respond.

"Do you need anything?" Jeanne repeated. "At the mall?"

"No," Del said, pouring lukewarm water over the powder in

the bottom of a mug. It was her father's favorite: a clay mug with a sculpted mustachioed face in one side. The spoon rattled against the clay, then Del hustled toward the staircase.

"Just let me know," Jeanne called hopefully. "If you change your mind."

With the lath and plaster removed in her bedroom, the walls were down to the bare studs. Del drank an unsatisfying cocoa, then went out to the shed for a ladder. It would be easier and perhaps smarter to continue removing the lath in other rooms, but that would require interacting with Jeanne, so instead she would take on the ceiling. Del climbed the ladder, lifted a shovel above her head, and swung. The plaster cracked. With another swing, the cracks stretched farther, and a large section of the ceiling began to sag. It was in the shape of Oklahoma. Del fitted the shovel's lip under the panhandle and pulled. Oklahoma fell to the floor and smashed to bits.

"Aren't you worried about asbestos?"

Billy stood in the doorway.

Del ran the back of her hand over her mouth. It came away damp with sweat and plaster.

"Not really. What are you doing here?"

"Mrs. Murrow sent me up."

"What are you doing here more generally?"

He walked into the room and viewed the work she had done. The room was bare to the studs and subfloor. Thick with plaster dust, the air hurt to breathe.

"Just wanted to make sure you hadn't died of septic shock.

Your hand looked pretty bad the other day, and then I hadn't seen you after that. If you weren't dead, I was just gonna say that a bunch of us are going to McClatchey's tonight."

Del stared at him blankly.

"Is that a no?"

She rubbed a sore spot on her knuckle. "I'm a little busy."

"At seven p.m.?"

"Pretty much all the time."

He shrugged. "Suit yourself. I just wanted to say the invitation's open."

Billy walked the perimeter of the room and then glanced out the window, where the tarp on one end of her lot had lifted in the strong winds.

"It seems lonely," he concluded.

The breeze coming from the broken window had a faintly metallic taste, and Del thought it might mean a flurry in the afternoon. She was glad of it: the temperature had been mild for the last couple of days, and it made her fear that the ice on the pond would fail.

Billy turned to her. "You're like those hermits who live in caves for decades and they discover their corpses with bird bones and stacks of old newspapers that they were using as toilet paper."

"I buy my toilet paper from you."

"Good. Hope your hand is better. See you later, if you want."

Del wasn't going to McClatchey's because it was a sports-themed bar with a liberal policy on checking identifications, so high school basketball players with wispy mustaches who were called by their last names went there.

When she came down at dusk, having removed the plaster and lath from the upstairs hallway, Jeanne was downstairs, sitting on the couch on top of a new wipe-clean outdoor chair cushion and digging through a plastic bag from a chain pharmacy.

She looked up at Del. "A guest?"

"Just the checkout boy at the supermarket."

"Oh, I know who he is. The Iverson boy. The youngest. I meant, who is he to you? A friend?"

"No. Just an acquaintance."

An Iverson. They were a big family of boys. Del was sure there had been an Iverson in her grade, though she couldn't remember his name. There seemed to have been an Iverson in every grade. There must have been at least six of them, all shaggy haired and heavy browed, like a sketch of a caveman. The Iverson boys were theater geeks, always organizing the plays put on by the local church, and Del, never a joiner, hadn't participated in that scene.

With Del's denial, the shadow of a smile crossed Jeanne's face, and Del hated it very much. Her interactions with Billy did not have a romantic undertone, but denial would only make it worse. Then her aunt pulled a bottle of sparkly blue nail polish out of the bag and tossed it to her. "Got this for you. Figured we could do a girls' night in. Manicures, all that. I got a deck of cards, too. We can play Spades."

"Don't you need to go home?"

Jeanne pulled the tab on the deck of cards. "In another day. Maybe two."

"Why not now? What's to fear? I mean, it isn't very nice here. Terrible bed. No showers. The maid service is just awful."

"Bed's fine, actually. And I've been showering at my gym. Though I might need to cut down on my membership soon. We're trying to save money. Me and Uncle Chuck are planning on buying a beach house. Somewhere warm that we can retire to, where the grandkids can visit."

Del snorted. "Well, that plan's shot now. Guess you can spend that money on a hotel instead."

Jeanne cut the cards and shuffled them back together. "Why's that?"

"Because you're plotting your escape with Johnny Christmaslights, or whatever his name is."

Jeanne frowned, confused. "I never said I was leaving Chuck. Why would I do a thing like that?"

"What?"

"No, no, no. It's just a temporary thing. We need to recommit to each other, as a family. We need some recovery time, then we'll come together again."

"Are you insane? People don't 'recommit as a family' after someone runs off with the president of the Christmas lights committee."

"Oh, Adela. Marriage isn't that simple. This is how it always happens." She bridged the cards, which smacked together into an even pile. "Also, he wasn't the president. I'm the president; he's the partnerships manager."

Those sleepovers with candy and movies. Finally, it clicked. They were Jeanne's affairs. That was why she had stayed with them. Del realized that her aunt wasn't looking after her mom—it was the reverse. Her mom had never said anything, had let Del and everyone else think that she was the lost cause, and none of it was true.

Jeanne sighed, tightened the pile of cards, and slid them back into the box. "Anyhow, let's not talk about it. Tonight is for fun. Girl talk." She pulled out a peach-colored polish from the bag and unscrewed the lid. An acrid smell filled the room.

Del put on her coat. "I need to borrow your car."

The plastic card that attached to Jeanne's key ring had the address. It wasn't difficult to find, set into a plaza on the turnpike about twenty minutes outside of town. Del flashed Jeanne's card at a girl who sat behind the front desk. The girl eyed Del's outfit with distaste, but quickly returned to the biology textbook on her desk.

The gym bathroom was three rooms, actually: one for toilets, one for showers, and a sort of powder room, like in movies set in New York in the 1930s. There were cloth-covered stools in front of large mirrors, and each station had a blow-dryer, hair spray, and various pots of cream.

Del took a towel from the stack and went to the showers. Unfortunately, because she'd left the house in a hurry she hadn't planned far enough ahead to pack another outfit, so she stacked the outfit she'd been wearing and placed it on a plastic chair outside of the shower cubicle.

After months of bathing with cool water in the tub, the shower's intensity felt uncomfortably sharp. Turning away from the pelt of water, she faced a tray of supplies. She ran a finger over the lettering on the refillable jugs. SHAMPOO. Even the word had grown exotic.

Without a comb, she used her fingers to try to untangle her hair, which hung in front of her face in thick hanks greased with conditioner. She broke through some of the knots, and that would have to be enough.

Stepping out, she wrapped a towel around herself, dried off, and put on her clothes again. A pair of jeans, almost worn through at the knees. An old gray T-shirt that advertised her father's auto body shop. His socks, patched at the toe. A green striped sweater, which she kept folded and placed beside her at the vanity station.

Another woman sat beside her. She smiled at Del but said nothing. Del watched the woman run pieces of her hair through an iron. The air reeked of melted plastic.

Once Del had been to a restaurant bathroom with a setup like this. It was a long time ago. It was her grandmother's birthday, and they had gone to an old-school Italian place.

Her mother put her cocktail down and sank into the upholstered chair in front of a mirror. She was in her midthirties; Del around eight.

Her mother glanced at her. "I had hoped you would be pretty. It makes life easier." In the mirror, she gently drew a fingertip across a fine line by her eye. "Oh well. It doesn't last. And it didn't matter anyway."

In the gym bathroom, Del pumped cream into her hand and sniffed it. Was it for the hair, the face, or the body? No telling. She put it in her hair, then pumped some more and put it on the rough red patches of her face. Now the lady next to her was really paying attention. Del flipped her hair over her face and set the blow-dryer to full blast. The heat cooked her skin, and she tugged the collar of her T-shirt open so that the stream poured down her breasts and torso.

Her hair was dry, and she had a pleasantly baked feeling, as if she had lain in the sun.

"Do you know if there's deodorant?"

A rabbity twitch from the woman's mouth. "Maybe the lost and found basket?" She motioned to an unlocked cabinet.

Inside, Del found a plastic basket with two deodorants, a cheap brand of hair gel, a sample packet of Q-tips, a plastic fine-tooth comb, and several elastic hair ties of varying colors. She took them all.

"Thanks," she said on the way out.

McClatchey's was in a plaza out by Route 2, between a department store on its last legs and a discount shoe store. Del had been to the department store many times before. They offered a layaway option that her mother used for most Christmases.

When she walked through the door at McClatchey's, Del immediately saw Billy in a large green booth along with a group of people she didn't recognize. A guy on the end of the bench slid in when she approached.

"Glad you could make it," Billy said. "This is Del, everyone."

A man with frosted tips addressed her. "We were in the same year at school."

Del took a beer that someone had poured from a pitcher of piss-colored lager. She couldn't remember Frosted Tips at all.

The regional high school had had about eight hundred students drawn from all the small towns in the county.

"Mmm. Good to see you again."

Billy pointed to each member of his crew, starting with the one who had gone to school with Del. "These are my brothers Aaron, Eric, Jake, Adam. Adam's girlfriend, Sophie. Jake's girlfriend, Tess."

"Nice to meet you." She surveyed the scene. There were no TVs, no pennants. "I thought this was a sports bar."

"Used to be," Aaron said. "Then the sheriff's kid drove drunk after he was served here and smashed his car against a tree. No one had checked his ID. He's living on painkillers and a ventilator for the foreseeable future. The old owners got driven out of town. It's a losers' bar now."

"You live in town?" Sophie asked. "Haven't seen you before."

Sophie had very thick, very dark hair that hung like beautiful black curtains at the sides of her face.

"Just temporarily staying here."

"You work or are you in school?" Sophie continued.

"Neither. I'm moving out west, actually. But I had to stop in town to wrap some things up first. Family business." Del hoped the final statement sounded agreeably boring.

Aaron reached for the plastic basket full of microwaved, cheese-covered nachos. "Did you move and finish high school somewhere else? I don't remember you at graduation."

Del shifted in her seat. She wasn't used to being the center of attention, and she didn't like it.

Billy glanced at her. "This isn't *60 Minutes*. Let's cut out the Q&A period."

"Sorry," Eric said. He looked to be the eldest Iverson, and he had a jolly, pink-cheeked face. "Mostly people move one way: out. We're just a little overexcited to meet someone who has breathed the air outside. Tell us what it's like."

Del shrugged her shoulders and fixed her gaze on an indeterminate spot on the wall. She wished there were a TV so that there would be something to look at instead of her.

Eric tried again. "We just got back from doing the sets for *Guys and Dolls*. It's the spring production."

"I wish someone had told me it was such hard work," Tess complained.

Del took a nacho that Aaron had offered. "You all still do church plays?"

She remembered the plays as being the affairs of weird teenagers who didn't drink and wanted their parents to like them. Her father hated the local theatrical season. She remembered one production that they had gone to see because her father had a customer whose kid was playing the lead, and at the end of the play—was it *The Importance of Being Earnest*?—the teenage cast ended with a rendition of "Comfortably Numb" that they sang with their arms looped around each other, in memory of a friend who had recently been killed in a swimming accident. Before the play ended, Del had joined her father in standing against the back wall of the church hall, and as he waited for the song to end, he impatiently tapped the pack of cigarettes in his jeans pocket.

"How maudlin," he said before they sneaked out the door just before the conclusion of the song.

"I teach at the middle school now," Eric said. "English. So I

direct all the plays, and my brothers still help me out a little bit."

Jake rolled his eyes. "A little bit. My splinters have splinters."

"My splinters have splinters have splinters," Tess agreed.
"They're forming a union and going on strike."

"It's a pretty much constant cycle," Eric conceded, counting
them off on his fingers. "There's a Christmas play at church,
the spring musical at the middle school, a summer drama camp
at church, and then a fall play at the high school that is usually
all hands on deck."

Billy smiled. "Good thing none of us had any ambitions or
goals to get out of this town so that we can continue to be your
unpaid laborers."

"Good thing my salary has been around to pay your rent
when you've been bumming around," Eric told him, eyebrows
raised.

The focus off herself, Del relaxed. The Iverson brothers
joked around for a while about a kid in the play who farted
whenever he got nervous.

Sophie got up to get another pitcher of beer and then sat
down by Del. "You know, it's nice to meet someone who isn't
an Iverson."

"I'm definitely not that," Del said. "What do you do?"

"Just got out of college. I'm looking for a job, but there's
nothing. My parents are old and I'm their only kid, so I didn't
want to move far, but . . ."

She blew a raspberry. No prospects.

"Yeah, it doesn't seem too promising around here."

"Tell me about it. I majored in history. I wish my guidance

counselor had told me what an expensive waste of time that would be. So you have family business? Is your family still around here?"

Del took a sip of her beer. The foam bubbled against her lip. "They've moved on."

"Lucky," Sophie said. "You're not stuck."

Del nodded.

Tess returned from a trip to the bathroom and joined Sophie and Del at the end of the bench. "Do you know Billy from work? Or from high school? Drama club?"

Del bit the inside of her cheek to stop herself from smiling. "No."

"Did you do sports or something?"

High school seemed like a very long time ago. Really, in the context of world history, they were basically still in high school. What Del did in high school was clear neither at the time nor in retrospect. Occasionally they went out into the woods and smoked and drank. Sometimes they swam in the river. Every once in a while, she attended classes. Not at any time had she participated in any organized activities of any kind.

"I was more of a loner," she told Tess.

Tess nodded. "You're looking at Regional's science fair grand champion of 1992. I did a year at the community college, but my dad got sick and I ran out of money. Now I move samples of blood from one room to another at the hospital."

"At least you've got a job," Sophie interjected.

"Maybe I should go back and give a speech at graduation. Let those kids know what life has in store." Tess ground a nacho between her teeth.

Del wondered about her friends from high school other than Frankie. What were they doing now? Were they in a different bar in another failing plaza at the other end of town? Did they ever wonder about her, talk about where she might have gone? Maybe they imagined that she had gone on to huge success.

The group remained at the bar for another hour. Del felt herself recede from their fascination and was surprised to find herself enjoying their companionship. As an adult, she had never had friends her own age, and it was interesting to see how they interacted. They were more enthusiastic than Tym and Dave, more eager to impress each other. It reminded her of a nature documentary about monkeys. Tess retrieved a trivia game from a battered pile of boxes at the end of the bar. Del's team won, and she scored several points in the movie category.

Eventually Eric declared the night to be at an end. He had to get up early to go to work. Billy had to start his shift at the supermarket in a couple of hours. The others were going to sleep. Some would wake up in the morning for jobs or school. Some would wake up for no reason at all. Del would wake up because there was only five weeks until her deadline, and she needed to start earlier, keep at it later, and not miss even a single day in order to meet her goal.

February

Chapter Twenty-Nine

A WEEK LATER, AND JEANNE REMAINED.

She had set herself up pretty nice in Del's parents' room. One night she had come home with a big bag of stuff from the superstore and unloaded a small TV, a massaging footbath, and an air-pop popcorn maker.

She held up the box of the popcorn maker. "Blast from the past. I didn't think they made these anymore."

"We don't have electricity," Del told her.

"You've got your power station over there. I can use that."

"I'm using it."

"When you're not using it."

"I'm always using it. It is here for the sole purpose of me using it."

A couple of days later, Del returned to the living room after a trip ferrying pieces of the house across the pond and found Jeanne on the couch reading a magazine. Somehow Jeanne's personal care hadn't faded at all. Her fingernails were painted, her hair still clean and flat as a laundered suit.

"Isn't anyone wondering where you are?" Del asked as she fixed herself a coffee. "Doesn't anyone care?"

"I left a note. Told Chuck I needed to do a little thinking. I'm sure he's just biding his time. He'll let me know when he's ready for me to come back. Things'll be better then. He gets really apologetic, treats me good."

Within the last few days, Jeanne's manic texting had lessened. It seemed as if Johnny Christmaslights was less interested in Jeanne, or that his appeal to her had faded. Ah well, there was always the next holiday season. Maybe by Halloween, when Del had long departed town, Jeanne would be having an affair with the pumpkin head from the town's haunted house.

"I see," Del said, and she took her coffee with her.

At the top of the stairs, she opened the door to her parents' room. On the floor by the radiator were several opened bags from Jeanne's daily shopping trips. Her clothes were hung in the closet. Del plugged the rotating saw into the powerbox and began cutting away the lath.

Moments later, Jeanne appeared at the door. "What are you doing?"

"Cutting the lath. Then I'm going to take out the bed and remove the floorboards."

"You can't do that. I'm sleeping here."

Del shrugged. "Find another place to sleep."

"Can't you hold off for just another day or two?"

"Nope. I'm down to the studs in every other room except the living room, and that's where I'm staying. This has all got to go. Then I'm taking out the trim and the window. It'll be pretty chilly in here with no window and the below-zero temperatures. If I were you, I'd probably find another place to stay, like a hotel. This is not a hotel. You'll know the difference because at a hotel you'll get a key to the door and the people will have to pretend to be happy to see you."

Jeanne sat on the edge of the bed. "Adela, I don't know what more I could do for you. I've been picking up food, running errands all over town, even getting a popcorn popper to make you happy. And yet you continue to be so selfish."

"Selfish?"

"Isn't that what you'd call it? After all I've done for you." She clicked her tongue and left the room.

Del knocked out the walls and cleaned the room down to the lath, then took Jeanne's clothes from the closet and threw them onto the bed in a rumpled pile. The sun was halfway down the horizon. It must have been late afternoon but still business hours.

Downstairs, Del plucked Jeanne's keys from the gold ring attached to the handle of a plum-colored handbag. "I'm borrowing the car."

She left before Jeanne could reply.

The roads were slick with black ice, and it took nearly fifteen minutes to crawl along what should have been a five-minute ride to Main Street. Del left the keys in the ignition and the door open, just in case anyone wanted to steal Jeanne's SUV. If they did, Jeanne would need to go to the police to report it, and then Del could nail shut the back door, too. She didn't mind crawling in and out of a window if that was what it took to get some peace of mind. You didn't appreciate how beautiful the quiet was until it was gone.

Inside the office, there was an older woman in a camel twin-set and pleated gray trousers sorting documents into a filing cabinet.

"Hello, darling," the woman said to her. "Can I help you with something?"

"I need to see Chuck."

The woman glanced at her watch. "Mr. Murrow doesn't have a meeting in his calendar for right now."

"He'll want to talk to me," Del said.

In the hallway of Murrow Construction, with the heat on full blast and the smell of leftover holiday potpourri heavy in the air, she somehow felt colder than she had outside. At the very least, she was more aware of the discomforts she had ignored: the damp at her ankles, the tender spot under her right rib where breathing had become difficult.

The woman in the twinset assessed Del.

"I'll ask," she said gently.

He was behind the desk in his office when Del was ushered in. He wore silver-rimmed glasses, which Del had never seen him in before.

"What can I do you for?" Chuck asked with a merry twinkle in his eye. "Ready to cry 'uncle'?"

"I need you to pick up your wife."

He frowned. She had caught him off guard.

Chuck reset his face to a neutral look. "Is that where she is? Who'd have thunk. Not the most obvious of choices. Helping you out, I assume?"

"I don't care about this weird little game you play. Just come get her. She's in my way."

Chuck put down the documents he had been reading. "Not my problem."

"It's your wife."

"So what?" He shrugged. "She's not my indentured servant. I can't make her go where she doesn't want to go. The laws have changed in that regard, you see."

These people were incredible.

"Don't you want her back?"

Chuck sat back in his chair. "I've been getting on alright, to tell you the truth. Noticed I was squinting a week back. That's the sort of thing I would have off-loaded to the wife: booking the appointment, hounding me to go. Instead, I go to the supermarket to pick up some frozen pizzas, and what do I find? They do glasses now! A whole rack of them, cheap as anything, take your pick." He lifted his glasses from the hinges and settled them back again gently on his nose.

They were sized, Del thought, for a child, or at least for someone who didn't have the face shape of an extra-large pizza.

"So that's it? You've been married for thirty years or whatever, and it's all over because you've discovered that you can buy discount glasses from the Sav-Mart by yourself?"

Chuck frowned. "I wouldn't say that's the only thing. But if she thinks I'm coming begging, she's wrong. I won't do it again."

Del was speechless. What a horrible mess these people were. And they thought that her branch was the pack of losers. They had shunned her father, been ashamed of her mother, never offered help to her when she most needed it.

Briefly she considered printing up a stack of fake tabloid newspapers, as she had done for an elementary school assignment, and distributing them to the neighborhood.

Headline: *Murrow Sex Scandal.*

Subhead: *Xmas Chump Wrecks Small-Town Trump.*

Chuck shifted through his papers and put several of them into a manila folder. "Slowing you down, is she?"

Del did not reply.

"Too bad," Chuck said, turning to his keyboard. "Just organized the clearing of your land today, actually. I'll see you in a month, either way. It'll be a nice view, straight down to the pond from the road. Might charge extra to whoever gets it."

He smiled as if the thought brought him more pleasure than the conversation had promised.

Del went to the diner, where she had a bowl of chili and six packets of saltines while she organized her lie, then she went home to deliver it. The waitress, who had learned her moods by this point, kept a respectful distance.

Several iterations of the lie were considered and dismissed before the final version made itself known. She couldn't say that she went to speak to Chuck—it raised too many questions. It would have to be a coincidence, that she bumped into him somehow. The cemetery, at her grandparents' grave? Too maudlin. The grocery store was the right level of pathos. Chuck aimlessly pushing an empty cart. Sallow. Bereft. Thinner—he was noticeably thinner. She had tried to avoid him, but he cornered her in the checkout line and asked if she had heard anything about his darling wife. Soon he would put up posters, call the police. There would be a countywide search. Sniffer dogs redirected from a murder investigation unit in the next state.

It didn't matter if the tale unraveled immediately when Jeanne and Chuck were together. It only mattered that Jeanne left, at which point Del could secure the premises and bar her aunt's return.

She drove back home and walked around the house to the sliding door.

"Auntie Jeanne," she said sweetly in the direction of the kitchen as she closed the door behind her. "I have the craziest story."

Eleanor appeared in the doorway to the living room. Just then Del noticed that all of the battery-powered lanterns were lit and there were two tin mugs and a half-empty container of nail polish on the floor. It looked like a postapocalyptic commercial for menopause vitamins.

Eleanor addressed her gruffly. "Del. Looks like I'm bunking with you and your auntie for a little while. It's a complicated situation, but it'll only be for a few days."

Del stepped backward, pressing herself against the sliding doors.

"By the way," Eleanor added, "did you know your front door is nailed shut? I should have thought of something like that myself, before my family came to visit."

Chapter Thirty

DEL SAT UP IN THE MORNING WITH THE TERRIBLE KNOWLEDGE that her nightmares were true. She had been invaded. Eleanor had slept upstairs, in her parents' bed. Jeanne was snoring loudly on the cushionless sofa above where Del herself slept on the living room floor. Every ten minutes throughout the night, Jeanne shifted position, mumbling about the metal coils pressing into her back, then reverted to snoring a few minutes later. Del had not slept at all.

She spent the early hours of the morning outside, alone, pushing broken pieces of wood and plaster across the frozen pond in the shopping cart. She had perfected the slow, careful crawl that was necessary to reduce the chance of slipping. Neither Eleanor nor Jeanne said anything to her, so she assumed that her lodgers either didn't pick up on or didn't care about her new path to her site.

When the sun was high and sharp across the icy tufts of snow that dotted the landscape, Del went in for a warm drink. Jeanne had gone off somewhere in her car. As the pot of water came to a full boil on the hot plate in the living room, Eleanor came downstairs in a rayon pajama pant set and an ankle-length silver fur coat.

"Brrr." Eleanor shivered.

Del stirred the coffee granules into the simmering water in silence.

"I had a very uncomfortable night of sleep, thank you for not asking," Eleanor continued.

Del shrugged. "This isn't a hotel."

"If it were a hotel, I would complain to the manager."

"Go to a hotel where you can complain to the manager."

Eleanor sat on the sofa and lit a cigarette. "No can do."

"Fine, go home."

"I can't do that, either."

Del dropped her mug to the brick hearth around the coal stove, where it landed with a clank. "Why not?"

"My family has come to stay with me. My brother and his wife. They said they wanted the winter experience back at the old homestead. Sunshine, they said, is boring them. They had wanted to come in the fall, for the leaves, and I put them off. I thought they would give up. Or die. My brother has a heart condition. The family curse."

"So what's that got to do with me?"

"I need somewhere to stay. I can't be with them. My brother talks at the TV. He just repeats exactly what's been said, in slightly different words, and his wife sits there bobbing her head like an idiot, as if she's hearing it for the first time. It's insane. I can't spend five minutes with people like that. I'll be convicted of murder. They just send old women like me straight to the electric chair. It's not worth feeding us and paying for all our medicine."

"Stay at a hotel, then."

Eleanor took a long drag. "It's crude to talk about money. But I am a woman of limited means. I haven't married as wisely as I should have. I'm living on the government dime. By the way, that's more accurate a phrase than you'd want it to be. A *dime*."

"Tell them they can't stay with you."

"Too late. They arrived this morning."

"And where do they think you are?"

Eleanor paused for a moment and smiled. "I left a note. Said I went to Florida. Said my lover is fronting a new casino and I had to be there for the gala opening."

Del couldn't believe it. "If you have no money, maybe you could get rid of some of those fur coats."

"These?" Eleanor gestured to the silvery tail. "I got them for peanuts at a tag sale. Dead women's children are always donating their old furs to the local theaters. But there are only so many villains, so the theater companies sell them and keep the cash."

Del ground her thumbs into her temples until she started to feel the bones pulverize to a fine powder. It was absolute insanity.

Eleanor poured herself a coffee. "You should really get nicer instant coffee. Just because you're a pauper doesn't mean you have to live like one. Where's the shower?"

Del took the big claw and began attacking the clapboards outside the living room, where Eleanor sat on the filthy sofa. She didn't speak to Eleanor, although they could have communicated through the cracked window. The message from Del was clear: this was the final stage of a demolition, and it would pause for no one. Del fit the big claw under one end of cracked gray wood and then another, teasing each warped board loose before tossing the pieces into a pile. Many of the boards snapped. She didn't care. It mattered that they were moved, not that they were moved whole.

It took the entire day to remove the clapboards from one side of the house. Throughout her work she listened to one of Tym's mixes on the loudest possible setting of the boom box and refused to enter the house. She pissed in the snow behind a clump of trees on the other side of the pond. The trees had thinned, and anyone looking could have seen her, but it didn't matter to her now. If they were disgusted, they could leave. It was the work that mattered. And the work needed to happen much, much faster.

By noon, she was up the ladder, and as the sun began to set she was finishing the final clapboard, up under the roof. Under the eaves was a small papery wasp nest. Del poked it with the claw. The face of the nest disintegrated and fell to the ground, revealing a dusty core of plugged cells. Pulling herself up the ladder, Del inspected the interior. Lodged inside one cell was a single wasp corpse. Poor thing. Hadn't any of the others told the poor fucker that they were moving? She swung again, and the nest collapsed to the ground. The sun sank below the trees on the other side of the pond, and she began to register the cold just as the final piece of clapboard fell to earth.

The convenient thing about the invasion of her home was

that she no longer needed to walk to the grocery store. Without speaking to anyone, Del plucked Eleanor's keys out of the pocket of a fur coat that was splayed across the floor like a rug, and left.

Driving the Lincoln felt like steering a cruise ship through a canal: the piled-up snow on the sides of the road came uncomfortably close to the windows. Del went first to a fast-food restaurant, where she ate chili, a baked potato with sour cream, and two orders of fried cheese sticks with marinara sauce at a corner table where no one could sneak up behind her. She had six refills of orange soda. There was no one else in the restaurant except for a tired young woman and two little kids who bounced on sherbet-colored horses in the small indoor play area. The cashier went outdoors for three smoke breaks before Del cleared her tray and got back in the car.

The supermarket parking lot was mostly empty, so Del pulled the Lincoln across two spots and cut the engine.

When the automatic doors of the market opened, she immediately spotted Billy at the checkout. He was talking to a young guy with very white teeth who left just as Del approached.

"Hey," she said to Billy.

He glanced at the clock above the meat department counter. "You're early."

She pulled one of the women's health magazines from the rack and wagged it at him. "I'm trying to get a solid eight hours a night. It's the key to optimum health."

"It was nice of you to come out the other night. It's been the same inside jokes since high school. Fresh blood is rare at this point."

Del picked up a discarded shopping basket out of the stack at the end of the lane. "Thanks for inviting me. It was nice to get out of the house."

"How is it?"

"How's what?"

"The house. Tearing it down. How's it going?"

She thought on the question for a moment before she answered. "It's OK. I've got less than a month now. I think I'll have it down to the frame and the floors in a week or two. So far, it's been hard work but pretty straightforward. When it's just the frame, I'm not sure how to take it from there. Also, I've got houseguests."

Billy's eyes narrowed as he tried to work out whether he was supposed to pick up on sarcasm. "Seriously? Why?"

"Yeah. It's like a horrible joke. Hard to answer on the 'why.'"

"Are they there to help you?"

"That I can answer conclusively. No, they are not."

"We could."

"You could what?"

"Me, my brothers. We could help you." He said it as if it meant nothing, as if he were offering to bring disposable cups to a party.

She flinched. "Why would you do that?"

"To be . . . nice? I mean, we can't come every day. We've got jobs. Some of us do, anyways. But I'm sure people would be willing to help. We build sets and take them down all the time. We've all got brawn. A few even have brains. I wouldn't include myself in that."

"You don't even know me."

He shrugged. "So what? It would be interesting. A story to tell the grandchildren. It's like, uh, what do they call it? What the Amish do?"

Del thought on what he might mean. "A barn raising?"

"Yeah, like that. But in reverse. An un-raising. A barn felling."

"That's really nice of you. I think I'm OK, though."

The idea of more people on her turf didn't appeal at all, even though she had actually liked Billy and his friends. She wasn't sure how to take out a floor or rafters, but she was nearly certain that she would figure it out. She was one hundred percent certain that the answer wasn't a troupe of semi-employed amateur theater enthusiasts.

"Sure. But if that changes, you know where to find me. We get together at the bar once a week, by the way. Always McClatchey's. In case you want to come by another time. Really, we're bored of each other. You'd be doing us a favor."

Del thanked him for the offer, then cruised the aisles shopping for the week. She didn't know why Billy was so nice to her, but she didn't trust it. She had not, for a very long time, had any friends her own age. Maybe the pizza delivery guy whom they had ordered from once a week was her friend. She had never asked him anything about himself or even made any small talk, other than the odd comment about the weather or what movie she and Tym were watching. Had he been delivering pizzas while he was in school? To support a crack habit? Details like that would have been good to know. She should have asked.

According to the meat counter clock, which was shaped like a joint of ham, it was only slightly past ten p.m. The aisles were sparsely populated, but there were other shoppers, unlike the times when she had gone at two or three in the morning. When she saw another person from the end of the aisle, she skipped it and came back later. Anyone who was shopping at unsociable hours was, she assumed, purposefully unsociable and, like her, probably wanted their space. It was a sign of respect to keep your distance.

Del had a yen for sour cream and onion–flavored chips, so she went to stand in front of the wall of options. Megapacks, giant bags, normal bags, multiflavored mixes. She lost herself in the multitude of choices. Above her, the ventilation system pumped down wave after wave of toasted air.

"Hi."

Greg. He wore sweatpants and a loose black coat. One of the coat buttons dangled from a broken thread like an eye loose in its socket. He didn't seem as if he had expected or particularly wanted to see anyone he knew. Del pulled her basket close to her chest, as if it were something precious she needed to protect, and began walking to the end of the aisle at a quick pace.

"Can you get a message to my mom?" His voice was loud, but he didn't follow her or even look directly at her.

She paused.

"Sure."

"Can you tell her, whatever my dad did, I'm sure he'll make it up to her."

Greg had no idea. Chuck hadn't implicated Jeanne in her crime. Maybe they didn't know about the earlier affairs, either. Maybe Chuck had kept it all to himself. It was a small-town episode of *Maury*. The audience would have jumped up from their seats at this point.

She looked at Greg standing there with his broken button. She could roll a grenade down the aisle toward him and watch his whole life explode. The Murrows had finally given her the power to destroy them. Always she had thought of them as connected, conniving and greedy, eager to treat her parents badly because they were vulnerable, and that vulnerability embarrassed them. Now, instead, Greg struck her as something pathetic. Perhaps not worthy of her care, but not deserving of her time, either.

Her hands gripped the thick plastic handles of the basket until the pattern imprinted into her skin.

"Sure," she said evenly. "I'll tell her that."

Greg stared at the wall of chips for a moment as Del lingered near the end of the aisle, by the salsas. He opened his mouth as if he would say something, but he didn't. A moment later, he snapped his mouth shut, walked away, and disappeared toward the front of the store. Del sensed her pulse slowing.

An idea came to her in the quiet, too-bright store. She thought about him standing there, saying nothing, his blankness and softness, and for no reason in particular, she thought about herself in the gravel parking lot of the gay bar with Frankie, the feeling that her heart and veins and everything that beat within her had dropped into the bowl of her hips and ceased movement, and that for a moment she was an empty shell, a doll built of newspaper strips glued around a wire frame, and that with a single word, a single flicker, she would immolate and disappear.

Pity, it was. She felt a pity for him that she had not felt for herself, and that no one had ever felt for her. It was an uncomfortable feeling, it made her throat feel tight, and yet she felt it anyway, all through the rest of her silent march through the store and up to the checkout lane, where reality came back into focus and she had to talk to Billy about how the spring production was coming along.

In the next week, she finished removing the clapboards from the house. Underneath the clapboards were wide pieces of flat timber held against the studs with old nails, many bent or broken. In many places, there were cracks where you could see clear through the house. Inside, it was colder than it had ever been, and the potbelly stove needed to be fed and stoked constantly throughout the day for the temperature to be at all bearable.

One day, in the late afternoon, as Del was rolling a shopping cart full of clapboards down to the pond, she paused in front of the living room wall. Eleanor and Jeanne were on the couch, the stove at a full roar.

"Hey, peepers!" shouted Eleanor. "I haven't been spied on since the Dixon's fitting room incident of 1968. Come back in ten—we're having beef stew out of the can. Dinty Moore's best. Half price!"

Del smiled and continued pushing the cart down the hill. The previous night, Jeanne had tried to cook from scratch on the camp stove, using what she had said was her mother's recipe for cheesy chicken noodles. The whole mess had boiled over, and the house stank of burnt milk as they wrapped up in blankets and played cards before bedtime. Canned beef stew seemed like a treat in comparison.

She came inside, went to the bathroom, wiped herself down with a damp washcloth, and dried off. By now she had learned that if she didn't wipe herself dry, the sweat seemed capable of chilling her in a way that the cold weather didn't. By the time she had finished, Eleanor had doled out three portions of stew into coated paper bowls and poured plastic cups of cheap Rioja. She handed Del a spork.

"How was work today?"

"Mm," Del grunted.

"How vivid. You sound exactly like my ex-husband."

"Which one?" Jeanne asked.

"All of 'em," Eleanor guffawed.

Jeanne and Eleanor had become an unlikely comedy duo. During the day, as far as Del could tell, Eleanor spent most of her time upstairs watching the kitchen TV plugged into the power box, while Jeanne was mostly away on unspecified errands. They seemed to come together in the afternoon and have coffee together in the living room and eventually would lure Del in for dinner.

Eleanor started in on Jeanne. "I think you should tell that shitweasel that you want to pack it up. Send you the paperwork, you're ready to sign."

"It's not as easy as that," Jeanne argued.

Jeanne could never hold her drink.

"I've done it five times," Eleanor countered. "And do you know what I can tell you? Nothing's easier. A million times over I'd rather divorce a husband than find another one to marry."

"Oh, you. You're just like her." She pointed to Del.

"Just like me how?" Del asked.

"You're meant to be alone. You like it."

Del shrugged. "Sure."

Eleanor wouldn't stop. "It's not just that. It's things, too."

"What things?" Jeanne asked.

"Your things. Your belongings," Eleanor said tauntingly. "The house, the car. The time-share, whatever you've got. You want all of it, just like you have now. Not half of it."

Del nodded in agreement. The chunk of beef was strangely smooth, like another tongue sitting on her tongue. She swallowed it whole.

"It's someone else's night for dishes," Eleanor said airily. "I cooked."

"I don't mind." Jeanne hopped up from the floor and collected the three paper plates, which she flung one after another out the sliding door, toward Del's trash pile. If she had thought they would fly there like Frisbees, she thought wrong. They flipped meat-side down and landed inches from the door.

"Silverware," Eleanor cautioned, raising her spork in the air.

Jeanne gathered the three utensils and ran them under the bathroom sink, returning them to a neat line on a paper towel next to the stove.

"What's on for tonight?" Jeanne asked, returning to the group. "Spades again?"

"Eleanor said I could borrow her car," Del replied.

There was no such agreement, but Eleanor didn't argue.

"Anything interesting going on?" Jeanne asked.

"Not particularly."

McClatchey's was busier than it had been the first time she came.

"Yo," the middle Iverson brother said as she approached the table. She couldn't remember his name.

"Milady," Billy said, moving aside to make way for her at the end of the bench.

They were drinking a horrifying concoction of beer and pickle juice.

"It has a name," Eric, the eldest Iverson, said, "but I forgot it, and now I really want to know it so that I can make sure I never drink this again."

The girlfriends weren't there. Del felt as if she might be interrupting an intimate family meeting.

Billy intuited what she was thinking. "Some more people are supposed to join us later. We're always first because we usually have dinner at my parents' place before we come."

"Coming to you Thursdays: Iverson family pizza night," Aaron said in a deep bellow, like a movie commercial.

"You eat at your parents' place every Thursday night?"

"Actually, most nights," Billy admitted. "My mom is a really good cook. My grandma, too. She lives above my parents' garage. And me and Aaron live with them."

"What do they make for dinner?" Del asked. It sounded like a TV show, not like anyone's life that she knew.

"A lot of pasta. Stuffed shells. Ziti. Pizza, too, but not thin crust. The thick type that's made in a pan. Old-school."

Del nodded as she took in the new information. She tried to imagine all the Iversons around a table with their parents and their grandma. The noise would be deafening.

"So I wanted to ask you something." She spoke quickly, before she was totally aware of what she was saying and could stop it.

"Yeah?" Eric asked.

Her mouth was dry. Her tongue made a weird clicking noise when she tried to speak again. "I wanted to ask for some help."

"What kind?" Aaron asked.

"Just with my house. I just needed some help taking the frame down over the next couple of weeks."

Aaron laughed. "God, that's good. I thought you were going to ask for a loan or something. I don't know why, you came across as really nervous or something, like you wanted us to invest in your small business."

Billy cracked a smile. "Door-to-door vacuum cleaners."

Del fingered the rough edge of the hair at her brow line. "Mobile hairstyling services."

Eric swirled the remaining pickle beer at the bottom of his glass. "Sure, we'll help. Can someone get us something else to drink? Literally anything else. Swamp water. Dog vomit. Anything."

The Iversons argued over what they should order next, and then had an even longer argument over who should pay. Billy squeezed out the other side of the booth and went to order a pitcher of IPA and some mini burgers for Aaron and Jake, who were still hungry after dinner.

Back at the table, he slid in by Del and began pouring from the pitcher.

"So they're going to do it?" she said to him quietly.

"Yeah."

"Why?"

He poured the final beer and slid it to her. "Curiosity. Boredom. Common human decency. A combination of the three?"

"Cool."

Tym used to make fun of her for saying "cool" when she didn't know what to say or when things got awkward. It was a deflection, but an effective one, allowing the conversation to slip over and past it as easily as water running over flat stones.

Later the bartender smacked the bell and Aaron claimed the sliders. He offered one to Del and she took it. Others joined: another teacher Eric knew from work; Jen, a woman whose sister had been in Del and Aaron's grade at school; and the nephew of one of Del's mother's friends. Because of the family connections, some faces looked familiar but lightly altered, as if her schoolmates had been drawn by a not particularly talented artist: there was the Italia nose, the Pulaski ears, the pitted cheeks of the Zubers, who, rumor had it, suffered from intergenerational cystic acne after cheating a Sicilian grandma in a game of cards.

They distributed packets of sugar with one pink package of fake sugar mixed in and played Killer. Twice, Del chose the pink packet and was the killer. She escaped after slaying the entire Iverson family, who must have had some genetic mutation that didn't allow them to blink properly, because no Iverson escaped from the investigators when he was the killer.

They wrapped up before midnight.

Jen Pulaski laid out her share of crumpled dollar bills for the food she had eaten. "Could anyone give me a ride? My car's in the shop; I had to have my mom drop me off."

"Del lives out by you," Billy said.

Del flushed and hoped it wasn't visible in the dimly lit bar. She remembered Jen's older sister well: she was the class secretary, and they had been in chemistry together. The sister wasn't popular, exactly, but traveled within a bubble of people with moussed hair who ran track and owned cheap hatchback cars they had been given for their sixteenth birthdays. She was not someone Del wanted to chat with about the good old days of Del's social exclusion after Frankie humiliated her.

She glanced up and noticed that everyone was looking at her. A response was required.

"Yeah. I've got a car. Fine," she mumbled.

"Not if it's any trouble."

Jen had given Del half of her nachos. She seemed like an alright person.

"It's fine," Del offered more convincingly. "I just have to get the car back, that's all. I borrowed it from someone."

"So you're from here?" Jen said after they shut the car doors and pumped up the heat in the Lincoln. The car made a deep, awful rumble, like a tsunami gaining strength.

"Yep," Del said curtly.

"What year did you graduate?"

Del told her what year she would have graduated if she *had* graduated.

"My older sister was in your class," Jen said, and looked at the passenger window, which was fogged with hot breath.

And then, to Del's surprise, Jen said no more about that.

Jen told her that she was taking an exam to be a dental hygienist. For the rest of the ride, Del told her about working in a dental office. They were the greatest hits she used to tell Tym's friends when they went out for drinks: the stage dad who brought his twins in for a cleaning every other month and insisted the dentist somehow make their milk teeth whiter; the Holocaust survivor who hid his top row of false teeth somewhere in the exam room during his visits and would smile gummily until the hygienist hunted them down in a room full of model teeth, like an evil game of Where's Waldo.

With her head tipped back in the car's teal leather headrest, Jen laughed so hard the bench seat shuddered. Her throat glowed under the phosphorescent streetlights.

"I had no idea what I'd be getting into," she said, wiping her eyes. "I thought I was just signing up to clean teeth. I'm just on the left here after the lamppost."

Del pulled the Lincoln up to the curb in front of a three-story brick building just off Main Street. On the bottom floor were handwritten signs on butcher paper notifying the public that the greengrocer had gone out of business.

Jen reached into the footwell for her backpack and scarf. "Thanks for the ride. See you around?"

Instead of going straight back home, Del cruised around

town in Eleanor's car. The headlights illuminated the municipal pool she'd last gone to when she was seven, the entrance
to the state park where during summertime teenagers drank
beers and lay in the sun by a low waterfall that spilled over a
basalt shelf, a closed fast-food shop that had sold fish and chips.
Without thinking she was headed any particular way, she
wound through town, crossing her own path several times,
until finally she headed out of town, past the stone quarry, and
to the closed gate.

It was past midnight when she arrived. There was no lock
on the gate, just a loop of chain link. Del lifted and dropped the
loop, which clanged down over the metal bars. She pushed both
sides of the gate open, then drove through.

There was no artificial light in the graveyard at night, but
in the full moon, the white stones glimmered above the ice-
crusted snow. Del left the engine running in the car. The snow
hadn't been shoveled, nor had it melted for weeks, so she sank
down to her calves, and with each step the thick shelf of ice cut
into her leg. She had forgotten her gloves—where were they?—
so, bare-handed, she wiped the mucus that ran out of her nose.
It left a trail across her cheek.

"Hello," she said. "I'm still here."

A strong wind shook the fir trees that delineated the edge of
the cemetery, and a shower of loose needles salted the earth.

"I'm leaving soon, though. I won't be back."

Far in the distance, a dim light grew stronger. Car headlights traveled slowly down the road, approached the cemetery,
and passed.

"I'm sorry how everything worked out. Dad is fine. You

probably know that now. Or maybe you don't. Maybe you're separate and that's best. Either way, everything's OK. I'm OK, too. I just wanted to let you know that you don't need to worry about me anymore."

Del put her hands in her pockets, bouncing slightly for warmth.

"Just to let you know, I tore the house down. I'm not sure if you would be mad or not. But Uncle Chuck is going to be fucking furious. Also, I know about Auntie Jeanne. It was the Christmas lights committee guy this time. It didn't work out. She's OK, though. I'm pretty sure you'd be happy about the house coming down. And about Chuck being mad. I know you would."

She placed her hand on the tombstone, felt the cold curl up through her fingers into her palm, and then returned to the car.

Chapter Thirty-One

SHE HAD AGREED WITH THE IVERSONS THAT THEY WOULD ARRIVE in eight days and work over the next weekend. By the Saturday they arrived, she wanted to have the house down to the frame and floors only. If they helped her dismantle it on Saturday and Sunday, it would leave her only with the foundation left to tackle alone over the remaining week before Chuck claimed the land.

What was left of the house? She got out of her sleeping bag early on Friday morning and stepped quietly around Jeanne, who was sleeping on the couch, to survey what was needed.

In every room, the walls had been stripped back to the vertical studs. Only the thin siding nailed to the exterior of the studs kept the outside chill at a bearable level, despite the fact that the coal stove was running all day long and Jeanne picked up a fresh bag of coal every other day. Del, Jeanne, and Eleanor wore their coats all day long and slept in them, too. The chimney was crumbled at the top where Del had ripped out the crown with Greg's truck but was otherwise intact. The Iversons, hopefully, could help topple the rest of the chimney and remove the heavy iron stove. Some rooms still had a lath and plaster ceiling cover-ing the joists. The sink and the toilet in the bathroom would need to be removed. Down in the basement, she found the packed dirt floor and the stone foundation as they ever were, as well as a few boxes that she had forgotten to remove earlier.

She got her ladder and began to take apart the plaster and lath in the kitchen.

"Good morning, sunshine." Eleanor appeared in the kitchen door with a dirty mug and a pack of cigarettes. "What're the plans for today?"

Del dusted the plaster out of her bangs. "Not much. I'm go-ing to take off the siding. Can't decide whether I want to take out the toilet before or after. There's something appealing to me about taking a shit inside a bare house frame."

Eleanor smiled wryly. "At this point, I'm forced to take my adieu. My family's visit is over."

"You don't have to go. You, too, can take a shit within full view of our beloved townsfolk."

Eleanor put a cigarette between her lips and clicked the lighter. "Oh, darling, I've done that before, many times."

Eleanor looked around at what was left of the house. "I really miss your mom sometimes. She didn't have it easy. But she tried."

"I know," Del said. She climbed down from the ladder. "It's been nice having you. Just leave the sheets and towels where they are; the housekeeper will come and pick them up later."

"I wouldn't dream of doing anything else. Thank you, Del."

Eleanor set her dirty mug on the floor where the sink would have been and went back to her room to get ready to leave.

Del would miss Eleanor. She was an asshole at times, but she was Del's kind of asshole: one who was always funny and occasionally meant well. Also, without her, Del was stuck alone with Jeanne, and Jeanne gave no evidence that she intended to move on despite the incompatibility of her surroundings with her desired way of life. Eleanor had redirected Jeanne's chummy energy toward her, and that had meant that Del could observe at a safe distance. With Eleanor gone, Jeanne would focus on Del again.

Why was Jeanne still here? And how could Del get her to go? The questions plagued her as she continued stripping out the kitchen ceiling.

Late the next morning, Del heard the sliding door and assumed that Jeanne had gone out on an errand. She went into the living room to begin taking apart the ceiling there and saw Jeanne standing in the backyard alone, looking out over the pond. She wore her flying toaster pajamas and no coat. Her pale feet were bare. The snow drifted down at a pace that was both gentle and insistent. Just in the course of the morning, two more inches had fallen to lay atop the existing pile. Jeanne stood close enough to the door that Del could see her roots, a pale grayish brown, starting to creep up under the blond dye.

Del slid the door open. "What're you doing?"

Jeanne didn't turn to look at her.

"I said, what are you doing?"

Nothing.

"It's warmer inside," Del continued. "Slightly."

"He's not coming, is he?"

Every cell in Del's body told her to lie, to spin a tale in such a way that would propel Jeanne to get into her SUV and re-unite with her awful husband and awful children, leaving Del alone in the wonderful silence.

Del took a step forward. The snow crunched under her boot. "No," she said. "He isn't."

Still, Jeanne didn't turn. "Guess I waited it out too long. Or maybe it was one too many times. Everyone thinks they know the rules. Then things change, and you don't realize it until you've fucked it up."

Del had never heard Jeanne swear before. Now was the time to come up with some words of comfort. Something that would make Jeanne feel better about the fact that yes, she had torpe-doed her marriage, and of course her sons would be furious when they found out. Small towns hated a harlot, and yes, it would probably mean a real decline in her standard of living.

"So what?" Del said.

A gust howled north over the frozen water and hit Del like the back of a hand.

Finally Jeanne turned. Her face had gone colorless. She wore no makeup, and she was strangely fragile without it, like some-thing just hatched and still tender.

"So what?" Jeanne said angrily. "So what?"

"Yeah. So what. So you have to start fresh? So what. You know how many people are in fucked-up situations? Can I tell you about the number of my friends who have died? I lost count. Most of them died alone, too. Their parents wouldn't even fucking see them at the hospital. The ambulance driver said my mom was probably conscious for ten or fifteen minutes after the crash, before they arrived. And you want me to feel sorry for you? I don't. So what. This is your fault. You played a game and you lost. Now deal with it."

"I liked being married," Jeanne said, a quaver to her voice.

"Not very much, apparently."

Jeanne's mouth contracted to a withered little coin at the bottom of her face. "Who are you to tell me anything?"

"I'm no one. But here you are at my house, so I'm the one doing the telling."

Jeanne said nothing, looked back over the pond, ground the snow beneath her left foot with her toes.

Del went at her again. "Why even bother going back? For your stuff? Your party room? Your stupid dog, who you haven't even mentioned once? Forget about those things."

"Things are important," Jeanne shot back. "You wouldn't know. You've never had anything."

Again the wind whipped across the frozen pond. Del's face burned with cold.

"I've had plenty. Just not the stuff you wanted."

A thin lace of snow was beginning to gather on Jeanne's hair. The temperature was unbearable to Del, and she was wearing a coat and shoes. She breathed deeply and tried once more.

"I need you to come inside now."

Jeanne made no attempt to move.

"You're going to need to come inside, Jeanne. It's not safe for you to be out here."

The wind sang through the trees, through the clashing branches, down the hard throats of birds. Anything with two brain cells would bury itself in a hole and stay for a month.

"I need your help," Del said.

A slight movement in Jeanne's head. Just a flicker, easy to imagine or ignore.

"Organizing," Del continued. "I need to organize the rest of this. Some friends are coming to help me in a week. A lot needs to be done before then."

A slight, ever-so-slight inflection of the head.

"If I can get everything done before they come, they can help take the frame down. Then I've just got the foundation. I need to be down to the foundation before they leave. They're big old stones. Heavy. I'm not sure I can get to that point without some help. If you help, I can finish it. And then—and then Uncle Chuck loses. I win. He might yell at you or something if he knows you helped. But at least he'd talk to you."

Jeanne drew her arms across her chest and turned around.

"Fine," she said. "I'll help you. But don't talk to me like you know anything."

Eleanor had evaporated as if she had never existed, leaving only a crumpled pile of sheets on Del's parents' bed and a mostly empty jar of an Italian brand of dissolvable coffee crystals.

After Jeanne came inside and sat on the couch, Del went upstairs and took apart the bed. It was a hollow metal frame, painted white and chipped in parts that revealed it had earlier been painted sage green, and before that black.

An hour later, Del hulked the mattress up on its side and pushed it to the top of the staircase, then shoved it down. It flopped toward the banister and caught for a moment before continuing its slide down to the bottom, where it rammed into the front door.

Jeanne appeared at the bottom of the stairs. "Some warning would be nice."

"Sorry."

"I've made an assessment. You're right, you've got a lot to do. The bed isn't a priority. Stop working on that."

"I'm almost done."

"So what? You would do it much faster if you had help. You need to be more methodical."

Del frowned. "I have been doing this for months now."

"Yeah, and I think you would have been finished by now if you had been more organized in how you approached it. This is actually a pretty simple structure. A child could have built this house. Children probably did. They didn't have labor laws in the 1800s."

"And you're qualified to know any of this how, exactly?" Del inquired.

"When Murrow Construction started, how big a staff do you think we had? It was two people working full-time: me and Chuck. I've seen every part of a house go up; I've operated every piece of heavy equipment. I married your uncle when I was nineteen, did you know that? I drove a backhoe before I got my driver's license. And then I went home and took care of the house and the boys, so I am, if I do say it myself, an effective manager of both people and projects. This project isn't that difficult. It's only gone so slowly because you weren't using the right tools and you probably did everything in the wrong order. You keep telling me that I don't know you, with your new name and your stupid haircut. I'm sure you're so interesting, so *complicated*. But you don't know me, either."

Del stared down the staircase at her aunt. Jeanne wouldn't budge. Del had only asked for her help so that Jeanne didn't do something crazy like walk barefoot onto the pond and die, which would undoubtedly have resulted in Del being sent to jail for the rest of her life because that's how things happened on *48 Hours*. She didn't think Jeanne was actually going to take charge. But this was the Jeanne who commandeered every committee, from school cupcake fundraisers to the Main Street better environment project. That other version of herself was just a flash, a moment of weakness.

"OK," Del said curtly. "Where to now, Mrs. Murrow?"

"Come downstairs. I'll show you what there is to be done."

Jeanne had sketched out the plans in her camel-colored leather planner. They sat together on the sagging couch as Jeanne reviewed with Del the bulleted list of what had to be done, how, and by when. Jeanne touched a fingertip to her tongue, then flipped the page and revealed a plan for the next week. In each day's section, Jeanne had laid out the to-dos for that day, and each task had a small penciled-in box next to it.

"So you can tick the box when you're done." Jeanne reached into her handbag for a set of colored pens. She uncapped a green pen and ticked the box next to "move mattress." That task had been planned for Tuesday.

"It's very satisfying," she added, recapping the pen.

Del shook her head. "Why didn't you tell me any of this before?"

Jeanne looked at her levelly. "You didn't ask. The tasks with red stars next to them are critical. That means if you don't do them on that day, it screws up everything that comes next. So do them. On those particular days."

Del sat back on the couch. Well, shit. In trying to pull Jeanne back from the edge, she had invited the town's most notorious committee leader into her project. Worse yet, Jeanne's plan made sense. Del rescanned the page, looking for something she could argue with, but the plan had a beautiful logic.

"Fine," Del said, pushing herself up. "What's next, fore-man?"

Later Jeanne went out to run errands that Del assumed would involve the gym or the hairstylist, but instead she returned with a second ladder, more tools, and a bag of fast food.

In the living room she handed Del the bag, which was hot with grease.

"I never eat this stuff." She frowned.

Del pulled out a sleeve of fries and offered it. Jeanne took one and placed it gingerly on her tongue.

"It reminds me of when the boys were little. We used to do their birthdays at the fast-food places so I didn't have to clean up. Remember that?"

Del didn't.

"The birthday boy got a free paper crown. Simpler times. I can't wait for grandkids."

Del thought back to Greg and the last time she had seen him in the grocery store.

"What about your kids?" she asked Jeanne. "Maybe you should check in on them."

"Oh, they don't need me now. They're grown men, making their way in the world. They don't want to hang around their mom."

"I think you'd be surprised," Del said. "Greg especially."

"I'll give him a call. But I wouldn't be surprised if he doesn't return it. Here's the thing, Del: you pour all of yourself into your children. Then they grow up and they want to pour all of you out again."

Jeanne lit the battery-powered lanterns and sat on the couch while Del ate her fried chicken sandwich. Jeanne picked at a tuna wrap she'd bought at the supermarket. "I'm going to sleep on the box spring upstairs. Couldn't be worse than this."

"Added bonus, I won't have to breathe your breath."

Jeanne raised her eyebrows. "Added bonus: I won't have to smell you. Showering should not be an optional addition to your week."

Del threw more fries down the hatch. "Will do. Tomorrow."

Jeanne grabbed her pillow and made her way to the door. "Not tomorrow. Tomorrow you finish the ceilings and have to start on the bathroom."

"Next day, then."

"Then you finish the bathroom. It's a critical juncture."

"When, may I ask?"

"Potentially you have one hour free on Wednesday before we start the roof."

"OK, just let me know."

"Will do. Lights out by nine. You need to be up early."

Chapter Thirty-Two

THE NEXT MORNING JEANNE WAS ALREADY WORKING BY THE TIME Del got up at sunrise. Del found her on a ladder in the kitchen, removing the remaining section of lath and plaster that made up the ceiling. Unlike Del, Jeanne seemed to have selected clothing that was suitable for the job. She even wore a hard hat and a mask.

Pulling down the mask, Jeanne accepted the mug Del offered her.

"At any point did you wear a mask so that you weren't breathing asbestos?" she asked Del.

"Nah. Didn't really think about it until I had almost finished."

"That's a shame. I've never done an abatement project myself, but it's quite an undertaking from what I understand. I'd guess that's ten years off your life."

Del shrugged. "Seems like they're the worst ten years, anyhow."

"My parents had a nice retirement," Jeanne said. "Seaside

house in warm weather. They spent every day walking on the beach. My mom made picture frames out of shells."

"And then where are they now?" Del asked.

"Well, now they've passed. My dad got Parkinson's, and my mom got cancer."

"Exactly. I'll take the skip card."

Jeanne held up a hunk of plaster that had a long strand of black hair curling from its edge. "A lot of the house has been renovated, but there's some original work here, too. Horsehair in the plaster."

"I wonder if you could charge extra for that, if you were selling the house?"

"You would absolutely find a way to charge extra. Character. Historical flavor. 'All the rustic charm of a Federal-style farmhouse.'"

"Not too bad. Maybe you should have been a real estate agent."

"I think you're right. It wasn't something I considered. Teacher, secretary, nurse. Guess I ended up being all three. What about you?"

"What about what?"

"What did you want to be when you grew up?"

"I wanted to be Debbie Harry."

Jeanne dug the claw of the hammer into a piece of wood. "Seems like it worked out for both of us."

With two people working, the ceilings were bare before noon, and they began to work on the floors. Del did her own bedroom, and Jeanne did Del's parents' room. Jeanne piled floorboards outside, and Del dragged them across the ice every few hours when she had built up the strength. The snow on the pond was thick and feathery, an easy surface to walk across. Del was surprised to find herself impressed with Jeanne. She was determined and efficient, and most importantly, she didn't chat very much when she was focused on her work.

"Cocoa break," Jeanne yelled out the back door after Del's third trip to move the boards.

Just as Del sat on the couch, the phone in her pocket buzzed. There was no need to guess who was calling. Tym was still the only person with her number.

Jeanne's eyes flicked to Del. "You have a phone? When did you get a phone?"

"Recently," Del mumbled.

There was no way she was giving Jeanne her number. The entire town would have it within days. She'd get a barrage of unwanted calls on her birthday, Christmas, Easter, even Presidents' Day.

She pressed the button to listen to a voicemail, then folded the phone shut again.

"Anything interesting?" Jeanne asked.

"No."

"Hm, that sounds interesting. A boy? A particular boy?"

Del put her mug on the floor. "The cold's getting to me. I'm going to get back to work."

At the back of the house, she lifted a half dozen floorboards and started to drag them down the slope to the pond. She followed her own tracks, a depression of six or so inches in a line down to the water that curved gently like a spine. The path had melted and refrozen, leaving a hard crust of ice over the prints from her boots.

Six was more than she had taken before, and the load was heavy. Somehow, though, Del knew that Jeanne was watching her, and because of this she was unwilling to shuffle the pile or drop any of the boards to pick up later. She walked slowly down the path, hugging the wood under her right arm. Her side ached; her whole body ached. She breathed deeply, gathered her strength, and moved forward.

Tym was going west for a funeral. Their friend Dave had died. Another one, one of many, but Dave was different. He was her father's best friend. Dave and her dad had dated very briefly before deciding to be friends. Tym knew Dave from high school and had introduced the two of them. He was the kind of guy the bartender always remembered, and it usually meant at least one round on the house during their annual Christmas visit to the old-man bar. Dave had played high school baseball and worked as a wine salesman. He was one of three brothers and, unlike many of her father's friends, his family had loved and embraced him, even after they found out he was gay. She tried to remember the names of his brothers, but she couldn't. She hadn't known he was sick. Maybe he had been sick for a long time. She hadn't called him, hadn't sent a postcard. She had simply assumed that she would see him again, next Christmas when she was settled somewhere and could fly in as well, but instead Dave had died. Another one.

Tym would fly there for the memorial service and wanted

to let Del know, in case she wanted to come. He told her that he knew she was still at home. If she needed money for a flight, he could lend it to her. His tone was strange, factual and cool, very unlike him. Del remembered then that Tym and Dave used to sleep together, a long time ago. Maybe Tym had known for a while and not told her. Maybe Tym was worried. Maybe it was something else entirely.

Del stepped onto the ice. The feeling of Jeanne's eyeballs on her back pushed her forward. Her shoulder screamed with the weight of the load.

Gingerly she moved forward until the back end of the floorboards dropped from the bank onto the ice. She pulled forward, one step, then another. The phone buzzed in her pocket. A text this time. She hoped that Jeanne was back in her own room by the time she returned to the house. This wasn't something she wanted to talk about. Jeanne couldn't understand. To her, Del's father's friends were just a pack of fags. Del had no appetite for Jeanne's opinion. There was no use in discussing it. Even if Jeanne said nothing, Del would sense the disapproval in her eyes, and she would hate her aunt with such a passion that the roof of the house would collapse and the frozen pond would implode and spit fire.

She stepped forward again, but the boards didn't follow. She pulled hard, but there was no give. The bottom of the pile was caught on a skip in the ice. She placed the front half of the load down carefully and then retraced her steps to investigate and free the tail end, which was near the center of the pond.

"Be careful."

Jeanne was up by the back door of the house, just as Del had expected. She was holding her mug in both hands, with her anti-asbestos mask hanging loose by its straps at her neck.

Del didn't respond. She nudged the pile of wood with her foot, but it didn't shift. She placed the ball of her right foot low on the pile and shoved it. The top three boards flipped over and fell softly into the snow. Carefully, Del placed her foot on the three remaining boards. She kicked. The wood came loose too easily and swung away from her. She lost her balance, tipped backward, and saw the sky as a gray flash, then lunged forward and landed hard on the ice, knees first, before collapsing face-down. Her right cheek lay against the snow. Her arms and legs extended out like a child making a snow angel.

"Are you OK? Del? Are you OK? Are you OK?" Jeanne's voice grew nearer at each asking.

"Stay back!" Del ordered.

"I'm going to call 911," Jeanne shouted.

Del couldn't see her, but she hoped that Jeanne had stayed off the pond.

"No!" Del placed one palm down. Bare ice that had been cleared by her fall. She pushed up and winced.

"I'll go get my phone. I'll call the fire department. Mac's got to be working. He'll come. It'll only be five minutes."

"No!"

Del placed her other palm down and pushed her torso up. She was about to get up on her knees when she felt it. Water. With her left boot, she gently explored. The ice by her foot was free and loose, bobbing in the water in a gap that had been opened by her fall. In a moment, she knew that she would die here and that Jeanne would be watching.

"Did the ice break?" Jeanne yelled, and then there was a pause. "Oh, god, it broke."

Her death, narrated. Del let her head drop back to the ice, felt the melting snow against her cheek, and closed her eyes.

"I'm going to call 911," Jeanne threatened again. "I need to go inside and get my phone. Don't move."

"I said no." Del pushed up and pulled herself forward, toward the edge opposite the house, which was closer.

"Don't move, I told you! Why don't you ever fucking listen?"

Del wiggled forward slightly, one inch and then another. She brought her knees up to her hips like a frog. Her left foot was soaked through.

"You need to roll," Jeanne ordered.

"What?"

"Roll toward the edge. It spreads out your weight. If you're not going to wait for help, you need to roll."

Her knees up by her hips, Del squirmed forward once again. Behind her, the ice split, and her foot went under again.

"Stop being a stubborn asshole! Listen to me: roll! Roll! ROLL."

Del scooted forward slightly, enough so that her foot was on solid ice again, and rolled. Once, twice, three times. She landed clumsily each time, back in the snow, looking up at the stone-colored sky. She rolled a fourth time and then a fifth. On the sixth turn, she saw tree branches above her. She reached over and felt a frosted crust of soil.

"Get up!" Jeanne shouted. "Get away from the water."

Del shimmied up the edge and stood. In the center of the

pond, she saw a dark patch the size of a beach ball. At its border, loose chunks of ice floated in the water.

Jeanne stood on the opposite edge. "Are you alright?"

Del nodded. Her foot was frozen through, and her knees felt like she'd been beaten with a baseball bat. She was stunned, cold, and scared, but that was all.

"Wait right there," Jeanne ordered. Del watched her go back up to the house and pull a few floorboards out of the pile. She dragged them down toward the pond, then walked along its edge until she reached the creek that fed it. Del joined her and observed as Jeanne laid the boards side by side over the water.

Jeanne dusted her hands on her knees. "I think that'll do. Come on over, we need to get you inside and warm."

Del touched her dry boot to a board laid across the creek. It wobbled and tilted to the left. "This isn't going to hold my weight."

"It's the best we've got."

The creek was frozen at the edge but still running. It was no more than three feet across.

Del dropped to her butt and scooted down to the water, then walked across, knee deep in water.

"You've got to be kidding me," Jeanne said.

"I'm going to fall in and break my leg otherwise."

Jeanne sighed and took Del's hand, pulling her up. "Get inside. Come on, let me take a look at that foot."

Though Del wasn't seriously injured, she was painfully cold. The skin from her toes to her calf was gray and mottled where the water had soaked through. Jeanne set her up next to the stove and chucked an entire bag of coals inside, then made a hot drink with a spoonful of hot chocolate mixed into dissolvable coffee crystals.

"Call it a mocha," she said, offering it to Del.

Del sipped. "Thanks."

"I'm glad you're not dead."

"I'm glad I'm not dead, too."

Jeanne watched her. "You don't seem happy, though."

"I can't just walk across the creek every time. Also, my knees are fucked and I might have twisted my ankle."

She lifted her right leg and gingerly touched her toe to the floor. A shock of pain went through her foot.

"Is that all you can think about? You didn't die. That's amazing. I don't think I'm out of line to call today a win by any reasonable standards."

"I've been working on this too long to give up. You don't understand."

"You're right, I don't understand. You're not dead. That seems like a pretty good reason to me to count your blessings. Look at what you've done. This is so far beyond what I expected. You know what Uncle Chuck said after he came home the night you made your agreement? He said you wouldn't last a week. Well, you showed him. You don't need to show him anymore. It's just plain arrogance at this point."

"I need to finish this. I do. I can't explain it. It just means something to me. It's the only thing, big thing, I will ever have done. It's the only job I won't have walked out on. It's the only thing that everyone thought I would fail at, and then I didn't.

I can't walk across the creek every time I need to get to the other side."

"No, that's not going to work," Jeanne admitted.

"So what am I going to do?"

Jeanne stood up and walked to the sliding glass door. She considered the view for a long time while Del finished her drink.

"We build a bridge," her aunt said finally.

"Huh?"

"I didn't do a good job with my first try. To quote a famous philosopher, 'So what?'"

"Do you know how to build a bridge?"

"No. But your dad did that first one. I have much more construction experience than he had, and he figured it out."

"My dad was a mechanic."

"I know a lot more about wood than your dad did."

More than anything, Del wished that Tym could be in the room with them to give one of his classic looks.

"I'm sure you know plenty about wood. Fine, so we build a bridge. What else? How are we going to get the rest of the house done if I'm limping around?"

Jeanne set her mug down on the single floorboard that was left in the living room. "If you're so set on doing this, you need to quit it with the what-ifs. What if the roof collapses on us? What if a blizzard hits? What if a sinkhole opens under us? We'll spend our time worrying about the things that aren't happening. It's time to get to work."

Jeanne explained that she'd start work on the roof while Del began on the siding. "Leave the siding in the living room last. We'll need it."

Del hobbled outside and watched as Jeanne placed a ladder to the right of the front door and began climbing.

"You're just going to . . . take the roof off?"

"Yeah," Jeanne said from the second step from the top, a hammer dangling from her belt. "And you're going to take the siding off. Get to work. Like you said, we don't have spare time. Take it easy on that leg. Go inside when you need a break. But not too many."

It took the rest of the day for Del to remove the remaining siding on the front and on the west side of the building, where the kitchen and her bedroom were. She didn't get to the back or the east side, where her parents' bedroom sat on top of the living room. All the while, she could hear Jeanne up on the roof, and every few minutes she watched pieces of wood shingle fly off and land softly on the snow.

A little past four p.m., the sun was beginning to set.

"Everything OK up there?" Del asked.

Jeanne's head appeared over the edge of the roof. "All fine. I'll be down in five."

Del went inside, turned on a lantern, and had started to load the stove with coals when Jeanne joined her in the living room.

"I think I need some real food and a real cushion to sit on for half an hour," she said. Flakes of dust and wood clung to her hair. "I'm too tired to drive. Can you?"

"Sure thing."

"I should have asked before: do you have your license?"

"Not technically speaking."

Jeanne shook her head. Wood chips pattered onto the subfloor. "What's new? OK, fine. But drive very carefully."

Chapter Thirty-Three

JEANNE DIRECTED DEL TO A VAGUELY FRENCH RESTAURANT ABOUT a thirty-minute drive away, in an upscale town overlooking the river.

"Very discreet," Jeanne said as she settled into the cushioned high-backed chair and glanced around her.

Del wasn't going to tell Jeanne, but she still had flakes of wood in her hair, despite having spent the entire car trip adjusting her face and hair in the sun visor mirror. The restaurant was small, only ten or so tables spaced far from each other in the back room where they were seated, with another two tables in the windows up front.

Finally, Jeanne's word choice clicked.

"Oh my god. Is this where you conducted your affairs?"

Jeanne recoiled. "*Conducted?*"

"Well . . ."

"Yes, I've had dinner here before. But you don't need to say it in that tone of voice, like I'm some kind of serial . . . affair-haver."

Del flipped through the pages of a battered leather menu. "But that would be accurate. Because you are."

"Mistakes were made," Jeanne said lightly, running her finger along the top of her water glass.

The waiter arrived to take their drink order. Jeanne put on her usual chirpy exterior, but the act looked slightly askew when paired with her dusty sweatshirt and overgrown roots. For the first time maybe ever, Jeanne didn't fit in, but she didn't seem to know it and acted as though she had a cocktail dress and a fresh blowout. The waiter leaned over her while she pointed to one of the wine listings on a laminated page. Del suspected that in Jeanne's mind she might as well have been in Paris or Rome, fresh as a bride. She wanted to say something, bring her aunt's attention to how ridiculous it all was, but she knew that it would deflate Jeanne's buzzy energy.

"You OK with that?" Jeanne asked.

"Huh?"

"Bottle of red from Chile?"

"I don't care."

Jeanne cozied up to the waiter. "Leave it to me, the snob."

Her aunt ordered for both of them: melted cheese pricked with rosemary, fried mushrooms dripping in butter, and a thin piece of fish cooked in cream. Finally, an almond-flavored mousse.

"I have a little secret to tell you," Jeanne said.

"Oh?"

"I called Greg. He told me something and told me not to tell anyone else. But I know you won't say anything, because who would you say it to?"

Del waited.

"He's going to start taking some college classes in the fall."

"Huh," Del said, her tone even.

"I was genuinely surprised. I thought he was all-in with the family company. But he said he just wanted to try something new. He's going to keep it quiet from Chuck, for now, just to see if he likes it. So that'll just be our little secret, just the two of us."

"The three of us."

Jeanne licked the back of the dessert spoon. "I guess you're right. What are you going to do when we finish?"

Del was dumb with wine. "Dunno."

"That's it? Your plan is 'dunno'?"

"What's your plan, Jeanne?" Del asked tartly.

"Dunno," Jeanne returned with an exaggerated shrug. "Guess this calls for another bottle of wine."

"No, thanks. I need about seven cups of coffee before we drive back."

The waiter stepped through the heavy claret curtain that divided the front room from the back. Del glanced over Jeanne's shoulder at the couple entering the room, then back down quickly.

Jeanne detected her inattention and immediately turned.

Frankie, her husband, Sal, at her side, paused at their table. Frankie's black dress, ruffled at the knee, highlighted her roasted salmon tan.

"Sal, do you remember Adela from school? We were little buddies back in the day."

Sal was done up in his Sunday best: ironed chinos and a V-neck sweater over a button-down shirt. He stuck out his hand.

"Been a while," he said as he shook Del's fingertips. "I wouldn't have known ya."

Frankie took in the wrecked plates on their table. "We're here for our wedding anniversary. Four years, two kids, can you believe it?"

Jeanne piped up: "It goes by so fast."

"Too fast," Frankie agreed.

"Not too fast," Jeanne corrected. "*So* fast. Yet somehow . . . exactly the right speed you need to get through it."

A brittle smile from Frankie. Sal eyed the empty table in the corner where the waiter stood by with two menus.

Del raised her empty wineglass: "Many happy returns."

The couple moved along and took their seats.

"What does that even mean?" Del pondered. "Many happy returns."

"The way you said it meant 'screw you,'" Jeanne offered. "But when I've said it, I usually mean 'I might never see you again, but best of luck.' Anyhow, quit worrying about those cheapskates. I always tried to get the deli to donate to the school raffles. You know what they'd give? Day-old cannoli."

"The nerve."

"Absolutely! Oh, you're picking on me again. I see, I see. Your little wisecracks aren't flying past me now."

"Jeanne, you're drunk."

"What's your excuse? You're like this all the time. So one-note," she said, mimicking Del's flat tone. "Back to what we were discussing: what you're doing. Going to do. Your future. I feel like I have to be the parental wisdom here."

"I don't need that."

"But you do. Clearly. You're aimless. That's what the parent is supposed to do. Point in the right direction."

"How'd that work with the boys?"

"It worked out fine, actually. They're all employed and happy. Taxpaying citizens. You can needle me about a lot of things, Adela. But not my boys. I'm proud of them."

Jeanne waved for the check.

Frankie had gone to the bathroom, and Sal sat alone at the table. While Jeanne settled the check, Del went over to Sal's table.

"Hey," she said curtly to him.

He looked up drowsily from his phone. A thin smile played across his inadequate lips.

"I saw you fucking someone else in a hot tub. I'm sure you think you're very suave about the whole thing, but if I know, other people know, too. So do me one little favor and wrap it up, huh? They have extra-small in stock at the Stop and Go. I'll have them hold one behind the counter for you."

Sal's eyebrows lowered, and he looked ready to launch into an attack, but then his eyes flickered to the bathroom door, which swung open. Frankie joined them at the table, glancing first at Sal and then to Del.

"Just saying goodbye," Del told her. "Such a delight, as always."

Out in the parking lot, Jeanne and Del crunched over the snow to the car. Del put on the knit hat that Jeanne had fished out of the back of the SUV a few weeks earlier and given to her. It was

white and had a giant pom-pom on the top. Jeanne stepped
toward her. The back of her aunt's thumbnails pressed into
Del's cheeks as Jeanne adjusted the angle of the hat. It felt
strange, being touched.

"There," Jeanne said, admiring her work in the dim light
cast off by the decorative lantern in front of the restaurant.
"Now that looks very nice."

Chapter Thirty-Four

BY FRIDAY NIGHT, FOLLOWING JEANNE'S PLAN, DEL HAD ACCOM-
plished more than she had expected. Jeanne had single-
handedly removed the shingles and sheathing from the roof,
which was nude down to the rafters. Del had disassembled the
bathroom and put the toilet out in the snow by the pond. ("No,
thanks," Jeanne had said, and drove off in her car to take care
of business.)

For the past two days, Jeanne had slept in her car while Del
slept in a tent inside the living room, which was the only room
with a subfloor. When she unzipped her tent on Saturday
morning, she looked past the cold coal stove, still sitting on a
brick hearth, and saw through the empty house frame the
thicket of woods that divided her land from the Francises'. Their
house was long gone, the land scraped bare and ready for the
new development.

As she plugged the hot plate into the powerbox and started
to boil water for coffee, she wondered where all the parts of the
Francis house had gone. The cracked wood, split bricks, the blue

ceramic tiles in the kitchen. Mrs. Francis's framed needlepoints, photos of their wedding in silver-painted frames, the shuffleboard cues. It was all at the dump probably. Crushed, burnt, a whiff of smoke rising from the steel throat of the incinerator.

Down the slope of the backyard and across the pond, she saw her land, the land that would continue to be hers even after the handover. Even though she hadn't been able to move anything across for several days, and there was a large pile of shingles, wood, and even the bathroom sink at the crest of the hill, the tarps were pleasingly full of her belongings. Flickers of electric-blue plastic were visible at the edges, but elsewhere the tarps were piled high with everything Del had removed from the house. A purple piece of fabric—a dress? her mother's?—rose and fell in the wind.

"Good morning, sunshine."

Jeanne stood outside where the front door used to be, holding out a bag.

"I thought you were still asleep," Del said.

"No chance. Big day. I went out at five a.m. just to get my head clear. Did a run on the treadmill at the gym, showered, went to Lucky Donuts to write down the plan for the day. They're the only place in town open before six a.m. How many people did you say were coming? I budgeted for four."

Del took a glazed ring from the bag. "The Iversons, so that's five, maybe, but I'm not sure which ones will come."

"They're good boys, the Iversons."

Del agreed.

"Any one of them in particular you're friends with?"

"All of them."

"Uh-huh. Well, eat up. I got you a coffee, it's in the holder in the car. You need your energy. We've got a lot to do today."

Around nine a.m. three cars pulled into the driveway. Eric, the eldest Iverson, opened the hatchback of his car and brought out a tool chest.

Aaron got out of a late-model butter-yellow sports car and gaped at the rafters.

"Jesus Christ," he said. "You did all this?"

"I did. A little help from Jeanne."

Jeanne was dusting the snow off the hood of her SUV and laying out her plans to show the team. "Actually, I did quite a bit."

All the Iversons were there, as well as Tess and Sophie, whom Del had met at McClatchey's, and another kid who helped them with set design.

Tess wore a zipped red parka and a blue pom-pom hat. She pulled a dried apricot out of a Ziploc bag in her coat pocket and chewed it while looking at the skeleton of Del's house.

"This is going to be the craziest thing I've ever done," she said to no one in particular.

Billy tapped Del on the shoulder. "We're here. Just like we said."

"Just like you said," Del repeated.

Jeanne clapped her hands over her head. "OK, guys, I'm going to need you to join me over here. There's a lot of work to get done, but I'm really confident we can pull together and do it, as a team."

Eric looked from Jeanne to Del. Del shrugged.

They gathered in a semicircle around the snout of Jeanne's SUV as she ran through the plans with them. It was a top-down operation, rafters first, which obviously needed to be done by people who weren't afraid of heights. Volunteers could identify themselves with a show of hands. It was a strength exercise, with pry bars, so strong young men would be great at it, really the strongest men, so if anyone happened to be the *strongest* they should volunteer. Great, with that sorted out, the rest of them could get to work on the bridge that would be needed in order to ferry the pieces across the creek. This was an engineering feat, not a strength exercise, so only great minds need apply. Three people should be able to figure out a simple bridge in a few hours, don't you think? Here were some quick sketches of what might work, but really if you're an en-gineering genius, feel free to add your own little touch just as long as it adheres almost entirely to the plan right here. By that time, the rafters and dormers would be down and piled by the worker bees who would sort all the framing into piles by what could be carried across by an average person. Then everyone could work together on the joists, and they'd just continue like that, wall by wall, until the entire house was demolished. Tar-get time of completion: two p.m. on Sunday, if the schedule was followed to a T and lunch was limited to a short, scheduled break with only one team member traveling to pick up the piz-zas Jeanne had already ordered from Lil Sebby's. You heard that right: two p.m. Sunday, give or take half an hour.

Jeanne finished her speech and paused for a deep breath. Tess raised her hand.

"I'll go get the pizzas," she offered tentatively.

Jeanne made a note on her plan. "Great, I've got you down for that. There's cash in an envelope on the passenger-side visor. Two-dollar tip for the jar. Keep 'em sweet, or you don't know what kind of extras we'll have in our pizza tomorrow."

Eric, Aaron, Jake, and Adam projected a mental space that was somewhere between amused and nonplussed. Billy was, Del noticed, completely unfazed. He must have gotten used to Jeanne's style from her patronage of the Stop and Go.

Aaron and Jake got up to work on the roof, supported by Eric, who stood at the base of the ladder and shouted supportive instructions along with the occasional warning that someone was about to fall and die. The others went down to the creek with a toolbox and some discarded wood to assess Jeanne's sketches, which Jeanne rolled under her arm and carried down to the creek with her like a general preparing for battle.

After Jeanne handed over the plans to Del and went down to join the group standing at the bank of the creek, Del took a closer look at them to see where she fit in. Sophie appeared by her side.

"This is wild," Sophie said. "I was imagining, like, a shed. This is an actual house."

"Yup."

"Billy must really like you," Sophie continued. She checked Del for a reaction.

"He's a nice guy."

"I mean. He must really *like* you. His brothers are happy

he's met someone. They'd almost given up. It's not that easy in a small town."

Del ran her fingertip across the edge of the paper. It was thick and heavy, like oaktag from elementary school art class. She swallowed.

"Billy's a really nice guy," Del said.

Sophie didn't respond.

Del joined the group at the bridge site. A couple of strong pieces of lumber from the house had been placed side by side in the dirty snow by the edge of the creek, and Tess was laying pieces of two-by-four on top of the lumber supports.

"It's not enough," Tess said. "A lot of the wood is weak or damaged. We can't use it."

Billy jingled his keys. "I'll go get more."

"I'll go, too," Del offered quickly.

She saw Sophie shoot a knowing glance at Adam.

"Cool," Billy said. "Anyone need anything else?"

Billy had a dented blue Chevy Nova with the odometer stuck on 999,999 miles. He pointed it out to Del as they lurched forward from the red light on the entrance ramp to the highway.

"Does your family know?"

Billy checked the traffic over his left shoulder. "Know what?"

"Do they know?"

He glanced at her, then back at the road as he merged behind a silver sedan.

"I don't get it. Know what?"

"Sophie said something to me. She said your brothers think you're interested in me. You're not, so why do they think that?"

Billy tapped his fingers on the steering wheel. They passed three exits before he said anything at all.

"They don't know," he told her.

"Why not?"

"They wouldn't understand."

"Have you tried explaining?"

"No."

"Well, should you?"

Flustered, he signaled left and floored the gas to leap ahead of another car in the passing lane.

"They like how things are. They like it when they understand things. If they thought that I was like that, they . . ." A click of the signal, the engine opening up, their car puttering back into the travel lane. "They just wouldn't like it."

"You won't know that unless you tell them. Your brothers seem like nice guys. They might understand."

"If I tell them, it won't be the same."

"Even if the same is a lie?"

He shook his head. "I don't want to talk about it. You don't get it. That's fine, you don't need to. But it's personal, and I don't owe you an explanation."

They didn't speak for a while. Billy continued to drum his fingers on the wheel, avoiding Del's gaze.

Finally, he looked at her while they were waiting at a red light.

"Is there something about me? That made you think?"

"No. Nothing like that."

"How did you know?"

"Just a feeling, I guess. Most of my friends are gay. But sometimes feelings are wrong."

"Not this time."

"No. Not this time."

They went to a big chain hardware store, and when Billy went to talk to one of the guys in the lumber aisle, Del lingered back by the entrance. She slipped two coins in a machine and twisted the handle. Out popped two gumballs, one pink, one yellow.

In the aisle where Billy was waiting for the clerk to cut the wood down to size, she opened her hand to him.

"Your choice," she said.

He lifted the pink gumball and popped it into his mouth. She took the yellow one. Her damp palm was tinted with the candy coating.

"I'm sorry," she told him. The gumball was enormous, and the words came out funny.

He opened his mouth and delicately removed the gumball. "It's OK."

"I shouldn't have said anything. You're right that I don't understand. I've never had a family like yours. I don't know what it would feel like."

Then the clerk arrived, wheeling over the sliced wood stacked high in a cart, which they pushed up to the checkout lane. Del breathed in the bouquet of sawdust. When they got to the top of the lane, Billy took out the credit card that Jeanne had given him.

The checkout clerk glanced at the card. "The Murrow account? Ten percent discount on custom materials, fifteen percent on packaged merchandise."

"Yeah, that's us," Del confirmed. "We actually needed to add some packaged merchandise, so thanks for reminding us."

She seized some boxes of candy from the checkout display and put them on the conveyor belt.

"For the workers," Billy told the checkout clerk. "Gotta keep 'em sweet."

As they pulled into the driveway at Del's house, he kept his hand on the stick shift after cutting the engine.

"Don't say anything," he said. "Please."

"I wouldn't do that."

He exhaled. "I'm glad we're friends. I was lucky to meet you."

She looked out the windshield. Eric and Sophie were up on the roof now. Half of the rafters were on the ground with Aaron and Jake, who shouted instructions up at their replacements.

"I'm glad we're friends, too."

By Saturday at dusk, exactly in accordance with Jeanne's plan, the roof was off, the staircase was out, the rafters had been carried across the new footbridge, and the top floor had been partially disassembled.

After the Iverson clan drove away, Del and Jeanne stood at the top of the slope in the backyard and observed what had been done. It was a mild day, a hint of early spring in the air.

The black spot where Del had crashed through the pond had never refrozen and became larger each day, like a dash of wet ink creeping across a page.

"We're going to finish it," Del said.

"Yup, we are. We're a good team."

Del walked the circumference of the house while Jeanne organized something in her car. The light was nearly gone, and the snow all around the property had been trampled flat over the course of the day. A blue metallic candy wrapper scraped across the snow and caught in the depression of a footprint. The old coal stove sat by the near side of the pond, and the chimney lay on its side by the house, like an arrow pointing toward the neighbors' property. The four sides of the house were still upright, but the interior walls, staircase, and all the flooring components had been removed down to the shallow, stone-walled cellar. It wasn't anyone's house anymore. It wasn't a house at all: it was materials. Del pressed her hand to a piece of swollen gray timber in what had been the living room. The wood felt cool and damp, as if it had come out of a fever.

Jeanne touched Del's shoulder.

"I'm gonna head out. I'm exhausted. I think tonight's the night for a hotel room. Want to come? We'll get Chinese delivered."

"No, I think I'd rather stay here."

Jeanne gestured to the piles of broken wood. "Where is there to stay? Are you a beaver?"

"I'm set. I've got all my camping gear. It's not too cold anymore."

"Do you want to get dinner first?"

Del shook her head. "I'm not hungry."

"Too much pizza for lunch. Carb overload."

"Must be that."

Jeanne jingled her keys. "I'll see you tomorrow, then. Bright and early. Should I leave the plans with you, in case the boys arrive earlier than I do?"

Del shot her a look. "No one is going to arrive earlier than you do."

"You're right. I'll hold on to them, keep them safe. See you in the morning."

Earlier in the day, Del had moved her tent outside the house and left it in the strip of woods between her house and the neighbors'. It was where she used to play as a child, in a clearing by a low, flat rock on which she had had lunch parties with her stuffed bears. In this clearing, she had built stick men, made a cat toy out of wild turkey feathers, buried marbles for pirates to unearth.

After Jeanne's SUV disappeared, she went to find the spot. By the time she arrived, the daylight was nearly gone, so she clicked on one of the electric lanterns to finish setting up the tent and unrolled her sleeping bag inside. She brought the lantern inside, as well as *The Cowboy Code*, one of her father's books, which she had taken from the pile across the pond. The pages had gone yellow and fat and were mildewed at the edge. She took off her hat and shoes, got in the sleeping bag with her coat still on, and picked up the book to read. The chill from the ground crept up through her back and legs. She closed her eyes, tried to focus on anything other than her discomfort, and then a minute later sat up and put her hat back on. If only she had thought to bring another set of socks, or a blanket to put on the ground between the sleeping bag and the thin, plasticky tent fabric.

She flipped through the swollen pages of her father's book and landed randomly on chapter seventeen. A cowboy rode back into the town that his enemies had burned. The saloon, the hotel, the dry goods store: all ash, all destruction. A child's bonnet trampled in the road. Even his horse cried to see it. The cowboy dismounted to follow the path to his sweetheart's house. His walk was slow, pained. Del felt a twinge in her own injured knee. The cowboy arrived and found among the charred wreckage a cobalt bone china teacup, perfectly intact.

She shut the book. Tomorrow, with the Iversons and Jeanne, she would take down the frame, and slowly, together, they would take it across. After that, the rest of the job would be up to her. It was strange. She hadn't wanted Jeanne's help, or sought out the Iversons' assistance, but she had liked, briefly, being part of something with them. She liked listening to the Iversons pick on each other and seeing how they pulled their friends into their jokes. It made sense, Billy wanting to remain part of that.

Still, though, she couldn't help but look forward to her last week, alone.

Chapter Thirty-Five

DEL WOKE TO THE SOUND OF A BIRD SINGING. IT WAS A STRANGE kind of birdsong, low in pitch, and as she blinked awake, trying to pin down the migration that brought this sound, she realized that it was her name being called.

She sat up and unzipped her sleeping bag. Everything cracked: her legs, her knuckles, her back, even her neck.

"I'm coming," she shouted into the woods as she stepped out of the tent.

Standing by her SUV, Jeanne wore a navy puffer vest over a cream turtleneck and bootcut jeans. She could have been an advertisement for soap and good health.

"I feel like a million bucks. It's incredible what sleep and a hot shower can do for you."

"Mmm." Del worked her fingers through her hair. It was knotted in the back where her head had lain on the ground.

"Well, you look . . . up and at 'em, anyway. Do you think I got enough food?"

Jeanne gestured to the hood, where there were two mega-boxes of bagels. It was enough to feed an entire T-ball tournament.

"I think that will be fine," Del said.

Undoubtedly the Iversons would have eaten before they showed up, but they didn't seem like the type to turn down free food. Del helped herself to two bagels, one onion and one sesame, and tried out two of the spreads, a pink one and the other flavored like chives.

"Let's go through the plans for today." Jeanne opened the passenger-side door and unrolled the paper over the seat. She and Del examined the to-dos for a second before Jeanne sniffed and reached into the coin well for a metal tin of mints, which she placed delicately on top of the paper by Del's hand.

"Onion bagels a mistake?" Del ribbed.

"I think we might get rid of that one before the boys arrive. And the other one is . . . ?" She raised her nose and sniffed at the air.

"Fish, I think."

"Right, well, I'm never ordering the 'Everything and the Kitchen Sink' again. We're not going around stinking of fish and onions all day. Plus whatever your hygiene situation is."

"My hygiene? Have you seen your roots? You could be in a documentary about the last days of Stalingrad, after they'd shot the hairdressers."

Jeanne narrowed her eyes. "I don't know what that means, but I know it was evil."

"It was."

An ever-so-slight tilt from the hip. "The master bows to the student."

"The master should make an appointment at Hair by Marco as soon as is feasible."

Jeanne flipped down the passenger-side mirror and leaned in to look at herself. "Maybe I'll go to the city. Take myself away for a few days. Get dolled up and see what the world has in store for me."

"Are you going to tell Chuck?"

"Nah. He seems to keep paying the credit card bills. So I might as well take advantage while I can. If there's something you learn in life as you get older it's that one day, the bills always come due for whatever it is that you've done. But I don't think today is that day."

Del looked at Jeanne with a kind of tenderness. "You'd be nice as a redhead."

"You think? Hm. Yeah, I can see that. I was always more of a Ginger than a Mary Ann."

Jeanne stared in the mirror, lost in thought, and Del imagined that she was trying on personas for who she might be next. Ginger, a real estate agent, a bachelorette living in a high-rise in the city with a doorman who signed for all of her packages. Jeanne was going to be alright.

The gang arrived just before nine.

"Thanks for coming," Del told Eric.

"No, this is great," he said, pulling off his fleece jacket. "Gets me out of taking our grandma to church."

"You go to church every Sunday?"

"Yep, we all do. Not Billy, if he has to work. Sometimes Jake and Adam don't go if they've been out too late. We were all altar boys, though."

"I couldn't keep that up. Too lazy."

"Grandma thinks we will literally be stewed in a big pot by the devil if we don't go. It's easier to sit through forty minutes of Mass than forty weeks of her telling you in Sicilian all the ways that you're going to be tortured for eternity for not going. Also, there's donuts and coffee in the basement at the end. It's not so bad."

With that, he grabbed a bagel and went to join Aaron at the east side of the house.

By eleven, working all together, they had removed the first wall, broken it into pieces, and carried it across the pond. Del's ankle and knees remained tender, worse probably for sleeping on the ground overnight, so she was on the sawing team along with Jake and Adam, cutting the pieces of frame into portable sections.

Jeanne blew a silver whistle to indicate that a ten-minute rest break would commence. The Iversons went back up to Jeanne's vehicle to pick through the remaining bagels and edited selection of spreads.

Del drifted down to the pond's edge and took her phone out of her pocket.

"How's it going?" she asked when Tym answered.

"Nice to hear your voice. It's fine. I flew in yesterday. The memorial service is on Tuesday. It's too *pleasant* here. I don't like it. It warps the brain. All these people walking around like dopes with smiles on their faces."

She told him about the progress on the house, about the help she got from the Iversons and Jeanne.

"Think you can send them over to me?" Tym asked.

"Why's that?"

"I'm helping out his family with the house. They've got to go back to the farm. It's going to take a while to organize everything, so I think I'll be here for a month. The pharmacy cut the photo counter, so I'm out of work anyhow. They're giving me thirty percent of the proceeds of the estate sale, which is nice."

But for Dave he would have done it for free. She knew it, but he wouldn't say it.

"I'll come. I'll help you. I can't come in time for the memorial service, so let me do this."

"How?"

"I'm finished here in a week. Sunday. After that, I'll get on a bus. It'll take me three or four days to get there, but I'll help you. I'm basically an expert now."

"PhD in Construction Science. Dr. Del."

She smiled. "Exactly right."

A whistle blew behind her. She turned and saw Jeanne pointing at the next wall they'd take down.

"I've got to go," she told Tym. "But I'll call you when I get the bus ticket. I might be there by next Wednesday."

"Love you, darling."

Her throat was rough. "Love you."

She flipped the phone closed and walked up the hill, careful about her ankle, to join the others.

They finished at 2:12 p.m. Del thought Jeanne would be pleased by how close they were to her initial estimate, but before she

drove off to her hotel, Jeanne had laid out the plans on the hood
of her vehicle and was trying to piece together where she had
gone wrong. One break too many, she muttered, then rolled
the documents and tossed them in the back seat.

Eric, Aaron, and Jake drove back to their parents' house to
wash up before dinner. Del thanked them and waved goodbye.

Billy and Adam stared into the crater, and Adam cracked open
a beer out of the six-pack he had brought back with their pizzas.

"I must say," he said after taking a sip. "I'm impressed with
us. We took apart an entire house in forty-eight hours."

Billy corrected him gently. "Mmm, I think quite a bit of
work might have been done before we arrived."

"Nah," Adam said. "It was about ninety percent us. Ninety-
five maybe. But it was a good start, Del. Good prep work. I'm
impressed."

She rolled her eyes at him.

"What's next?" Adam asked.

"With the house? I'm going to move the foundation."

"Sounds horrible. Mule work. I didn't mean that, though. I
meant big picture."

"Oh. I'm going across the country. Getting a bus next Sunday. I have a friend who needs help with a project. He's got a
house and needs to get rid of all the stuff in it."

Adam looked at her like she was crazy. "Is this a service you
offer now?"

"Definitely not."

"Good. I think this was a one-time-only offer from Clan
Iverson."

"I appreciate it."

He downed the rest of the beer and crunched the can in his fist. "Billy, I'm gonna make a call in the car. See you in five."

"Honestly, I didn't think we'd be able to do it," Billy told her.

"I did."

"Why?"

She looked across the foundation and the pond to the pile of house materials on the other side. "I don't know. Because I wasn't willing to stop, I guess."

"Did you mean it, about taking a bus across the country, or are you just flagrantly lying like you do sometimes?"

"Yeah. I talked to my friend. He needs me."

"I'll go."

"You're going to take a bus across the country with me?"

"No, I'll drive."

"It's not like a sightseeing-type deal. I've got to leave on Sunday and get there as soon as I can."

"We'll get there faster by driving. Buses have to stop, and you'll have to change. Also, I don't smell like a bus passenger. Although I guess for you that isn't a problem."

She laughed. "But what about your job?"

"I work part-time in a grocery store. That's exactly the kind of job you quit to drive across the country. Or not even quit. Just never show up again."

"What about your family?"

"There are so many of us, it'll take them days before they even recognize that I'm gone, and by then I'll be back." Now it was his turn to look across the pond. The ice had melted, and the water had turned a muddy green. "Or maybe I won't. Maybe I'll stay. Who knows?"

"Why would you want to do something like that?"

He looked at her. "I'd do it for you, because we're friends."

The car horn honked. Adam gestured impatiently from the driver's-side window.

"Billy, you're the best person I could have met."

"Same. Pick you up next Sunday morning," he told her as they walked up the hill together. "Try to take a shower before then."

Chapter Thirty-Six

A STORM PULLED IN AFTER MIDNIGHT. DEL LISTENED TO THE sound of the trees clashing as the roof of the tent sucked in and pounded flat until the gales stopped. Jeanne had left her with a box of granola bars and a case of bottled water, so eventually she sat up, turned on the lantern, and ate a granola bar while reading the rest of her father's book. The cowboy found his girlfriend, and then he was shot.

When she got out of the tent before dawn, the storm was over. A few steps away from the tent, an old elm tree had toppled and lay across her path. A near miss. She looked up, past the branches with pale-green buds, and saw that the sky was blue and free of clouds.

The rainfall had melted the last of the snow. The ground was muddy, each step tugging at her boots. She dropped her tools onto the basement floor and then lowered herself down.

The walls came up to neck height and were lined with field-stones pointed with cracked gray mortar. When she was a kid, the basement had flooded every spring. Her father had bor-

rowed a sump pump from Mac MacIntosh at the fire department to drain away the water, then spent the next month
repointing the mortar. Looking over the walls, she could see
the lighter sections that he had repaired and the crumbling
fragments that had been repaired earlier or never at all.

She lifted the pickax and swung at a weak section of mortar,
which broke into chunks and crumbled to her feet. She swung
again and again until the hunk of stone wobbled free at the
base. Placing her hands under it, she lifted. No luck: it was
stuck somewhere. She dug through the pile of tools she had
dropped down to the muddy earth floor and got the big claw.
With the big claw under the stone, she pushed down, and the
stone lifted at one end. She bent at the knees, hugged the stone,
and then heaved it over the top of the wall to the ground above.
Looking at her phone, she saw that the entire process of freeing
one stone had taken forty-three minutes.

She put her hands at the top of the wall and scrabbled up.
On the east side of the house by the copper beech tree was the
pile of power tools she hadn't returned to Murrow Construction quite yet. Out of respect for Jeanne, she had put them
under some plastic sheeting she'd found in the shed so that they
wouldn't be ruined by the elements. Out of respect for herself,
she hadn't said anything to Jeanne about what was under the
plastic sheeting or when, or if, it would be returned to the company inventory.

The backup power box that she'd stolen after the first one
died was going to be needed, and she selected another few tools
that might be handy. She dropped a ladder down into the basement and in a couple of trips brought everything down with her.

The reciprocating saw was a no-go. Tiny pieces of stone flew out from the vibrating blade, grazing her cheek. Del touched her face and scrutinized her finger. Blood, but not very much. She placed the saw down on a piece of plastic in a corner of the basement and plugged in a little chisel. A buzz filled the air when she flipped the switch on, and it grew even louder when she pressed the tip into a section of loose mortar. Within minutes it broke away, and the fieldstone, fat and clean as a new baby, was ready to be lifted. She should have asked Jeanne for her protective gear before she left. Goggles, gloves. As she turned to the next stone and applied the chisel to the mortar at its base, she saw that her knuckles were cracked and bleeding already. Tym would be disgusted when he saw her.

March first was a Sunday. She hadn't agreed to anything in particular with Uncle Chuck. Just that she'd get her money then. Presumably work started on Monday. How would the money work? Did he intend to give her a check? A series of checks? Where would he send them? She should have dictated what she wanted in advance. There was no room to negotiate now. Chuck seemed like he wanted things to be quick and clean. He'd see, then, what she had accomplished. How his doubts were misplaced. She had done everything she said she would, in perfect time. It hadn't gone exactly as she had planned, but what did? It would be a good story for Tym when she saw him again in a week and a half.

She pondered her hands again. When she flexed her knuckles, the lines of dried blood came alive and leaked again. She would need to clean up before she rejoined society as a functioning human being. She had lost so much weight that her period had stopped. Her hair hadn't been cut since the first time she tried, but it didn't seem like it was growing as fast as it used to anyway. She found herself talking to herself at times, too. Encouraging herself, pointing out her accomplishments. You couldn't do that out in the world, or people would think you were a nutjob.

She lumped another stone up over the wall onto the grass, then picked up the chisel again. After three more stones, she pressed her foot into the wall and raised herself up to ground level. She had hidden the stolen Stop and Go cart in the woods in case one of the Iversons pinned it on Billy and ribbed him about it for the rest of his life. Now she pulled it up to the side of the cellar, loaded it with stones, and threw her weight behind it to guide it along the muddy path down to the new bridge.

By the water, she noticed a slight movement in the mud. She lifted her hands from the cart and watched. Another low flicker by the water. She barely breathed so as not to scare it. A snapping turtle the size of a roast turkey raised its head at her.

"Hello," she whispered.

It placed a thick foot forward, followed by another, then disappeared into the water with a splash. The water rippled and then was still. Del went back to the cart, crossed the bridge, and dropped the fieldstones at her site. There was no more room on the tarp, so she piled them alongside.

By dusk she had finished half of a wall. She wore just a T-shirt and jeans though it was only around fifty degrees. She wished she could take a dip in the pond to cool off, but it would be too cold, and there were the turtles, which were big enough to bite off a toe.

She was beginning to cross into the woods when she heard a car pull into the driveway and turned to look. It was Billy.

"Hey," he called out as she approached. "Figured you might want some company."

"That sounds nice."

He surveyed her, from her matted hair down to her filthy outfit, and then fished for something in the glove compartment. He raised a pair of keys. "Good, I've got them. One stop first."

Over the summers, he always worked at the public pool as a lifeguard, and he never returned the keys. They parked on the far side of the lot, where no one would see the car from the road. He fumbled the key at the door, looking over his shoulder repeatedly to make sure they weren't spotted.

Finally, the door opened and they went inside.

The corridor had a green tile wall and a cement floor. Though it was five months since the pool had closed for the season, it still smelled of chlorine.

"I haven't been here since I was a little girl."

"It's exactly the same. I don't think the town has done any improvements at all. They diverted all the funds to the new sidewalk project."

He took her to the staff room. In a drawstring sack he found a stack of towels and handed them to her. "Not freshly laundered but good enough. There's a lost and found in the blue locker behind you."

She took what he gave her and went to the women's showers. Here the tiles were pink, many of them cracked. The metal grates in the floor had rusted. The plastic curtains that divided the shower section from the changing area were ripped and bloomed with mold. Turning the valve all the way up, she stepped under the showerhead. Just as she remembered, it only came to lukewarm in temperature and intensity. There were five showers along the wall with no dividers between them. She turned them all on and walked back and forth under them, feeling the water pulse over her and then go dry for a second before she arrived under the next showerhead. By her feet, filthy water swirled down the slope of concrete into the rusted grates.

Finally, she turned off the showers one by one and wrapped herself in a towel.

Billy was in the office playing Solitaire on a very old computer.

"Can I go for a swim?" she asked him.

"The water hasn't been treated, and the cover is on. Also, I hope you don't mind me saying this, but you don't smell terrible for the first time in a really long time."

"No offense taken. Can we just sit outside for a while?"

White reclining chairs sat in a stack under an awning. Billy grabbed two off the pile and placed them in front of the pool, which was covered with a charcoal PVC sheet.

"Feeling better?" he asked.

"A lot."

They sat in comfortable silence, looking out over the scrubby farmland on the other side of the pool. The sun was setting, and Del began to feel a chill. Billy handed his fleece jacket over to her.

"Can I ask you something?" she said.

"Why not?"

"Why haven't you told them? They seem like good people."

Billy closed his eyes.

"When I was twelve, I got pneumonia. I had to miss Mass for a month, which, if you know my family, is a really big deal. I couldn't walk, just lay in bed like a corpse. It was summertime, and everyone kept saying how weird it was, for a kid to get pneumonia in summer. I had been to camp, sleepaway camp, and they did this exercise in the pond where the counselor flipped your boat over, to show you how to right it in case you capsized out on open water. I was in the boat with this kid Ben. The counselor flipped us, and we went overboard. Under the water, I opened my eyes and Ben was right there. I grabbed his ass. He probably thought it was just grasping blindly. He never said anything to anyone. But I got pneumonia and had to go home. I thought I was going to die. And I thought I deserved it."

Del didn't say anything because there wasn't anything to say. She reached over to him and placed her hand on top of his. They lay like that, staring out over the crumpled dead grass in the old cow field, until the light was gone.

"What was your dad like?" he asked her.

"It's funny. Going through all their stuff, I thought I'd get to know them better. I'd find something, and it would all make sense. It hasn't, though. It's just stuff, and they were just people. My mom, I guess, I never got to know. I do, a little, now. When she died, I was really angry at her. I understand some things about her that I didn't before, maybe because I'm not a teenager anymore. My dad, I got a little more time with, and honestly, I'd say that in the end he was peaceful. He had found his place and his people, and I got to see that. He got to see me, too, not just as a kid. My mom never got that. I wish she had."

"That sounds nice," Billy said.

"Yeah. Yeah, I think it was."

"Do you want to go and get something to eat after this?"

"Sure."

"What day was it you need to leave?"

"Sunday."

"OK. I assume you're going to be at home? Should I just drive by and pick you up when I'm packed?"

"Yeah. Actually—you can call."

He sat up. "You have a phone?"

"Yeah, I just—I've barely used it. I guess I never think about it."

She reached into her jeans, which were by her feet, and felt for the phone in her back pocket. She flipped it open and pressed every button until she found the screen that showed her number.

"Here it is." She showed him.

"Cool. I'll write it down in the car. I can call you when I'm on my way over."

Back in the woods, when she got in her tent, she took out her phone again and dialed.

Tym had gotten a sunburn. He had eaten watermelon rolled in powdered chili. It had made him sneeze. He had put his feet in the sand and stared at a different ocean. He met some of

Dave's West Coast friends, and though some of them were nice, none of them had a sense of humor, which he thought was a result of too much sun and exercise. The memorial service was the next day, in the afternoon. In the morning, he would buy a suit that he could return a day later.

"When did you know he was this sick?" she asked him.

"I didn't. The drugs were working for a while. Then it happened fast. When I heard that he quit smoking a few weeks before he died, I thought things were serious. Who quits the five minutes of enjoyment they get in life if they're going to die?"

"What a joke."

"Absolutely. But I'm not laughing anymore," Tym said darkly.

Chapter Thirty-Seven

BY THURSDAY AT NOON, SHE HAD TAKEN DOWN TWO WALLS FROM the foundation. Removing the stones and mortar had loosed the groundwater that had been held back by the wall. Now the water came up to the toe of her boots. She sank the ladder into the mud to start work every day and had to keep her pile of tools and the power box above her, at ground level.

Each stone must have weighed twenty pounds. Thirty, even, for the big ones. At noon she took a lunch break to eat three granola bars and drink a bottle of water from the case that Jeanne had left her. Then she lay in the grass by the pit, letting the sun fall on her. New shoots of grass were tender against her cheek. There was a softness to the soil and to the light filtering through the dogwood tree, and to the pale-green buds on the tree that would soon burst open into small pink flowers. She would be long gone by then. She breathed in the mulchy odor that lifted off the pond and let her eyes shut. She thought about fishing off the small bridge her father had built over the creek.

Pulling up rainbow trout with her purple rod, asking her mother to take the hook out of the fish's mouth. The smell of onions frying in the pan before her father rolled the fillet in flour and pepper. The sound of beers cracking open and of potatoes rumbling in boiled water.

She got up, because there was more work to do.

She sprinkled some coffee granules into her father's clay mustache mug, poured bottled water on it, and sloshed it around. The granules didn't dissolve and left a bitter film on her teeth. She drank it anyhow.

Billy had left her the keys to the municipal pool. It was almost an hour's walk, but by midafternoon she was too tired to work anymore, so she went there to shower and sit on the terrace. When she eased herself into the chair, every bone in her body cracked. She remained there, her eyes closed, her palms facing up, until the sun set and it was too cold to stay outside in just a towel.

The diner was never busy for dinner service and only stayed open until six p.m., which suited her perfectly. She arrived just before five. The place was empty. Del had seventeen dollars left, all in wrinkled dollar bills in her jacket pocket.

"How are things going?" the waitress asked after taking her order.

"Almost done."

"Congratulations. I expect we won't be seeing you around?"

Del watched as a club sandwich platter was delivered into the serving window.

"No," she said. "I think this is about it."

The waitress frowned. "I, for one, will miss you. It's nice having someone pleasant to talk to. One of the vets tried to pinch my ass last week. Can you believe it?"

Del couldn't.

She ate, paid, and left a five-dollar tip.

On Saturday, Eleanor came by.

"Good morning, princess," she said, leaning over the pit.

The water was up to Del's ankles.

Del squinted up at Eleanor. The sun was a ball above the old woman's head. "How's it going?"

"Fine, fine. I had to sell one of my furs at a consignment shop for twenty dollars. I'll probably buy it back for forty dollars in the fall. But that's how it goes. I should have had children so that they could pay my bills when I got old. Oh, I met a potential for a future ex-husband. Says he's a pilot. One of his eyeballs looks fake."

"I'm impressed," Del said.

"By the eyeball?"

"That you keep trying."

Eleanor offered to take them out to lunch. She had a coupon that meant her proceeds from the fur coat sale would cover them both for lunch, but Del had too much to do. Instead Eleanor went out and came back with a bucket of fried chicken that she placed on the grass at Del's eyeline.

Eleanor poked at a foam cup of slaw dripping with mayonnaise and watched with approval as Del reached into the bucket and pulled out a drumstick that she gnawed to the bone almost instantly.

"Never thought I'd say it, but you could use a couple pounds on you."

Del wiped fried crumbs away from her cheek with the back of her hand. "That means a lot."

"Your mother would have been proud of you."

"Maybe," Del said.

"Oh, I'm sure of it."

"What are you going to do when the fur coat money runs out?"

Eleanor thought about it. "I've got more to sell. An opal ring. Some war stuff that belonged to my second husband. The house, eventually. I'm not worried, though. I hope to die in my sleep at a ripe old age of eighteen months from now, before I'm destitute."

Del shook her head.

"Listen, kid, my hip's too bad to keep standing up here like this, and I've got to go pay the electricity man before he shuts my lights off. Can you believe my brother and his bride kept the heat running at Florida temperatures the entire time they were staying at my place? The insolence. Come and see me before you go, my darling. And if you can't? Well, this is our adieu." She blew a kiss to Del and left.

March

Chapter Thirty-Eight

ON SUNDAY AT DAWN, THERE WAS STILL WORK TO DO. DEL FIG-
ured that she would finish up and then walk into town to Murrow Estates to pick up her check. She dropped into the pit. The
water came halfway up her calf. Fifteen stones left. She would
be done around one p.m., if she skipped lunch. She would pick
up her money and then call Billy, and they'd be on their way.

When seven of the stones were free, she heard a car pull in.
Whoever was there didn't get out immediately. She began to
suspect that she was going to have to climb up the ladder, but
then Chuck's face loomed above her.

"You've done it," he said.

"Almost."

He contemplated her new plot of land. She knew what he
was seeing: the enormous pile of broken wood, tiles, and pipes.
The potbelly stove. The toilet. It looked like a very compressed
junkyard. Not the best view from his new high-class development.

He shook his head. "Pretty pointless, if you ask me."

"I didn't."

He smiled ever so slightly. She knew, at some level, that he was impressed.

"Can we get this wrapped up?" he asked her.

She climbed the ladder and came to stand beside him. He glanced over at the power tools with Murrow Estates labels on them lying in a haphazard pile on the ground. They were caked with mud and grit. The chisel had stopped working the day before—Del had busted the bit and didn't have a replacement. Chuck didn't say anything.

"I've got everything here for you."

He handed her two envelopes: one a clasped manila envelope, the other letter-sized and blue.

The manila envelope was heavy. She opened it first. It was cash, stacks of hundred-dollar bills held together with rubber bands.

"That's per our agreement," Chuck said.

"I thought it was going to be a check or something."

He smirked. "No way. This was not an aboveboard operation. Honestly, I thought you would quit immediately, and if you didn't do that, it was a pretty safe bet that you'd either die or get mangled. I wasn't going to get sued by whoever would sue me."

She opened the blue envelope. It was a smaller stack of hundred-dollar bills, maybe a thousand dollars in total. "What's this?"

"Graduation present. Realized we never gave you one. We gave the same to all the nieces and nephews, a thousand dollars fair and square. Your auntie Jeannie called me and told me to do it. It's only fair you got yours, too. She's had to go to the city on business. But she said to tell you 'many happy returns.'"

"Thanks." She put the blue envelope inside the manila envelope.

"Want some advice?"

"Not really."

He looked at her sternly. "Too bad. I think you need it. Work hard. Invest in yourself. Don't gamble. Don't make friends with losers. Don't lend money to anyone, ever. A tip is ten percent, any more is a handout. What I'm giving you is a lot of money. It's a new start in life. Don't screw up. Build, grow, learn how to be independent. *Invest.* You saw what happened to your parents. They got handed this house, and what did they make of it? How did they improve their investment?"

She looked over the pond to the pile of stones and wood that would soon disappear.

"Nothing." Chuck answered himself. "They made nothing."

"Do you know where Greg is?"

"He's at the office this morning. Got some paperwork."

Chuck turned and looked again across the water, at the broken remains of his childhood house.

"You know, I thought of this all the time when I was a kid. Getting up at four a.m., milking the cows, feeding the pigs. Being whipped with a switch if I ever got up late or missed a day. Never getting anything, never going anywhere. I thought when I grew up I'd knock it down or burn it down. I would have lit the match myself. But I never thought it would actually happen." Then he clapped her on the shoulder. "We're starting construction tomorrow morning at nine. Don't be here."

He got back in his SUV and drove away.

Del pressed the envelope of money under a fieldstone and dropped back into the pit.

The last stone was underwater. As she bent to lift it, she thought of the snapping turtle she had seen, its smooth, glossy shell.

She didn't have enough energy left to hurl it up over the wall, so she carried it under one arm as she pulled herself up the ladder. It just fit in the shopping cart along with the others.

It was the last time she would transport the house across the water, so she took her time. The wheels of the cart fit into the grooves set by earlier trips. All around her, she saw the evidence of her work: the bent grass, the muddy path, the tree branch she had snapped off because it brushed her head one too many times. When she was gone, it would begin to repair itself. Within a month, maybe less, Chuck would have filled the foundation pit, new grass would grow, and it would look as if she had never been there at all, except for the broken house across the pond. That, too, would disappear as the swampland closed in around it, and the land and what it meant would become a secret that only she would know. She wondered if the children in the new development would go exploring, if whole tribes of them would set up forts in the woods as she had done, would fight with stick swords and paint their faces with pokeweed berries, if they would find her house and believe they had discovered a new continent and new people. They would play with the hairbrushes and the music boxes, the broken paperbacks and plastic checkers, and they would see it for what it was: treasure.

She piled the stones along the edge of the site, then went back to her tent to go through her stuff. There wasn't much to take. Most of her clothes were unusable, worn through, stiff with mud, and destroyed by overuse. She changed into the least bad jeans and least ripped T-shirt and switched from her mud-soaked boots into sneakers and a pair of her father's striped green socks. Then she took the tent and the rest of the clothes across the water and shoved them underneath a piece of lumber poking out the side. In her pocket, she kept the St. Christopher medal she had found in her mother's bedside table.

That was it. Done.

To the north side of the pile, she saw something that she had placed there earlier. It was on its side, but she recognized it all the same. She stepped over the speckled purple buds of skunk cabbage and leaned across the kitchen cabinets to reach it. It was the part of the bridge where her father had carved their initials. s l a. She traced the damp letters with her index finger. Then she put it back on the pile and walked away.

It took a long time for the door to open after she knocked. Greg opened it just a crack. Behind him, the lights were off in the hallway.

"Yeah?" he said.

"I did it."

"I heard."

"I just wanted to say thank you," she told him. "For your help. Even though you fucked me over sometimes, too."

He opened the door a little more. He was in his Sunday

gear: sweatpants and a T-shirt. There was a pen tucked behind his ear.

"I'm waiting for a catch," he said.

"There is none. Just thanks and good luck."

"Do you need anything?" he asked her.

She didn't.

"I wasn't surprised, by the way. That you did it. I thought you would. Just out of sheer stupidity, I guess."

"Thanks."

"Well, this . . . is goodbye."

He put out a hand and she shook it.

An hour after she called him, Billy arrived to meet her at her house.

"My stuff is in the trunk. You can put your stuff in the back."

She held up the fat envelope of money. It was all she had.

"I travel light."

"Cool. I'm sorry, but we're going to have to stop by my parents' house. Just for two minutes. I didn't get a chance to say goodbye to everyone."

They drove over to the opposite side of town, near the river. The Iversons lived in an old 1960s ranch with a narrow front yard that unspooled down to the street. Billy put the car in park and went out to talk to his parents and his brother Adam, who were gathered at the front door.

Del was lost in thought, picking through the dirty pennies in the coin well, when there was a tap at the window. Eric, the eldest Iverson. She rolled down the window. Outside smelled of sunshine and laundry.

"Excited for your trip?" he asked.

"Yeah, I am."

Eric looked up at Billy, who was hugging his grandma, a very old woman with a walker and a tiny pom-pom of silver hair on the top of her head. "Do me a favor?"

"Sure, what?"

"Look after Billy. He's always had someone looking out for him. He needs that. He's a kid still. He doesn't understand how people can be."

Mr. and Mrs. Iverson surrounded Billy in a group hug. "I'll do that."

Billy jogged down to the car and said goodbye to Eric. In his hand was a St. Christopher medal attached to a yellow ribbon. He draped it over the rearview mirror and then reversed down the hill.

"Present from Grandma," he said.

"Funny. I have one of my own." She took her mother's medal, which was attached to a thin chain, and hung it on the mirror alongside Billy's.

"When did you tell them that you are coming back?"

"I said maybe a month or two. Like an extended spring break. I dunno. We'll see."

He didn't say anything else, just drummed the wheel. Excited but also nervous, Del thought. She left him to it. Billy steered the car down to the road by the river, which led out of town to where they could pick up the interstate.

"Can we just make one more stop?" she asked him.

"Pee break?"

She gave him directions.

She had Billy pull up to the mailbox at the end of the drive-way. The envelope of money was heavy on her lap. She took out the small blue envelope and put it on one leg and left the fat manila envelope on the other leg. She pressed one hand over each envelope until her damp prints appeared. Then she stuffed the bigger envelope into a rusted mailbox and put the faded red metal flag up. She asked Billy to beep the horn, which he did until Eleanor appeared at the door wearing a pink terry robe.

"Special delivery!" Del shouted out the window.

Eleanor blew a kiss. They drove away as she started down the path to the mailbox.

"Ready ready?" Billy asked as they returned to the intersection that led out of town.

"Ready ready ready."

They picked up speed as they headed toward the highway. Del rested her face against the window, with Billy's balled-up hoodie cushioning her neck. Her eyes drifted low, and the rocking of the car set her almost to sleep until there was a jolt and her eyelids flew open. They were just past town, headed west, among the old tobacco fields. Del knew this place. To the left was a faded red barn where corn and strawberries were sold by the roadside in the summer, behind a hand-painted sign.

One winter when she was a child, they were driving out to see a friend of her father's who lived in the middle of nowhere. It was late afternoon, dark, the roads slick with ice. They were in their old orange station wagon, and when the car went down the incline alongside the barn, the back wheels spun out of control. Adela was strapped in, in the middle of the back seat, while her mother slept up front in the passenger seat without her seat belt on. Her father, the driver, reached across the car and pinned her mother to the seat with his arm, his other hand holding the wheel straight.

The station wagon swung wildly to one side and the other. She watched a metal fence come into view through the back window, then disappear again. Her mother woke and cried out: she was scared of the dark, had always been haunted by terrible dreams. Her father held the wheel. Del watched his hand, knuckles firm, and she knew he would not let go.

Billy twisted the knob on the radio to find the one station with reception and turned it up to maximum volume. Classic rock. A bad moon rising. The sun beat down on them and warmed the fake leather seats. Both of them were silent, contained by their own thoughts.

In another year or two or five, things would be different. They would have jobs and apartments and 401(k)s. They would have first, last, and security. They would go out for work drinks with people they merely tolerated and vomit discreetly in wastepaper baskets the next day. They would log in to see their bank statements and their friends. They would receive postcards every six months reminding them to get their teeth cleaned. They would review the labels of pasta sauces to see how much sugar was included. They would watch the news and if a bubble burst, they might care. They would observe their soon-to-be-ex-boyfriend take his last shirt off a hanger, throw it in a bag, and call a taxi. They would swear against love, but they would always, always do it again.

For now, though, they had none of those things. They had an '88 Chevy Nova, a quarter tank of gas, a stolen Murrow Construction corporate credit card, and the light just turned green.

Acknowledgments

Thanks to my agent, Cathryn Summerhayes; to my editor, Jen Monroe; and to Jess Molloy and Candice Coote for their assistance.

For research help, I'm indebted to Brad Guy and the book he coauthored with Bob Falk, *Unbuilding: Salvaging the Architectural Treasures of Unwanted Houses*. Also, to Ryan Donovan and Edward Azuar for speaking with me about AIDS in the 1990s and pointing me to work by Paul Lisicky, Edmund White, Sarah Schulman, Marie Howe, and Mark Doty, and to the ACT UP Oral History Project.

I'm grateful to my workshop mates Maria Adelmann, Christin Rice, Sharlene Teo, Nathan Grover, Gillian Haigh, and Anna Harvey, and to my teachers Jonathan Barnes, Fred Leebron, and Kathryn Rhett.

Thanks to Syndyze Maxhuni, Jackie Roberts, Lilias Hoskins, Helka Cross, Babs McCoid, Suzie Feldstein, and Cat Lincoln for their support.

Thank you to seat 2244 in the British Library.

Thank you most especially to Philip.

Housebreaking

COLLEEN HUBBARD

DISCUSSION QUESTIONS

BEHIND THE BOOK

READING LIST

Discussion Questions

1. Think about Del's reaction to finding out the house she now owned was going to be torn down. Why do you think this was a tipping point for her in the novel?

2. Throughout the novel, Del thinks of her mother a lot. What do you think the deconstruction of the house represents in relation to her memory of her mother?

3. Del discusses why she stuck to tearing apart the house she inherited. Thinking about this, why do you believe she chose to keep the house in the first place?

4. With Del's memories of her parents, there seems to be a running theme of escape. Considering your answer to the last question, do you think that tearing the house apart offers an escape? For whom?

5. Jeanne's life is unraveling at the same time Del's house deconstruction is taking place. Why do you believe the author

chose to have this happen? Do Jeanne and Del have any similarities?

6. Discuss Del's relationships within the novel. Do you think her views on family have changed by the end?

7. Did the novel play out in a way you expected? What did you think was going to be the outcome of Del's housebreaking?

8. Could you relate to Del and her struggles with family? Why or why not?

9. Do you think how Del handled her problems was the best way? Would you have changed anything she did? Why or why not?

10. Discuss the ending of the novel. Do you think that Del finds some new purpose after the story's events? If so, what do you think that is?

Behind the Book

Housebreaking came into being one afternoon in London. There was a gap between selling our old place and moving into a new one; during that weeklong period we stayed with our friend Keith. One afternoon, I pulled from Keith's shelf of paperbacks a history of Shakespeare by Bill Bryson. In the book, Bryson describes Shakespeare's company moving an entire theater building over the frozen Thames one night.

The image of moving a building over ice hooked into some part of my brain, and for many months afterward I wondered how it might happen on a domestic scale. The gestation of the book was slow—I worked full-time at a hospital and never found time to write. More than a year after staying at Keith's place, I joined an evening writing workshop in London and submitted about ten thousand words of what would become this novel. I paused when work got busy, and then looked at those first few chapters again once I was on maternity leave with my daughter. I had twelve months off work and decided to complete the manuscript during that time.

If that sounds like the goal of a sane person, don't be fooled: I had postpartum depression, which was coupled with, or perhaps caused, a sense that my identity had somehow dissolved. I wanted nothing more than an objective that felt inadvisable.

In his book *The Art of Fiction*, John Gardner said that fiction ought to create a "vivid and continuous" dream. I don't know what is more like a vivid and continuous dream than the early days of taking care of a baby, with their insomnia, intensity of feeling, and repetition. Everything felt heavy with symbolism and meaning. It wasn't difficult to stay in the mindset of the book—I was always in a subaquatic stupor through which the characters felt as real as I did.

The final stretch of writing began in November 2019, two months after the baby had arrived, and finished in May 2020. Before the COVID lockdown in London, I worked at the British Library at desk 2244, feasted on spicy noodles at a Chinese restaurant near Euston station, then went back to the baby.

Del's story seemed then, as it does to me still, like an arrow loosed from a bow: the people had their own sense of direction and momentum. I didn't feel I was inventing a story so much as telling one I had heard. Tym and Del's relationship, the side gig at the Christmas tree farm, *The Judy Garland Show*, the initials carved into the bridge—all of it came together as if I were telling you about something I'd heard about a neighbor.

The book is a work of fiction shot through with vague memories. As a child in New England, living on what was overgrown farmland originally owned by my immigrant great-grandparents, I spent a lot of time in the woods, where I found bits and pieces left behind by earlier inhabitants whose belongings were, for whatever reason, abandoned: empty photo frames, cracked mirrors, a tortoiseshell hair comb alongside a paperback spoiled by rain.

Who knew what sort of person had left behind what seemed, to a child, like treasure? I am much too lazy and not confident enough to take on a project like Del's, but I could place myself as one of the children who followed her into the woods, uncovered her plastic ponies and her jigsaw puzzles, and was glad that she'd been there before me.

Reading List

I was surprised to find the immediate postnatal period a rich time for reading. In the middle of the night, I held my daughter upright after feeding her to prevent her from being sick, and while she slept, I read.

What do the books have in common? They are full of vivid language and economical sentences. Many are funny. All of them are short.

The Magician of Lublin by Isaac Bashevis Singer

The Magician of Lublin, which I bought at a used book-shop near my house, was so enjoyable that I actually looked forward to being awake at four a.m. to read it. In the book, a traveling magician in 1880s Poland who has a wife and several mistresses questions the meaning of his life. What could possibly go wrong?

How to Write an Autobiographical Novel by Alexander Chee

Some books make me wish I was friends with the author. This series of essays by Alexander Chee is one of them. If you enjoy nothing more than the sensation of righteous anger, you will particularly enjoy the passage in which one of Chee's fellow writing students asks why anyone should care about the lives of the "bitchy queens" in Chee's stories.

O Pioneers! by Willa Cather

Living outside the United States, I miss the sense of vastness in the landscape, which is unlike anything I've seen in England. I've read this book a few times before and particularly wanted to read it during this time for its portrayal of the American landscape and of the complicated dynamics among a farming family.

West by Carys Davies

A big story in a compact package, this is a classic American frontier novel that manages to feel fresh and surprising. A Pennsylvania farmer travels west to find the monsters that are the source of newly discovered fossils and leaves behind his ten-year-old daughter for what he promises will be a two-year journey.

Mrs. Bridge by Evan S. Connell

A series of vignettes about a well-to-do housewife in Kansas City who tentatively touches the edges of her life of comfort and boredom. There's something very Betty Draper about Mrs. Bridge, yet Connell creates a sense of compassion and sensitivity for a woman who isn't terribly admirable.

Sorry to Disrupt the Peace by Patrick Cottrell

It must be the nightmare of every writer to discover that someone already wrote your book and theirs is better, as is the case for me with this novel about a difficult young woman who travels home to understand a fracture in her family. It's a dark, funny, and moving exploration of identity and grief centered on Helen, a Korean adoptee who returns to the Midwest to understand why her brother, also a Korean adoptee, died by suicide. I can't remember a contemporary novel I enjoyed more than this one.

My friend Ryan Donovan, a scholar of theater history, suggested the following resources from his culture survey course at the School of Visual Arts when I was looking for information about the experiences of people with AIDS in the 1990s:

"1,112 and Counting" by Larry Kramer
The Gentrification of the Mind: Witness to a Lost Imagination by Sarah Schulman
What the Living Do by Marie Howe
"The Way We Live Now" by Susan Sontag
Later: My Life at the Edge of the World by Paul Lisicky
TheAidsMemorial Instagram
Not-About-AIDS-Dance (video) by Neil Greenberg (1994)

A native of New England, **Colleen Hubbard** now lives in the UK with her family. She wrote her debut novel, *Housebreaking*, while on maternity leave from her job with the NHS. She graduated from the University of East Anglia's MA program in creative writing, where she earned the Head of School Prize with a distinction.

CONNECT ONLINE

ColleenHubbard.com

Ready to find
your next great read?

Let us help.

Visit prh.com/nextread

Penguin
Random
House